# IT
# WOULD
# HAVE
# BEEN
# ENOUGH

# IT
# WOULD
# HAVE
# BEEN
# ENOUGH

## *Manny's*
## *War & Peace*
## *Book II*

## David Brown

AESOP Modern Fiction
Oxford

AESOP Modern Fiction
An imprint of AESOP Publications
Martin Noble Editorial / AESOP
28 Abberbury Road, Oxford OX4 4ES, UK
www.aesopbooks.com

Second edition published by AESOP Publications
Copyright (c) 2014 David Brown

A catalogue record of this book is
available from the British Library.

Second edition 2014

ISBN: 978-1-910301-15-9

*If he had split the sea for us*
*And had not taken us through on dry land*
*It would have been enough…*

*Dayenu* – *It Would Have Been Enough*
(Passover song)

*To all the men and women
who gave their lives
so that we could have
A Better Tomorrow*

David Brown

# Cast of main characters

| | |
|---|---|
| **Manny Grenfeldt** | Austrian Jew |
| **Rita Grenfeldt** (née Krantz) | Manny's wife |
| **David Grenfeldt** | Manny and Rita's son |
| **Miriam Grenfeldt** | Manny and Rita's daughter |
| **Susan Grenfeldt** | Manny and Rita's daughter |
| **Saul Grenfeldt** | Manny and Rita's son |
| **Josephine Grenfeldt** | Manny and Rita's daughter |
| **Daniel Krantz** | Rita's father |
| **Hannah Steinberg** (née Grenfeldt) | Manny's sister |
| **Isaac Steinberg** | Hannah's husband |
| **Barry Steinberg** | Isaac and Hannah's son |
| **Jacob Steinberg** | Isaac and Hannah's son |
| **Joshua Grendfeldt** | Manny's brother |
| **Freda Grenfeldt** (née Grossman) | Joshua's wife |
| **Abraham Grenfeldt** | Joshua and Freda's son |
| **Sam Grenfeldt** | Manny's cousin |
| **Sarah Grenfeldt** (née Faulkner) | Sam's wife |
| **Michael Grenfeldt** | Sam and Sarah's son |
| **Lily Grenfeldt** | Sam and Sarah's daughter |
| **Zachary Bergman** | Manny's friend |
| **Dominique Bergman** (née Gonzales) | Zachary's wife |
| **Harry Bergman** | Zachary/Dominique's son |
| **Abraham Bergman** | Zachary/Dominique's son |
| **Daniela Bergman** | Zachary/Dominique's daughter |
| **Joe Rosen** (Joseph Rosenblatt) | Broker; Manny's friend |
| **Marlene Rosen** (née Shulman) | Joe's wife |
| **Adrienne Rosen** | Joe and Marlene's twin daughter |
| **Anne Rosen** | Joe and Marlene's twin daughter |
| **Mr White** (Israel Herzolwitz) | Works for Haganah |
| **Mr Amber** (Abe Goldberg) | Works for Haganah |
| **Helga Friedman** (née Mäeller) | Manny's friend |
| **Hans Meyer** (was Mäeller) | Manny's friend |

# Foreword: Manny's War & Peace

S OMEONE once wrote: All that is needed for evil men to triumph is for good men to do nothing. *One Only Kid* and its sequel, *It Would Have Been Enough*, combine truth with fiction. Both books are about people living through a brutal war, where normal human beings can become cold-blooded killers.

### *One Only Kid*: a brief look back

In Vienna, sixteen-year-old Manny Grenfeldt's life changed dramatically with the emergence of Adolf Hitler's Social Democrat Party, and its persecution of Jews, who lived with the ever-present threat of being beaten or killed.

At school Manny and his siblings were physically and verbally abused by other children. Because of this, Manny attended self-defence classes run by the Haganah, where he was taught the art of self-defence, and how to use everyday items, like pens and keys as weapons.

Manny and his siblings were then sent to stay with their aunt and uncle in London, while his parents tried to sell their properties in Vienna. After some months with no communication from his parents, Manny, tall for his age, blond and blue eyed, pleaded with his uncle to let him return to Vienna and find out what had happened them.

Back in Vienna, Manny found out that the only way he and his parents could leave the country was by obtaining affidavits showing they had jobs in England. While waiting for the affidavits to arrive the Grenfeldts' shop was attacked by Nazis, one of them being an ex-employee, Conrad Meinhoffer. Father and son defended themselves, and although badly beaten, survived.

Manny's father, David, was taken to a concentration camp and tortured, but released with the help of Manny's friend, Hans Mäeller. The affidavits arrived too late as David was taken away again, but this time he was murdered. On hearing of her husband's death his wife Martha committed suicide. Because of laws passed by the Nazis, Conrad Meinhoffer seized the Grenfeldts' shop and apartment. Manny avenged his parents by killing Meinhoffer and then went to live with his friend Joseph at the Zionist camp until his affidavits were processed and he could leave Austria.

He enlisted the help of Joan Withers, a secretary at the British Embassy in sending some papers through to England and they eventually became lovers. As Manny and other congregants left the synagogue after Sabbath services, they were surrounded by German soldiers and taken to Mauthausen concentration camp and the guards committed atrocities against the prison inmates. With the help of a baker, Daniel, Manny escaped from Mauthausen, but not before taking revenge and killing a sadistic SS-officer. Crossing into Switzerland he met up with Joan and eventually returned to London.

On the outbreak of war, Manny, with other Austrian and German Jews, was interned on the Isle of Man, where he met and befriended Isaac Steinberg and David Wasserman. There was a special bond and humour in this friendship. While there, he came in contact with a professor of economics, Joseph Rosenblatt, who had a gift for making money, and the pair formed a business liaison.

Tragically Joan was killed in a bombing raid. After many requests to the authorities by an angry Manny and others on the Isle to be allowed to fight the Germans, the British Government relented, realising that German-speaking men could be invaluable, and the three friends were allowed to enlist in the Parachute Regiment. On their first leave home, Manny met Rita, and although frightened of another relationship, eventually realised that he was in love with her. Against the backdrop of war there were softer, loving moments.

A meeting with Manny's cousin, Sam, a Commando officer, brought the three friends in contact with Zachary Bergman. Because of their linguistic skills, the three friends, with Sam and Bergman, were sent on covert missions behind enemy lines. On their return, Manny was promoted to sergeant, David and Isaac were made corporals, and put in charge of a platoon of Jewish soldiers of Austrian and German descent.

Dressed in German uniforms, the group were sent to rescue an American colonel whose plane was shot down. The American Officer knows the Allies' plans for the invasion of Europe. By sheer bad luck, Sarah Faulkner, an agent sent to rescue him, who also happens to be Sam's fiancée, was also captured. Both were being held in a Bremen prison. After rescuing the pair, the group fought their way out, reaching their rendezvous in time to meet the aircraft taking them back to England.

Now read on ...

*David Brown*
*Great Yarmouth*
*May 2014*

# Prologue

*A*FTER *a week's recuperation in Reading, and not being able to get to London to see the girls, Manny and his men were bored with lazing around and wanted to get back into action. He visited his four wounded men and was told they would be rejoining him in a couple of weeks.*

*Before leaving, Manny, Isaac and David, visited Sarah who was recovering from her ordeal at a nursing home in Hertfordshire. Sam was with her, having been granted two weeks' compassionate leave.*

*Sarah's face still showed a faint hint of bruising.*

*'The doctor said she might be able to go home in a week,' said Sam.*

*'How come you were captured so quickly?' Manny asked.*

*'I went to the Wüstestätte where I was to meet my contact.' She shrugged her shoulders. 'Just my luck, a boy from my old school recognised me, the bald-headed Gestapo agent. He followed me and I was arrested, thankfully before I met my contact. He told me the only reason he was in Bremen was to pick up an American colonel for interrogation.'*

*Her voice quivered slightly as she added, 'I tried to walk casually away, but he grabbed me, wanting to know what I, a Jewess was doing in a place like the Wüstestätte. I told him it's for the music, he just laughed. The rest, as they say, is history.'*

*She stood kissing the three of them on the cheek. 'If you hadn't come to rescue me, I don't know what else they would have done to me. Thank you.'*

Sam moved to her side, placing a caring arm around her waist. *'We both thank you. I owe you one.'*

*'Don't be stupid,'* said Manny. *'You don't owe us anything. As Isaac once said, we're family; this was what families do for each other.'*

He smiled, *'We'd better be on or way.'* He kissed Sarah on the cheek, hugged his cousin, whispering in his ear, *'Is she OK?'*

Sam whispered back, *'Yes, she's stronger than you think.'*

# PART I

# Chapter 1

*22 May 1944*

THERE was a hubbub of noise as Manny and his men, with the rest of the company, waited for their CO to appear.

'Company, attention!' yelled the company sergeant major. There was a scraping of chairs as the men obeyed the order.

The room was silent except for the sound of Captain Fry and his officer's boots marching in time as they headed towards a raised platform. Fry moved quickly to the centre of the platform, looking silently for a moment at the sea of faces in front of him and smiled. 'At ease gentlemen, be seated, smoke if you want.'

There were whispered words by the men as they sat, and in the silence that followed, the striking of matches. Cigarette smoke rose like a cloud towards the already-nicotine-stained ceiling. There was an air of expectation and a little tension, as the captain moved to one side of a cinema screen and nodded. The lights go out and an aerial picture of a beach appeared. The camera panned slowly across it and out to the countryside beyond.

'This was an aerial picture of the Normandy beaches,' said Captain Fry, 'where, within the next month, British, American and Allied forces would be landing.'

A large-scale map appeared on the screen. 'The 6th Airborne Division, that's us, with the 1st Canadian Parachute Battalion and Glider Troop, have three primary tasks before the seaborne landings begin.'

He paused for a second to take a drag of his cigarette. 'The first of these tasks is to capture the bridge at Benouville and hold it until commando reinforcements arrived.' He tapped a pointing stick at the bridges before continuing.

'The second is to destroy the guns at the Merville battery so they can't fire on the landing forces. The third is to destroy the bridges over the rivers Dives, Verville, Robehomme, Bures and Troarn.' He pointed at each different place with his stick.

'This is to stop German reinforcements coming from the East, and...' he paused to smoke the last part of his cigarette outing it on the floor with his boot '... place a protective net around the Eastern flank where the British second army was to come ashore.'

He slapped the pointer once again on an area of the map to emphasise his meaning. 'Our job is to capture and hold this long ridge and forest area here, at Bois de Bavant and the crossroads between Breville to Troarn until the infantry can reach us.'

'This ridge is very important as it overlooks the landing beaches. If the Germans gain command of this ridge, they could halt the invasion and we would receive heavy casualties.' He paced up and down the stage like a caged lion, head turned towards them.

'We would not let that happen.' He stopped pacing to look at the men. 'Would we?'

There was a muted response of 'No, sir.'

'Would we?' yelled Fry.

'No, sir,' they yelled back.

He stood in the middle of the stage, pointing stick held in both hands across his thigh. 'We begin training for this drop bright and early tomorrow morning. Officers and other ranks, without exception, will take part in briefings and practices, and as from now all leave is cancelled.'

There was a low disgruntled murmur from the men. Fry waited for the hubbub to die down, looking around at the young faces in front of him. His voice softened. 'I know that not being able to see your families is hard on you, but secrecy is paramount. One slip to the enemy could cost many lives, even your own. That's it. See you all bright and early in the morning.'

*

Training was stepped up, with map reading and individual briefings in a room with replica models in amazing detail of Normandy towns, villages, and roads, including ditches and trees, down to the amount of houses in a street and their individual numbers.

The men were questioned over and over again on how they would go unobserved from one village or town to another, even from one house to another.

Manny's twenty-fourth birthday was spent training. He pushed his men to the limit, with special emphasis on unarmed combat. At the end of May they were moved at night to a transit camp in Southern England. Security was tight, the men sealed off from the outside world. All letters written home were censored.

Suddenly, without warning, they moved from camp to an airfield in Hampshire.

'This is it,' said David.

'That's been said before,' Isaac quipped.

'Care to make a small wager?' David took out his wallet. 'Say two-pounds?'

Isaac laughed. 'I won't play cards with you, or make any sort of wager – you always win.'

*

At last the waiting was over. A heavily laden Manny climbed aboard the Dakota C39. He, like his men, carried 150lbs of equipment that consisted of 150 rounds in clips for his Sten gun, grenades, a commando knife; rations for twenty-four hours, a water bottle, plus trenching tool. In a holster strapped to his right thigh was a Colt .45 revolver with two spare clips of bullets.

The pilot, an American, with his co-pilot, headed towards the cockpit, saying in a Southern drawl, 'Hi, how yah all,' to the men, who were checking their weapons and gear as he passed.

The Dakota's engines roared into life and they moved, following a line of other Dakotas as they taxied towards the end of the runway.

At 2327 hours on 5 June 1944, Manny's aircraft left the tarmac, reaching for the dark, moonless sky.

The flight across the Channel was smooth and uneventful until they reached the French coast; when suddenly, above the drone of the engines, there was a loud bang of exploding shells plus lines of red and orange tracer bullets arching slowly up towards them.

The red warning light came on. Manny ordered the men to stand and hook up their parachute lines. A crewman opened the fuselage door as each man checked the equipment of the one in front of him.

Manny stood by the open door, holding on to the inside of the fuselage, waiting for the green light to come on, the cold wind tugging at his clothes. He blinked, as bright flashes of exploding flak lit up the darkness like a giant firework display.

His eyes, behind goggles, had a glint of anticipation; which suddenly changed to one of horror, as the Dakota beside and slightly ahead of them was hit, and couldn't help but look as it dived in a ball of flame towards the ground, exploding on impact. He swallowed a little nervously, turning his attention to the red light, willing it to change to green, then glanced around to see another aircraft going into a shallow dive, one engine on fire, seeing clearly the pilot in the glow of exploding shells and flares struggling to keep the aircraft up as it spewed Paras, then without warning blew up. The last Para to jump followed the flaming aircraft to the ground, his chute on fire.

Suddenly, Manny and the men were thrown to the floor as their pilot took violent evasive action. The crewman grabbed the door to close it.

'What's going on?' Manny yelled against noise of the crump, crump of ack-ack.

'The pilot said he's turning back, he can't identify any landmarks. It seemed the Germans had flooded the area around the Orne and Dives rivers.'

Manny unhooked his line, moving back along the fuselage towards the cockpit, as his heavily laden men helped each other back onto their seats.

David knew something was wrong by the expression on his friend's face as he passed, entering the cockpit. Manny pulled the Colt from its holster as the pilot looked around to see who it was.

Placing the tip of the Colt against the pilot's temple, Manny said coldly, 'Turn this plane around and head back towards the drop zone, or I'll shoot you,' pulling back the hammer.

'OK, pal, it's your funeral,' the ashen-faced pilot said, turning away from Manny to bring the aircraft around.

'No funny business, otherwise I'll come looking for you, and believe me this ack-ack would be child's play to what I would do to you.' Still pointing the gun at the pilot he yelled through the open door, 'Everyone take your places.'

Saul Friedlander, another of the men under Manny's command, who was usually the next to jump after him, moved to the entrance. The crewman once again opened the fuselage door and the red light flashed on.

Manny looked through the cockpit window to see searchlights piercing the night like spotlights on a theatre's stage moving across the sky; stopping when they found a target, following it like a wild animal that won't let go its prey, as the aircraft in its beam tried unsuccessfully to escape. Manny suddenly realised how vulnerable he and his men were as another shell burst close to the aircraft, the whistle of metal flying through the air adding to the noise.

Returning the colt into its holster, Manny turned back to sees the red light change to green and Saul leapt into space, followed closely by the others, who took no notice of the shrapnel and hot tracers flying all around them.

Manny hooked up behind David, Isaac's in front of him. Moshe was about to jump when a shell burst close to the aircraft, throwing them onto the floor.

'We've been hit,' the crewman yelled. White smoke trailed behind the port engine.

Manny and the others got to their feet. 'Let's go,' he yelled above the noise in and around the aircraft.

Moshe stepped quickly to the door and out of the aircraft, the others close behind. There was the familiar adrenalin rush as Manny's chute opened. He looked down, dimly seeing the others just below him and then up to the right of the canopy of his chute.

In the brightness of shell bursts, he watched the Dakota, white smoke trailing from its port engine turning for home; then looked down once more eyes searching the darkness below for the enemy as the earth comes to meet him. He quickly released the parachute, Sten gun ready for action. Above them aircraft unloaded their human cargo, gliders unhooked from towing aircraft glided silently towards the ground. Some were hit, going down in flames with their human cargo still inside.

Manny knew they had landed in the wrong place. It was anybody's guess as to where the rest of his men were. 'Hide the chutes and let's get away from here,' Manny ordered.

Having covered some distance from where they landed, Manny stopped under a clump of trees to study his map, the others looking over his shoulder.

'Bloody heck, we're miles from our DZ,' said Isaac.

'There was a strong cross wind when we jumped; by my reckoning we're here.' Manny pointed a finger at the map. 'At least thirty miles, maybe more, from where we are sup—' He was interrupted by someone shouting in German.

'They've found our chutes,' David said.

'We need to move west,' Moshe, commented pointing in that direction.

'Yep, I agree,' Manny acknowledged. 'Let's avoid the road and travel across country, I'll lead off—' pointing to Moshe '—you and then Isaac with the Bren, David you bring up the rear.'

They moved off with the thunder of German ack-ack, and the sound of small-arms fire in the distance. Manny set a fast-but-cautious pace, covering ten miles in the first hour; much slower than their practice marches. High hedges and walls surrounding the fields could easily hide German soldiers, slowing them up.

Passing through a hedge into an adjoining field, Manny's arm swung up and down as he spotted the silhouettes of three German soldiers walking in a line towards them. The middle one grumbled to his companions, 'Here am I, away from the cold of Russia and supposed to be in a warm bed with that stupid baker's daughter, not out here looking for British paratroopers.'

Manny moved over to Isaac and whispered, 'Cover us with the Bren.'

Isaac nodded in reply. Turning to the other two, Manny motioned with his right hand a snaking movement. The two men nodded, sliding their packs from their backs and with Manny in the lead, slithering quickly and silently through the grass passing to the right of the enemy.

Isaac waited till they were in position then called out in German. 'Over here.'

The three soldiers turned to see who was calling. Manny and his two companions rose from the ground like ghostly spectres. The man in the middle of the three started to turn and was about to yell a warning but was too late, dropping his rifle, hands clutching the knife in his throat, mouth moving, but there was no sound as he gradually fell to his knees, the bodies of his two comrades dropping to the ground beside him, their eyes open in death.

A big grin spread across Manny's face; noticing that one of the Germans had a Russian Tommy gun, he picked it up, searching the body for extra magazines.

'What do you need that for?' asked Moshe.

'This—' Manny pointed at the weapon, as they returned to Isaac '—is the best Tommy gun in the world.' He picked up his pack, 'and Moshe, when you see what it can do, you'll want one too.'

With Manny in the lead, having decided to take to the road and make better time, they left the dead Germans hidden in a ditch under a hedge covered with leaves and branches.

Manny hoped to come across some of his men who were somewhere in front of him.

'Let's go,' Manny ordered. This was what he'd been asking for these last few years, to kill Germans. There was a grim determination to succeed in his quest of vengeance for his parents, Joan and those he left behind in Mauthausen. He looked across at Moshe, whose entire family were taken to a concentration camp. He was lucky, because that very afternoon he'd taken a chance and gone to the cinema.

Manny looked at his watch – 0130 hrs – and for a moment wondered if their pilot reached England. He moved cautiously forward, searching the area in front of him, stopping abruptly, arm up, bringing the others to halt. He crawled towards an open gate, looking into the field, eyes coming to rest on a glider, and then gradually moving around the field – it was empty.

Manny moved back to the others. 'There's a glider in the field. I can't see any movement, but just in case someone's still alive in there, we should check it out.'

Covering each other, they entered the field, fanning out, weapons ready. Manny entered the glider through a gaping hole in the fuselage just behind the right seat, where an officer, a lieutenant, was slumped against a shattered window. Isaac found four dead soldiers still strapped into their seat.

'He landed it before he died,' David whispered, looking down at the pilot, a sergeant.

'Help me get them outside. We'll bury them beside the glider,' Manny suggested, opening the crew's blood-stained jackets, taking one of their dog tags, dropping one into the pocket of his camouflaged smock, and leaving the other to be placed where they buried them.

'There's a jeep back here, spare ammunition and other equipment,' Moshe told them.

'Before we sort that out, let's see to these men first,' Manny ordered, gently lifting the pilot from his seat.

They dug shallow graves, marking them with the men's dog tags before turning their attention to the interior of the glider.

Miraculously, neither the jeep nor its fuel had been hit, but the tyres on the trailer containing spare ammunition and a Piat anti-tank weapon with six shells was beyond repair. They pushed the jeep out of the glider, loaded it with as much ammunition as they could take, plus the Piat with its six shells and six cans of petrol.

\*

With Manny behind the wheel, they drove out of the field onto the road. The tall hedgerows sped by as they ate up the miles, the sound of sporadic small arms fire ahead. It seemed they were not the only ones who had landed a long way from their drop zone.

They raced round a bend; Manny slammed his foot onto the brake as they came face-to-face with a group of SS-grenadiers having a brew-up beside the road.

For a moment both parties stared at each other in surprise. Moshe and Manny were the first to react. Moshe fired his Sten-gun into the group, yelling abuse at them in German as Manny put the jeep into reverse, firing his Russian Tommy gun with one hand, zigzagging the reversing jeep back around the bend, with David and Isaac leaning precariously over the side, their weapons shuddering in their hands.

The Grenadiers still alive dived for their weapons, confused by the four men in the jeep swearing at them in German.

Just before they disappeared back around the bend, an SS-Obersturmführer (senior assault leader) stepped from behind a half-track, feet astride, bravely firing his machine pistol at the same time yelling orders at his men, which were cut short by bullets from Moshe's Sten-gun.

Manny stopped the jeep by a closed gate leading to a field. David jumped from the jeep, opened the gate and leapt back on as Manny accelerated into the field, cutting across at an angle, hidden by the tall surrounding hedges.

A half-track, with grenadiers on board, roared into the field behind them, its tracks cutting deep furrows into the ground as it raced in pursuit.

David yelled at Manny to stop, picked up the Piat jumped from the jeep, yelling for Moshe to load. Moshe grabbed a shell, loaded, tapped David on the shoulder and then hopped back onto his seat as David pressed the trigger.

Moshe leaped in the air, yelling happily as the missile landed on the half-track, which immediately exploded, sending its occupants flying through the air. David boarded the jeep and Manny put his foot down on accelerator crossing the field and through an open gate at the other end, emerging onto a road, leaving a smoking half-track and some ten or more dead and wounded Germans behind them.

Manny had a slight grin on his face; the excitement of contact so soon with the enemy had given him an adrenalin rush. He turned to David, 'Having fun?'

David smiled back. 'I knew you were mad, but the way you're driving, I know you're insane.'

Manny faced the front, letting out a roar of laughter. Suddenly out of the darkness loomed three Tiger tanks parked by the road side. Manny accelerated, swerving past them and before the Germans could blink they disappeared around a bend, quickly hidden by high hedges. Manny put the gearstick into neutral, switching off the engine, bringing the vehicle to a gradual stop.

'Come on,' he ordered, getting out of the jeep and picking up his weapon.

'Where are we going?' David asked.

'You saw those Tigers, we're going to try and make sure they don't get the chance to attack us, or our men.'

'With what?' asked Moshe.

'I have two adhesive grenades, do you have any?'

'I've one,' replied Moshe.

'I've two.' David showed them to the others. Isaac held up one.

'Six grenades, three tanks,' said Manny. 'I'll take the far tank with my two grenades; Moshe with Isaac's grenade take the middle tank, and David the tank nearest to us. Isaac will cover us with his Bren.'

He turned to Moshe and David. 'Place one grenade by the engine and the other the gun turret; right, let's go.'

*

The tank crews sat beside a Kubelwagen some twenty yards from the tanks. Beyond them were two motorcycle combinations, their riders also having a brew and smoke.

David waited by the first tank as Manny and Moshe snaked their way towards their targets. In the shadow of the second Tiger, Moshe watched Manny, his right index finger against the trigger guard of his gun.

Manny crawled behind the Tiger, hidden by the tank crews, and rose slowly to his feet; he pulled the pins from the grenades, placed one by the engine and the other on the side of the gun turret. He looked quickly around and then ran as fast as he could to Moshe, who pulled the pin on his grenades, and together they moved quickly in a crouched run towards David, who pulled the pins of his grenades, following on behind them as they headed back to Isaac.

A tank crewman walked a few paces away from the others; as he opened his fly to relieve himself he looked around and spotted the three running Paras. The man yelled, pointing in their direction, giving chase, pulling his pistol from its holster, fly still open.

Isaac opened up with his Bren, killing the yelling German. Manny yelled at the other two, 'Move over so Isaac has a clear field of fire.' Bullets kicked up the ground around them as they ran as fast as they could, Manny yelling over and over, 'Fuck, shit.'

They reached Isaac as the first grenades exploded, quickly followed by the others. The three men passed Isaac as he fired a long burst at the advancing Germans, then getting quickly to his feet, he walked backwards, finger on the trigger, sweeping the Bren from left to right until he was out of ammo.

Turning, he ran as fast as he could after the others, sliding the Bren onto the jeep and diving headfirst onto the rear seat beside Moshe as Manny gunned the engine and with sliding, screeching tyres drove away, not waiting to find out what damage they'd caused, with Isaac holding on for dear life, his legs in the air.

Suddenly there was a loud bang. Manny let out a whoop of delight at their success. Isaac managed to get back onto his seat, reloading the Bren, stopping for a moment to watch exploding ammunition from the tanks lighting up the darkness.

They hadn't gone far when Isaac looked back along the road yelling, 'Put your foot down, we've company.' Manny glanced round to see two motorcycle combinations closing fast, with a Kubelwagen behind them. Isaac fired a burst from his Bren, the German sidecar passengers returning fire.

'You'd better think of something quickly, otherwise we're going to be in serious trouble,' David yelled, firing at the enemy as they closed in on them. Without warning the Germans were suddenly engulfed in a withering crossfire.

The motorcycle combinations crashing into each other, the riders and sidecar passengers were killed instantly. The Kubelwagen veered to the side of the road, nose-diving into a ditch.

Six paratroopers appeared from either side of the road, running towards the motorcycles and Kubelwagen, weapons ready for action, shouting in German for the occupants to come out with their hands up, but there was no need, they were all dead.

Manny braked to a stop and with the others got out of the jeep, a look of astonishment and relief on his face.

Moshe walked slowly towards one of the Paras, a big smile on his face. 'Is that you, Saul?'

'Yes, Moshe it is.' Saul's teeth white against his camouflaged blackened face, smiling at his friend as they embraced.

'You're still as ugly as ever, but it's nice to see you're alive.'

'OK you two, that's enough banter. Don't you know there's a war on, and I intend to be part of it.' Manny said. 'By the way, thanks, we were in a spot of trouble there.'

'Don't mention it, Sarg,' a small, weedy man named Feidleberger said, giving a toothless smile.

'Are you all OK? No one injured?'

'We're fine, Sarg,' Saul replied.

Manny nodded, looked at the map in his hand. 'We aren't too far from our objective. Load your packs onto the jeep. Feidleberger, you drive.' He pointed to another of the men. 'Jacobson, in the back with the Bren.'

Carrying only their weapons, the Ten Paras, with Manny in the lead, headed toward the sound of gunfire. It was dawn when they reached Battalion HQ and Manny reported to his CO.

Captain Fry grimaced, as he automatically returned Manny's salute with a badly strained arm that he'd injured when landing in a tree, refusing to go to the first-aid station in case they sent him back to England.

He looked down at the map on top of a stack of ammunition boxes, gesturing for Manny to join him and pointing to a section on the map. 'As you know, we need to hold this ridge. It's bordered by hedges and woods that run south along the road to the Le Mesnil crossing, and to the Chateau St Come. Our main problem is we don't have enough men.'

Manny gave Fry a strange look. 'How many men do we have, sir?'

'At a guess, I'd say about two hundred and fifty.'

'What! There's supposed to be seven hundred of us.'

Fry sighed. 'You and I know that, so does the CO. The operation hasn't gone to plan. Because of a strong cross wind the Brigade, like you and your men, were scattered over miles of French countryside. For the last hour our men have been reaching their allotted objectives in ones and twos, or in small groups. I've attached some of your men that arrived earlier to Sergeant Smithers's section for the time being.' He winced from the pain in his arm pointing once more at the map.

'The CO gave orders for continuous patrols to the villages along the ridge, wanting to give the Germans the impression that we're a stronger force than we actually are, making them think we're at Brigade strength. It's vital, as you know, that we hold those positions. If the Germans capture that ridge it'll halt the landings and the troops on the beaches would be annihilated.'

'What do you want me to do, sir?'

Fry placed a finger on the map. 'Take up position here, linking up with Sergeant Smithers's group and pick up the rest of your men at the same time. You'd better collect some extra ammo. I'll notify you later about patrols.'

Manny stood to attention and saluted. 'Yes sir.' Turning, and without another word he joined his men.

'David, take Rosenblum and Hirschfeld and pick up some extra ammo. Isaac, you and Moshe get us some hot tea and any food you can scrounge, and then join us on the ridge.'

*

Manny led the rest of the men to their position on the ridge. There were shouts of jubilation and playful bantering when they were united with the other men of their unit, but within minutes they were down to the serious business of digging defensive trenches.

David arrived with extra ammunition and grenades, but Isaac and Moshe returned empty-handed.

'We were told in no uncertain terms to get out of the kitchen – well, what they called the kitchen – by Corporal McGee. He said as soon as he'd made some sandwiches and the tea was hot, he'd bring it up to us, and was quiet indignant when I said we could do it ourselves.'

Manny smiled. 'Wait till he needs someone to peel the spuds.'

While the men dug defensive positions, Manny and Moshe set up distance markers. Manny and the other sergeants were summoned to Fry's Bivouac.

'Just to put you in the picture—' Fry pointed the tip of his pencil at a place on the map '—as you know we're dug in here along the hedges. The password is "Cock and Hen" and the reply is "Guinea". Our troops will be landing on the beaches pretty soon, so we must keep the Krauts busy.'

Within seconds of the sergeants returning to their trenches they could hear a noise like an express train running along the track. Someone yelled, 'Take cover.' Then there seemed to be the sound of a scythe cutting through grass and then earth erupted around them, quickly followed by the bang of exploding shells, and hot shrapnel flew through the air, embedding itself in trees and flesh. Manny nervously licked his lips, crouching down in his foxhole thinking that he didn't want to be killed by a random mortar shell. The barrage seemed to last an eternity, and then suddenly, silence, followed by sobbing and cries of help from the wounded.

One of Sergeant Smithers's men poked his head over the lip of his trench then fell back; the crack of the sniper's rifle a second behind the hole that appeared in the centre of his forehead, a trickle of blood seeping from it.

Manny peeked over the edge, blue eyes searching along the ridge of trees ahead, but the sniper was well concealed. There was another shot. This time the Para was lucky, only a shoulder wound.

Manny crawled along the trench till reaching the best shot in his company. 'Goldstein, get you're rifle ready. I'm going to get that son of a bitch to fire at my helmet, see if you can spot him.'

Goldstein nodded, 'OK Sarg.'

Placing his helmet on top of a branch, Manny raised it above the trench. The helmet jumped off the branch falling to the ground, a dent in the middle of it.

'See him?'

'Not certain, Sarg. Could you try again?'

Manny moved a couple of yards along the trench lifting just the top of his helmet over the edge, and once again the helmet jumped off the branch, a hole a centimetre above the dent.

Goldstein snuggled his rifle into his shoulder saying, 'Got him Sarg,' and squeezed the trigger.

Moshe yelled, 'Well done, Arek,' as a body somersaulted off the top of a tree, to the cheers of the men in the trenches.

\*

It was a grey, misty morning in Normandy as Manny and his men ready themselves for the inevitable attack. Throughout the night, he and the other sergeants had periodically taken their men out on patrol; trying to con the

Germans into thinking they had more men than they actually had, and it seemed to be working.

'Take cover!' someone yelled, just before mortar shells fell around them. Manny swallowed back the bile, trying to stop himself from shaking. He yelled at the top of his voice, covering his ears with his hands against the continuous noise of exploding shells that threw earth and metal splinters into the air. They rained down around him, splattering against his helmet and he was violently sick. Above the sound of the shells could be heard the yells of scared men. Branches, like arrows, fell from trees, adding to the danger.

As quickly as it started, the barrage stopped and there was an ominous eerie silence, apart from the groans of the wounded; smoke and the smell of cordite drifted across their positions. Manny knew an attack was about to start when the barrage began again. Ten minutes later the barrage lifted. Manny chanced a peek over the edge of the trench.

There was a chilling silence as soldiers of the Waffen-SS, their lips drawn tightly together faces set with determination advanced slowly towards them, and then suddenly the quietness of the advancing enemy was broken by shouts of bravado as their pace quickened and they broke into a run, shouting anything that came into their heads, bayonets gleaming in the early morning sunlight. When the Germans reached the markers the defenders opened fire, beating the enemy back with heavy casualties.

The men were tired, but still, with a lull in the fighting, they went out on patrol, not wanting to let down those who were waiting to storm the beaches.

*

Around midday, as if by mutual consent, the battle came to a stop, and silence reigns once more over the battlefield. This respite enabled the men time to have a smoke, receive food and drink, and the slightly wounded attended too. Defences were strengthened, weapons cleaned and munitions replenished.

Manny and the other sergeants received information that Allied troops had landed and although meeting heavy resistance were advancing slowly towards their positions. Manny spread the word amongst the men, and suddenly the cloak of tiredness disappeared; smiles appeared, teeth white against their unshaven and dirt-streaked faces, and light-hearted friendly banter that was synonymous with men who had faced danger and fought shoulder to shoulder, brought laughter to the Paras' positions.

\*

Early in the afternoon the Germans attacked along the whole length of the ridge. Manny and his men received intense mortar fire, followed by a Brigade strength assault. This time the Germans breach the Para's positions and opposing forces were locked in hand-to-hand battle.

The Germans attacking Manny and his men were taken completely by surprise when they were verbally abused and sworn at in German, the men laughing and confusing them even more when reverting to Yiddish.

Manny gestured for a tall Waffen SS-corporal to attack him, goading him, saying softly, '*Ich bin Juden*; see my big nose.'

The corporal lunged at him with his bayonet. 'Join the whore you call a mother,' he shouted, hatred in his voice.

Manny sidestepped at the last minute; the bayonet brushing the side of his thigh, he plunged the blade of his commando knife into the German's body, whose momentum carried him another couple of steps before he fell to the ground.

Gradually, the defenders' determination and confidence forced the enemy to retreat amidst the taunts and jeers from the men with the Pegasus badge.

\*

The following days were a round of continuous fighting and patrols. The insidious stench of dead men, horses and cattle hung in the air. Leaves and branches of trees littered the area; brought down by mortar fire.

Manny received orders to report to Major Briggs at Battalion HQ.

Major Briggs, his black hair above the bandage around his head matted with dried blood, returned Manny's salute.

'Sergeant, I'm promoting you to Second Lieutenant.'

'What?' Manny was stunned.

Briggs gestured for Manny to come forward, stepping towards a map on a fold-up table.

'We've taken heavy casualties, especially officers. Your CO, Captain Fry, had been injured and evacuated to the hospital ship. He recommended you for the promotion.'

'But, sir, I … Sergeant Smithers was senior to me, as is Sergeant Bracken.'

'Bracken was killed on patrol this morning, and Smithers wounded. I want you to take charge of what's left of their sections.' The major's brown eyes softened as they looked into Manny's. 'Reinforcements should arrive today, if not by tomorrow morning at the latest. In the meantime…' He left the rest unsaid.

Manny nodded. 'I'll do my best, sir.' He saluted.

Briggs didn't return the salute. 'You'd better have these.'

In the palm of his hand were second lieutenant's pips. Manny took them from him. 'Thank you, sir.' Briggs nodded and without another word walked over to a signals corporal sitting by a radio. Manny turned and left.

\*

Manny's promotion was, as expected greeted with friendly banter from his men. He promoted David, Isaac, a corporal

Jones from Smithers's section, and Mackintosh from Bracken's section to sergeant. Within minutes of taking command, they were attacked once again, but were able to repel the enemy.

Searching the Waffen-SS soldier's pockets, they found orders from Hitler that no British parachutist or commando was to be taken alive.

There was little respite for Manny or his men, who fought courageously, sometimes bordering on madness, as the Germans attacked again, pouring men into the forest.

By evening, the attack had once again failed, and as usual, as soon as the enemy retreated, mortar and artillery shells rained down on the ridge in a continuous sound of explosions, whistling metal, and the cries of wounded men; the stench of burning trees adding to that of cordite and smoke that drifted across the battlefield. The barrage stopped and Manny yelled, 'Here they come again.'

This time, by sheer weight of numbers, the Germans got the upper hand. Manny requested some reserves, otherwise they were going to be overrun. Major Briggs sent the reinforcements requested, and bit by bit, they pushed back the Germans with heavy losses to the Paras who, this time, had taken an awful beating.

Manny knelt beside Saul, pressing a field dressing against his stomach, trying to stem the flow of blood, while Moshe gave him a morphine injection.

'Saul's face was ashen. He gripped Manny's arm. 'Manny, please say a prayer for me, I'm all that's left of my family.'

Manny nodded, looking at Moshe, who turned his head away, tears in his eyes. Saul let out a long sigh, and was gone. They carried him to the aid station, but not before the men said a prayer for their dead comrade.

Manny and his men were relieved by troops who had landed on the beach. After two days' rest they were once again on the move, as the Allies advanced towards Falaise.

The countryside was a scene of utter desolation, with trees uprooted, bodies and carcases of animals everywhere; some roads impassable.

The advance was slow through the narrow lanes and high-banked hedgerows, the Germans fighting for every inch of ground.

# Chapter 2

A FTER bitter fighting with heavy losses on both sides, Caen, the hub of twelve major roads, fell to the Allies, but there was still heavy resistance by German Panzer divisions and armoured battalions; a breakthrough by British and Canadian forces south-east of Caen left the road to Paris open.

Manny, face black with dust and grime, uniform torn, sat with his back to a wall, weapon leaning against his shoulder, hungrily spooning hot stew into his mouth.

He looked around at all that was left of his men, all carrying wounds of some kind, and gave a slight smile, remembering the conversation they had with Major Briggs who wanted to send them to the rear for a rest. However, disregarding Briggs's rank, they had ganged up on him, demanding to carry on the fight.

Calling them mad, Briggs reluctantly let them do as they demanded, saying to Manny, 'Who am I to stop you, but you must have three days' complete rest.' They had given into this order, but that was a week ago.

Manny looked up, tossing the can to one side as a corporal approached and saluted. Manny nonchalantly returned it.

'Beg pardon, sir, but Major Briggs asked if you could see him right away.'

The major looked up from the paper in front of him as Manny entered the tent, stood to attention and saluted.

'Stand at ease.' The major leaned back in his chair placing his fingertips together. 'How many men are left of your original platoon?'

Manny looked at Briggs, a puzzled expression on his face, wondering why the question. 'I have twelve, including me. Fourteen killed, four badly wounded, sir.' Manny took a pace forward, 'Excuse me, sir, was there a prob—'

Briggs held up a hand. 'No problem at all, except…' He slapped the paper in front of him with the back of his hand. 'I've received orders to send you and your men back to England.'

'Why? We want to stay here and fight.'

'Yes, I know all that, and if truth be known I'd prefer you to stay. You're a good officer and the men, not only from your platoon but the whole company, respect you, but this order comes from way on high, and is immediate. Get your men ready to move out. Don't say anything to anyone. If asked, just say you're going to the rear for a rest. Good luck.' Briggs stood up and held out his hand.

Manny took the offered hand. 'Thank you, sir, and good luck to you.' He let go the hand, stepped back, stood to attention and saluted.

*

A light shone into the interior of the lorry, and a voice yelled. 'Everyone out, wakey, wakey!'

Manny was instantly alert. Covering his eyes from the glare of the torch with an open hand, he yelled back, 'Put the bloody torch out, you idiot.'

The light was immediately extinguished. Manny jumped down to the ground, eyes quickly adjusting to the darkness after the glare of the torch. A sergeant major, two armed soldiers either side of him, stood to attention and saluted.

Manny returned the salute. 'Sergeant Major, point those weapons somewhere else, otherwise you'll find them up your backside,' he ordered angrily, adding harshly, 'What's going on here?'

Someone moved out of the shadows. 'Calm down Manny.'

Manny gave a wry smile on seeing Bergman, 'What are you up to now?' The two men hugged.

'I apologise about the reception committee, you and your men must be hungry. Line them up, leave your weapons here.'

'I'm sorry, Zach, but I'm not leaving this.' Manny held up his Russian Tommy gun. Bergman smiled knowingly. 'OK, where are Isaac and David?'

Manny gestured over his shoulder as the men jumped down from the lorry. The sergeant major marched up to them and gave a parade-ground salute. 'Shall I line them up, sir?'

Bergman looked at Manny, who nodded. 'Good idea, Sergeant Major, but take it easy, they're tired.'

The sergeant major turned sharply about and marched towards the men, coming to a halt in front of them, lifting his head back, took a deep breath and was about to yell instructions when Bergman ordered, 'Quietly please, Sergeant Major.'

'Yes sir. Everyone line up at the rear of the lorry, quickly now.'

The men obeyed the instructions as Bergman strolled over to stand in front of them, looked along the line, a big grin on his face when spotting Isaac and David. He walked over to greet them.

'What scheme have you planned now?' David asked.

Bergman laughed. 'Me? Planning something? Don't be silly. I'll see you both later.' He walked back to Manny.

'Why do we need guards?'

Bergman brushed the question aside. 'The sergeant major will take you over to the mess. Have a meal, shower and get a good night's sleep. We'll get together in the morning. There are some old friends here who are dying to meet you.' He patted Manny on the shoulder, turned and walked away saying, 'See you in the morning, goodnight.'

Bergman was right. He and his men were tired. They hadn't slept, except for catnaps, since leaving Normandy. They thought themselves lucky to have flown back to England, instead of crossing the channel by boat.

*

Later, after a light meal, Manny leaned slightly forward, arms outstretched, hands on the wall of the shower, letting the water cascade over his body. Turning off the shower, he reached for the towel, draped it around his waist and walking into the barracks he stopped for a moment to look along the line of beds. For the first time in days he smiled at the harmony of snores coming from his exhausted men. Letting out a sigh, he lay on the bed, knowing that if Bergman thought it urgent, they would now be at a briefing. His eyes closed and he fell into an exhausted dreamless sleep.

Someone shook Manny's shoulder. He opened his eyes to see the sergeant major from the night before bending over him. The sergeant major straightened up, stood to attention and saluted.

'Excuse me for waking you, sir, Major Bergman would like you and the two sergeants to join him for breakfast. He's left it to you to wake your men and send them over to the mess. The major also apologised about your uniforms, but he'll explain everything when you meet him.' The sergeant major looked at his watch. 'Shall we say in an hour, sir? The private outside will take you to the major when you're ready.'

Manny pulled back the covers, swung his feet onto the floor, glanced at the chair beside his bed; his uniform had become a set of fatigues. Wondering what Bergman was playing at, he said, 'Tell the major I'll be there as soon as I can.'

The sergeant major saluted and marched out of the barrack.

*

An hour later, Manny, Isaac and David, not too surprised, were being greeted by Bergman, Sam, Sarah, Mr White and

Mr Amber. Sarah kissed him on both cheeks, seemingly fully recovered from her ordeal. He turned to Bergman. 'OK, what's this all about?'

'I'm hungry, let's eat. How would you like your eggs?'

'Here am I dressed for cleaning latrines, and you want to know how I like my eggs? You're crazy; poached please.'

'How was it over there?' Mr Amber asked.

'Bloody, but we'll win.'

There was silence between them as two waiters served their breakfast. As he ate Manny looked at the people sitting around the table, but no one made eye contact with him. Fed up with the forced silence, he leaned back in the chair, placed the knife and fork on the side of the plate, the poached eggs half-eaten, and said, 'Anyone, by the look on your faces, would think someone had just died. Was there something you're not telling us, or do I have to read your minds to find out what it is?'

'Do we get twenty questions?' Isaac joined in a slight smile on his face wiping his mouth with a napkin.

'We want you to enjoy your breakfast before, ahem, before we ... well.' Mr Amber ran his fingers through his mop of hair, looking towards the others for help.

'What's this, a breakfast for condemned men?' David asked.

'We have another situation,' Bergman came to Mr Amber's rescue. 'Well, not a situation as such, but something you and your men are suited for. Secrecy is the word, that's why there are guards around this particular facility.'

'Zach, stop beating around the bush, it isn't like you. Just tell us why you dragged us from Normandy.'

'OK, if you insist, but eat your eggs; they're getting cold.'

Manny nodded, and continued eating.

Bergman took a sip of tea, and then said, 'On July 20th an attempt was made by General Von Schweck and his associates to assassinate Hitler. Unfortunately the attempt failed. Hitler was lucky, and as we speak the Gestapo are rounding up those who they know and think were in on the plot, including General Schweck.'

'Where do we come into this?' Manny leaned forward in the chair, fork poised in mid-air, pointing the knife at him. 'You're not thinking that we should—'

Bergman laughed, 'Assassinate Hitler? No, of course not, and, no, we're not going to try and rescue the General. He's already been tried, convicted, and shot.' Bergman's voice warmed. 'Finish your breakfast, then we'll go over to the ops room and I'll explain what we had in mind.'

The ops room was quiet, except for the slight humming of generators. A table with a tarpaulin over it took up half the floor space.

Manny, Isaac and David followed Bergman to the far end of the room where there were three rows of cinema seats in front of a stage. A map of Europe covered the back wall, with different coloured pins here and there.

Bergman gestured for them to sit and then walked onto the stage, with Sam following behind.

Bergman looked down at Manny who sat between Isaac and David. 'Five of Hitler's Army, SS Generals and Gestapo officers, will, in five days' time, be in the City of Regensburg, Bavaria. These men have ordered, and participated in, despicable acts against ours and allied servicemen, including Jews and the civilian population of the countries they've occupied.'

Sam stepped forward. 'At the moment we've a toehold in Europe, but the tide of the battle could turn at any moment. We've received information that these men are planning something that would defeat the Allies with heavy loss of life; what the plans are we don't know as the informant was killed before he could tell us.'

Sam took a cigarette case from his pocket holding it out to Bergman. 'Whatever it is, we are told, could change the course of the war.' He extracted a cigarette and lit it, letting the smoke trickle through his nostrils as Bergman took the offered cigarette from Sam, saying gravely, 'The men at Regensburg are some of Hitler's staunchest followers and would stop at nothing to win the war.'

'Where do I and my men come into this?' Manny asked.

'We need to stop these men from completing their plans, whatever they may be,' replied Bergman.

Manny leaned back in his seat and clasped his hands behind his neck, looking up at Bergman and Sam. 'And the plan is?'

'The plan is for us go in and kill them,' Bergman replied in a matter-of-fact tone.

'By us, you mean the five of us?'

Sam gave a glimpse of a smile, replying, 'Zach, me, you, and your men, but – and this is a big but – you'll have to volunteer for this job, because if any of us were captured – well, I leave the rest to your imagination.'

'I will tell you now—' Manny wagged a finger towards the stage '—and you of all people should know this; I and my men would jump at the chance of hitting the Nazis in their own backyard, but we're exhausted.' He stood and walked toward the stage staring at the map, then at Sam. 'I suppose you have a plan for this operation?'

Sam nodded in reply.

Manny turned to look at Isaac and David, both slumped into their seats, dark rings under their eyes from lack of sleep, and could feel the tiredness welling over him too. Turning back to Sam, he gestured towards David and Isaac. 'Can you give us a few days? My men and I need to relax, and sleep.'

'No problem, I'll get a couple of films in—'

'And some decent food,' Mr Amber chimed in.

For three days Manny and his men did nothing but eat, sleep and relax. By the fourth day, they were ready to fight once more.

Manny and his men walked into the operations room where Sam and Bergman explained their plan for Regensburg.

# Chapter 3

MEYER Zylberger, an architect from Berlin, had a faraway look as he described to the men about Regensburg. 'The city was on the banks of the River Danube. It surpasses many German cities with outstanding buildings,' he said passionately 'Most of its architecture dated from the thirteenth and sixteenth centuries and it's also famous for its Regensburger sausages, eaten with sweet mustard and sauerkraut.' He smiled. 'No good if you're kosher.'

He sighed, like a man talking about his lover. 'The Architecture of St Emmeram Romanesque Benedictine Monastery, where the Gestapo Officers and Generals were staying, was smothered with an exuberant decorative scheme by the aristocratic Thurn and Taxis family, who converted it into a luxurious residence. This family owned land in the Bavarian forest and the largest brewery in Bavaria, known locally as Death and Devil.

'The best view of the city's medieval skyline is from the twelfth-century Stone Bridge. When the bridge was built, it was the only safe and fortified crossing across the length of the Danube, turning the city into an international trade centre.'

Meyer extracted a cigarette from a packet; the men waiting patiently for him as he lit it, letting the smoke trickle from his lips as he continued, 'Legend had it, that the builder made a pact with the devil. If he helped him build the bridge, the builder would give the devil the first soul that crossed the finished bridge.' Meyer smiled. 'The builder tricked the devil, as the first living thing sent across the bridge was a donkey.'

Everyone burst into laughter at the story.

The lorry came to a stop. Bergman banged on the side yelling, 'Everyone out!'

The men found themselves in a darkened hanger with a black-painted Dakota transport in the middle of it.

Manny walked along the line of men, checking their equipment. Satisfied everything was OK, he said, 'Let's go.' The heavily laden men entered the belly of the aircraft.

\*

Bergman sat straight-backed in the rear seat of an open-topped Mercedes staff car. The silver threads on his shoulder tabs identified his rank as an SS-colonel. Around his throat hung the black and red ribbon of the Knight's Cross with silver oak leaves. Sewn on the chest of the tunic were ribbons of honour. On the cuff of the left arm that rested on his knee was the black Das Reich title. The silver Death's Head Totenkop, above the peak of his cap, caught the morning light. Next to him was Sam, an SS-major. Manny, with the insignia of an SS-captain on his epaulettes, was in the front seat beside Isaac, an SS-corporal, who was driving.

The rest of the platoon was in two Kubelwagens, following in line behind, driven by David and Moshe, both SS-sergeants.

They parachuted in during the night with their vehicles some thirty kilometres from Regensburger, close to the Bavarian forest during a diversionary bombing raid on Munich.

The three vehicles were brought to a halt at the gates to the monastery by a heavily armed guard of the Wehrmacht. A lieutenant walked over to the car, saluted smartly, saying. 'Papers, please, sir.'

While the lieutenant inspected their papers, a man of medium height, bald head sitting on his shoulders like a bowling ball, hands thrust into the pockets of his long black leather coat, walked from behind one of the guards towards the Kubelwagens.

He stopped beside each vehicle for a moment; unblinking lizard eyes stared at the occupants in turn, and then stepped a few paces forward to the car, coming to a halt beside where Bergman sat, who ignored him, looking impassively straight ahead. The man turned to face Bergman and gave a straight-arm salute. 'Heil Hitler,' then held out his left hand.

Bergman slowly turned his head, a gleam of contempt in his eyes, looked him up and down, and then lifted his arm saying quietly, 'Heil Hitler,' ignoring the outstretched hand.

'Your papers, you didn't give them to the lieutenant.'

Bergman turned to the man once again, eyes hard, face like thunder. 'When you address me, it's with respect,' he said authoritatively, 'you say, sir, and please.' He opened the car door, stepping down to stand in front of the man, who was at least three inches shorter than Bergman, still with his hand out.

'Your papers,' the man repeated harshly, avoiding eye contact by turning to look towards the lieutenant as if for help, but he had his back to him.

Bergman slapped the hand down, snapping his fingers, 'ID.'

The man reached inside his pocket, withdrawing a card as he said, 'Gestapo.'

Bergman looked at the card with the name – Captain Heinrich Schumann – then leaned towards Schumann, looking down at the Gestapo officer, his face inches away from him. 'You ever speak to me like that again in front of my men, I'll kill you,' Bergman said coldly, prodding him in the chest with his fingers. 'And don't think for one moment I won't.' He snapped his fingers at Manny, who opened a briefcase by his feet, withdrawing some papers. Manny alighted from the car, handing them to Schumann.

Schumann took the documents, looked at the signature at the bottom and with shaking hand returned it to Bergman.

Bergman handed the papers back to Manny, looked once more into the Gestapo officer's eyes, and couldn't help the cold smile that for a fleeting moment creased his face at the fear he saw in them. Harshly, in a barbed whisper, he said, 'I've fought all over the world for my country, including the Russian front.' Bergman slapped Schumann across the face; 'Don't cross my path again.' He turned, walking the two paces to the car and slid onto the seat, looking straight ahead as if nothing has happened.

The lieutenant returned to the car, saluted and handed the papers back to Sam. 'Sorry to have kept you, sir.'

They couldn't see the look of hatred in the Gestapo officer's eyes as he rubbed his cheek with the imprint of Bergman's fingers. As they drove through the open gate onto a gravel driveway that curved in a circle in front of the monastery door, Manny laughed, saying, 'You smacked him like a little naughty boy.'

He shook his head as they came to a stop beside the right-hand wall, covered in ivy, and the smile left his face.

\*

Sam ordered the men down from their vehicles, and silently they dispersed around the building. Manny and Bergman got out of the car, entering the monastery through two open arched oak doors where they were met in a stone-walled hall by a man whom Manny estimated to be around six foot four and built like a tank, attired in striped trousers and jacket, black bow tie and starched wing-collared shirt; the bulge under the left arm of his jacket unmistakable.

'Can I help you, gentlemen?'

'I'm SS-Colonel Bergman,' he added with a gesture towards Manny, 'SS-Captain Koning. We've orders to guard the … ahem … gentlemen staying here.'

'Please wait a moment and I'll get the Lieutenant Colonel.' The tall man turned and walked away, entering a room to his right. Within seconds a lieutenant colonel of the

Wehrmacht appeared, followed by the butler and two armed soldiers.

Bergman and Sam saluted.

'Orders,' the Wehrmacht officer snapped, holding out his right hand. The butler stood off to one side, hand inside his jacket.

Manny, took an instant dislike to the arrogance of the German as he opened the briefcase, handing the papers to Bergman, who stared straight into the lieutenant colonel's eyes as he presented them to him.

The Wehrmacht officer didn't look at the signature at the bottom, but moved slightly away from them, holding the paper up to the light coming through window, nodded, and moved back to Bergman saying quietly, 'Who's the Commander of Das Reich Division for Operation Spring Awakening?'

'SS-Lieutenant General Werner Ostendoff,' was the quick reply.

'Who's Otto Baum?'

Bergman smiled, and was about to answer when the lieutenant colonel pointed at Manny. 'You.'

Manny's facial expression did not change, confident of his answer. Bergman and Sam insisted they should know everything about the SS-Divisions and their commanding officers for just such an eventuality as this. Looking straight ahead, Manny replied without hesitation, 'Otto Baum was born 1911, served in Poland, France and Russia, where he was battalion commander of an infantry regiment. He won the Knight's Cross and was badly wounded earning the Oak leaves. He was in command of the Das Reich division a month ago.'

The lieutenant colonel smiled, handing back the paper with his left hand, holding out his right. Bergman took it. The Wehrmacht officer clicked his heels. 'Ernst Von Krüger.'

Bergman smiled back. 'Zachary Bergman.'

'That's a Jew—'

'Name – so I've been told on many occasions. If I were, would I be wearing this uniform?' He pointed to his medals and Knight's Cross. 'Or these?'

Krüger bursts out laughing. 'I suppose not.'

'My men and I are at your disposal.'

Krüger's face showed his displeasure at them being there, as did his voice. 'I don't see why you're here. I've more than enough men to guard the generals.'

'We're what you might call bodyguards, sir,' Manny said.

'Personal bodyguards, if you get our meaning,' Bergman added.

'OK, follow me.' They followed the lieutenant colonel into a prayer hall with ancient wall paintings. Bergman stopped to admire them, noticing the two guards in a gallery above.

Krüger turned. 'Beautiful, aren't they?' Bergman nodded, and walked on, following the officer with Manny mentally noting everything as he trailed behind them.

*

They entered a lounge with comfortable leather armchairs and sofa. Kruger came to an abrupt halt, clicking his heels to attention.

'Excuse me, Herr Field-Marshal Voch, General Von Schreiber. I'm showing these SS officers around. They're to be your personal bodyguards; orders from SS-Field-Marshall Baum.'

Bergman and Manny moved either side of Krüger, and saluted. Both generals, who had been in deep conversation before Krüger interrupted them, sat back, nodded and waved their hands as if dismissing them.

Krüger's face turned red at being dismissed in this way. He saluted and exited the lounge with Bergman and Manny following. They crossed the hall to a room opposite.

'This is the Officers' Dining Room. You and your officers may join us for dinner this evening, 1930 hrs. Your men can eat with the rest of the guards in the mess on the other side of the courtyard.'

'Thank you, sir.' Bergman bowed slightly.

Krüger continued to show them around the rest of the monastery and its luxurious rooms.

'Herr Krüger, we understand from my commandant that there are five generals here and two Gestapo officers. Is this correct?' Manny asked.

'That's right, plus the General's aides, making twelve in all. The Gestapo officers have their own men around the monastery and in the city.'

'Is there any chance of meeting the person in charge of Gestapo security so we could coordinate our protection?' Bergman asked.

'You met him on the way in.'

'Schumann?'

'So you've met that arrogant piece of – well, let's say he couldn't secure a dog on a leash,' Krüger commented bitterly.

'Yes, we've met him. I must say that on first sight I agree with you, Herr Von Kruger,' Bergman stated.

Manny said to Bergman, 'If you don't mind, sir, I'll get the men settled, and then I'll have a look around the area.'

'Good idea, send Brek back here.'

Manny saluted, marching smartly away. His pace back to the courtyard was slow, as he noted the guards' positions. Suddenly coming to halt by a door with a notice in bold letters, FORBIDDEN, he quickly looked around and tried the handle. It was locked.

With his body close to the door, he took a small knife from his pocket, opening the blade. Glancing quickly around, making sure no one was close by, he inserted the blade into the lock. There was a click, one more glance around, he opened the door just sufficiently for him to move quickly through, closing it silently behind him.

Manny stood with his back to the door taking a lighter from his pocket and in the light of the flame spotted some steps going downward. On the wall to his right was a piece of cord and he pulled it. A naked lightbulb lit up the cellar and he descended the stairs, stopping with one foot on the bottom step, the other on the floor, letting out a silent whistle on seeing what looked like metal oil barrels stacked against the walls.

He walked slowly over to them, eyes widening, stepping back in alarm. 'Oh! My God,' he whispered on seeing the skull and crossbones stencilled on them; other symbols and words had been painted over. He was sure it was poison gas or some other toxic chemical, and was in no doubt as to how it was going to be used.

Manny walked quietly up the stairs, switched off the light, opening the door just enough to look around, all clear. Grim-faced, he closed the door, hearing the lock click into place and walked away, knowing he must tell Bergman, but there were other matters to be dealt with first.

*

He didn't say anything to Sam as they once again went over the plan they'd practised for two days in a mock-up of the monastery back in England. All the men wore dogtags with their own names on them, as they wanted the Germans to know who they were if killed; capture wasn't an option.

For show the cousins saluted each other, and then moved in separate directions.

Manny found David and Isaac waiting for him by one of the Kubelwagens. The three of them left the monastery, driving to an aircraft assembly factory on the outskirts of the town, returning just before dusk.

Manny immediately went in search of Bergman; he found him in the officers' quarters. Sitting close to Bergman, he said quietly, 'Everything is ready, but there's a new development...' He looked around to ensure they couldn't be overheard, and then told him about the cellar.

Bergman's face hardened at the news. He paced up and down the room for a few moments, head bowed in thought.

'We can't blow the place up,' Manny pointed out quietly. 'The gas, or whatever it is, would spread very quickly, and we don't know how long it would take before it dispersed and the air becomes breathable again.'

'We'll go ahead with our plan,' said Bergman. 'If we had the time, I'd block up the cellar door, but we haven't. Let's worry about it later. Although it's important, we can't be distracted from our plans; otherwise we could jeopardise the whole operation.'

*

That evening, Manny, Bergman and Sam dined with the generals and Gestapo officers. Schumann sat next to Manny, trying to draw him into a conversation, but he ignored the Gestapo officer.

The main course has just been served when Isaac entered the dining room. He marched over to Bergman, saluted, bending slightly and whispering in his ear.

'All the guards and kitchen staff have been taken care of, except those outside the gate. David's in the gallery above if you need him. Do you want me to stay here?'

'No. Check that none of the staff are missing, and then get the men ready to move out.'

Isaac stepped back, saluted once again and left the room.

Schumann leaned towards Manny, who was sitting next to him. 'I wonder what that's all about,' he whispered in a suspicious voice.

'He's reporting that all's OK and going to plan,' Manny responded, not looking at Schumann but at Bergman, who undid the top button on his tunic; the signal that all was ready.

Manny's right hand moved inside his jacket, grasping the butt of a pistol with a silencer attached, tucked inside the waistband of his trousers. He looked across at Bergman, then Sam. Both nodded. Manny counted to five, threw the napkin onto the table and got to his feet, at the same time pulling the pistol from the waistband. Each of them had pre-arranged targets, and their aim was lethal. Within seconds all the men at the table were dead. Schumann, a look of astonishment on his face, uttered, 'What the...' before he died.

While Bergman stood guard, Manny and Sam walked around the table, making sure that no one was playing possum. Satisfied, the two men returned to Bergman, who looked up at David in the gallery, waved him away, and they left the dining room.

*

Earlier, Manny and Bergman had told Sam about the barrels of chemicals in the cellar. After a lengthy discussion they decided to leave them where they were, hoping that the only people that knew what they were and where they were going to be used were now lying dead in the dining room.

They passed various members of staff in different postures of death, including the butler propped up against the wall, and joined their waiting men. So far, everything had gone to plan.

Manny gestured for the men to board the Kublawagons and within minutes the three vehicles moved towards the gates where two Paras were waiting to open them. The dead Wehrmacht guards lay propped up against the wall.

In a line, they drove through the open gates, the last vehicle stopping to pick up the two men who closed the gates. The three vehicles sped from the monastery, passing tanks and armoured vehicles, their crews standing by the roadside, or sitting in their vehicles, unaware that the people they were guarding were dead.

Isaac pulled up by the aircraft assembly factory. Manny stepped from the car, walked to a small bush where they had hidden a detonator, its wires snaking through the undergrowth and under a barbed-wire fence to explosives placed around the walls. Manny pushed down the plunger and then walked quickly back to the car, slid onto the seat beside Isaac saying, 'OK, let's go,' just as the building blew up.

Now fitted with front-mounted machine guns, Isaac and the other drivers pushed their vehicles as hard as they could along the unlit country lanes that ran beside the River Danube. At the same time the men changed their German uniforms for camouflaged Para smocks, replacing helmets with the coveted red berets. Bergman and Sam put on their green commando berets.

They turned right at Platting with the river Isar, a tributary of the Danube, on their left, their objective the fighter base at Dingolfing.

So far Sam's plan had gone like clockwork. Isaac pulled the car into a lane two hundred yards from the air base, and while he and the other drivers changed into British uniforms, Manny, Bergman and Moshe, faces blackened, left the others to reconnoitre ahead.

They climbed the overgrown perimeter wall into the base, moving silently towards the entrance.

On the left, just before a one-bar barrier where two guards stood smoking and talking in low tones, was a guardhouse. Bergman tapped Manny on the shoulder, pointing to it.

Manny nodded, looked at the guards still with their backs to him and ran silently across the road, moving to a window at the side of the guardhouse and looked in.

A smoky haze drifted around the room where two privates and a sergeant sat playing cards. The sergeant's eyes, squinting from the smoke rising up from the cigarette dangling from the corner of his mouth, laid his cards on the table a big grin on his face.

The other players displayed various emotions as he scooped the money in the centre of the table towards him. Manny watched for a second more, then moved to the edge of the guardhouse and looked across at Bergman and Moshe, showing three fingers.

Bergman pointed to himself and Moshe, and the two guards, placing a finger across his throat. Manny gave the thumbs up sign

While Bergman and Moshe crawled towards the unsuspecting guards, Manny checked the magazine of his pistol with the silencer, then peeked around the guardhouse wall in time to see Bergman and Moshe rise like ghosts from a grave behind the guards and clamp a hand over their mouth.

In a second it was all over. As they dragged the guard's bodies into the bushes, Manny entered the guardhouse, slamming the door shut with his foot. The three men turned towards the door, a look of surprise on their faces, before they could say anything, or move towards their weapons, Manny fired three times. There was a slight sigh as the bullets left the silencer; the three soldiers were dead before falling simultaneously to the floor.

Manny strode over to the table to make sure they were dead, and as a matter of interest looked at the sergeant's cards. Blue eyes widened in surprise: he'd never seen a Royal Flush before.

'At least the sergeant saw the impossible before he died,' he whispered, walking out of the guardhouse towards Bergman and Moshe. 'I'll get the others,' he said.

Leaving two men to guard the gates, the three vehicles raced past the administration blocks, bursting onto the airfield where Messerschmitt 110s and 109s stood in a line.

Two soldiers appeared from behind an ME110, trying to unsling their rifles, but they were too slow and were cut down by a stream of bullets.

David headed across to the far side of the airfield, his machine gunner firing at the line of fighter planes, setting them alight. Amongst the noise of the machine guns, mixed with that of exploding aircraft and their armaments, could be heard the wail of an alarm. A group of airmen appeared from behind the barracks, running towards them, firing their weapons. They didn't get very far as the two men in the rear of Moshe's vehicle fired back.

Having reached the end of the line, Isaac turned the car around for another pass, but there was no need: most of the aircraft were either damaged or aflame. A river of fire flowed along the tarmac from ruptured fuel tanks.

'Where are the fuel dumps?' yelled Bergman.

'They're at the back of the hangars,' Sam shouted back, as more and more Germans spilled out onto the airfield, diving for cover as they were met by a stream of bullets coming towards them.

Bergman leaned towards Isaac, shouting, 'Go round the back of the hangar; let's find the fuel dump.' Without a word, Isaac drove across the tarmac towards the far end of the hangar.

Meyer Zyleberg leapt from the rear of the Kubelwagen and threw grenades into the hangar, while his friend Yaccov Rubinfeld fired the machine gun at the soldiers now entering the area.

Seeing Isaac heading towards the end of the hangars, Moshe yelled at Meyer to get back in the vehicle and put his foot down, following Isaac.

David, having destroyed three aircraft and a refuelling tanker at the far end of the field, turned his vehicle around to see what other damage they could cause. He saw the others, and headed in their direction.

The three vehicles raced around the hangar to be met by intense fire. Manny, his face set in concentration, returned fire, silencing the enemy, but two of his men were hit.

'There it is,' Sam yelled, pointing.

Isaac had also seen it.

'Make one pass,' Manny yelled, tossing two grenades in quick succession as they passed. Above the noise of gunfire and exploding ammunition, Manny yelled at Isaac, 'Let's get out of here.'

\*

Petrol gushed from severed fuel lines, sending flames leaping into the sky, adding to the black pall of smoke from the burning aeroplanes and the chaos they had caused.

They hadn't escaped unscathed. Two of David's men, Rosenberg and Fieldelberger, were dead, another wounded. Moshe had a shoulder wound, but ignored the pain as he followed Isaac. Meyer was hit and fell out of the Kubelwagen. Moshe started to brake, but Meyer waved him on, firing at the soldiers and airman running from the hangars, until he was unable to fire any more, slumping to the ground, blood flowing from a multitude of wounds.

Bergman was also hit, blood oozing from a thigh wound. Sam turned to help, but Bergman pushed him away.

A bullet grazed Manny's forehead just below the beret. They sped past buildings with the enemy hanging out of windows firing down at them. How their vehicles never sustain any fatal damage as they ran that gauntlet was a miracle.

They approached the barrier, which was now open. The two men left by the gates gave covering fire, and then leapt onto David's vehicle as he slowed down to pick them up.

Smoke mixed with red flame spiralled into the darkness as they sped towards their next objective, a communications centre at Mühldorf am Inn. With ten miles to go before reaching it, they pulled into a field to tend to their wounds, have something to eat, drink and refuel the vehicles. Some sat smoking, just wanting to be with their own thoughts, while others talked quietly about nothing in particular, just relieving the tension of battle.

Manny, a plaster covering the graze on his forehead, walked from man to man, saying a few words to each, ensuring they were OK. The men were happy wearing their own uniforms and red beret. The Germans would soon know who they were, especially when they saw Meyer's dogtags.

Manny looked across at Bergman and winked. Bergman smiled back at him, adjusting his green beret, while Rothman, their medic, dressed his wound.

Fifteen minutes later, having made sure everyone was ready, Manny ordered, 'Climb aboard.'

They crashed through the barrier of the communications complex, killing the guards and firing at anything that moved, coming to a stop at the entrance to the underground communications rooms.

Moshe and his group stood guard while Isaac and his men lay charges on the radio masts and aerials.

In the meantime, Manny, Bergman and Sam fought their way into the underground control centre, but the battle didn't last long. They destroyed equipment, while Manny placed codebooks and any other documents he thought important into a backpack. Sam and Bergman lay charges with a ten-minute delay and they left the building.

Thirty minutes after entering the complex, the three vehicles raced towards the next objective, a transport depot at Rosenheim, as the explosive charges went off.

*

It was just after 0120 hrs when they arrived on the edge of the depot. Trucks, tanks, and armoured personal carriers stood in lines, waiting to be delivered to troops.

For the next twenty minutes they reconnoitred the area to ascertain where the sentries were posted.

The men, each carrying a small backpack filled with explosives, paired off, melting into the darkness. Once they had taken care of the sentries, they moved along the line of vehicles, placing explosive charges, set to give them enough time to get back to their vehicles and drive away.

They had nearly finished their task when a siren wailed, and the compound was ablaze with light. Someone must have discovered one of the dead sentries.

Manny and his men fired at the lights, and once again the compound was in darkness, but not before they were fired upon.

Having laid his charges, Manny headed towards the exit, at the same time blowing a whistle. It was a signal for the men to return to their vehicles.

A German soldier ran around the corner; Manny fired from the hip, running past the dying man without slackening pace or giving him another look.

Moshe, with Rubinfeld draped across his shoulders, fired his weapon one-handed as he ran towards the gates.

David and Isaac joined Manny, and the three of them walked backwards, giving Moshe covering fire. There were similar battles around the compound as the Paras tried to extract themselves from the scene.

Manny hurled a grenade over the barbed-wire fence towards an oil tanker. It exploded under it, spilling a flame of oil that spread along the line of vehicles.

Reaching their hidden vehicles, Manny found Bergman and Sam with two of his men. Moshe knelt, laying Rubinfeld on the ground, ripped open a sterile pack with his teeth while pulling open Rubinfeld's shirt with his other hand, pressing the pack down onto the wounded man's chest, trying to stop the flow of blood pulsating from a gaping hole, but the wound was too severe and Rubinfeld had already lost a lot of blood. Manny knelt beside Moshe and gently touched his shoulder. Rubinfeld smiled at Moshe and then at Manny, his face now a pale, pasty colour. 'Thanks.'

'For what?' Manny asked.

'Revenge,' he replied huskily. 'You gave me the chance to pay them back for what they did to my family. Now I am content.' He let out a sigh and was gone.

They would have buried Rubinfeld, but there was no time as soldiers moved out of the depot towards them. The wailing of the siren had stopped.

Two tanks lumber out of the compound towards them. Saying a quick prayer for the dead, Manny yelled, 'Mount up.'

'Where's Jakowitz?' Isaac yelled above the noise of firing as the Germans advance. He moved behind the steering-wheel of the car and started the engine.

'He was killed as we came through the gates,' Sam answered, jumping on board and reloading his machine pistol.

There was a screech of tyres as Isaac pulled away, just as one of the tanks fires a round. The shell fell harmlessly behind them, hitting a tree that slowly crashed to the ground. They sped around a bend hidden by a hill as another shell crashed close by, splattering the vehicles with earth.

Two armoured cars appeared. Sam yelled at Isaac to put his foot down, while at the same time waving the others onward. A shell from one of the armoured cars landed at the side of Moshe's Kubelwagen.

Joshua Rothman, in the back of the vehicle, steadied himself against the seat, placing a Piat anti-tank weapon to his shoulder. His friend, David Koning, loaded as Moshe zigzagged along the road.

'Keep it steady for a moment,' Rothman yelled. Bracing himself against the seat, he took aim and pulled the trigger. The lead armoured car erupted in flames. Koning gave a yell of triumph, as the following armoured car crashed into the first.

As they raced onward, Sam looked at his watch; 0250 hrs. His lips forming a straight line; they might just make it. 'Isaac, pull in,' he ordered. The others stopped behind them and the men get out of the vehicles. 'Gather around,' Sam said.

Manny counted the men, and then looked quickly towards the vehicles to see if some were having a pee. He couldn't believe it – there were only eight of them left.

'We've two hours to get to the rendezvous. I suggest we refuel and leave the car behind.'

Bergman nodded. 'Good idea.'

Refuelled, and having destroyed the engine of the staff car, the group continued onward, turning left at Penzburg, heading for the combined skiing resort towns of Garmisch-Partenkirchen.

\*

The huge ski stadium, with its two ski-jumps and a slalom course built for the 1936 Olympics, could be seen miles away, standing on the outskirts of the town. Because of the location, it made this the best ski gateway to southern Germany and access to Germany's highest mountain, the Zugspitze.

They moved apprehensively through the combined towns, guns ready for action, and not taking any chances, removing their berets. Manny was sure that, like him, everyone was alert, although tired. He held his breath as tension mounted, expecting at any second to hear a shout of recognition, or someone firing at them. Then they were through and heading towards the Austrian border. Manny smiled, letting out a sigh of relief, but it was short lived as Isaac braked hard to a stop.

Ahead of them, the border barrier was guarded. Manny looked through his binoculars, letting out a groan of resignation; these were elite ski troops.

So far they had survived on adrenalin and the intensity and excitement of the last few hours, which gradually changed to one of: what next? Manny jaw tightened, lips set in a determined line, looking at the others as David moved his vehicle alongside Isaac's. As if by mutual agreement they gunned the engines and raced side by side towards the border with Manny and Moshe firing at the ski troops, who fired back.

The two vehicles smashed through the barrier, intense fire from the ski troops following them. Moshe was killed; both Rothman and Koning badly hit. David had a bullet lodged in his left leg but kept his right foot down on the accelerator, then let out a gasp of pain as he was hit once again, the bullet passing through his shoulder.

Manny was also hit, the bullet breaking a bone in his left arm. Somehow he reloaded his Russian Tommy gun one-handed and continued firing. He had been lucky again; blood trickled down the side of his face where a bullet grazed his forehead, knocking off his beret and leaving a long, open wound.

Sam's guns jammed; up to now he had led a charmed life, but was hit twice, not seriously, gritting his teeth as the road twisted around the mountain like a snake. Isaac, his face a grimace of pain, had a cracked collarbone. Every turn of the wheel was agony, but he was determined to continue driving.

Sam glanced at his watch. Fifteen minutes to the rendezvous. He looked up. In the East the night sky was welcoming in another new day.

Suddenly an armoured half-track appeared in front of them. Bullets whizzing past, some pinging off the vehicles as David, who had followed Isaac along the winding road, brought his vehicle beside them.

'We're running out of time,' David yelled over the noise of the diesel engines.

'Someone must have radioed ahead,' said Manny, blood running down the side of his face, looking across at David, blood oozing from his right shoulder. Behind him, Rothman's camouflaged smock was red; his friend Koning pulled himself one-handed up from the bottom of the Kubelwagen, giving Manny and the others a white-faced smile, yelling across, 'This was fun.'

It seemed they were all carrying wounds of one kind or another. 'Can you fire the machine gun?' Manny asked.

Rothman lifted the machine gun from the front mounting, placing it across the top of the front seat, the butt against his blooded shoulder, turning to Koning and saying something to him. His friend nodded, loading the machine gun with a spare magazine.

'One last charge and we're there,' Manny shouted across at them.

The three men nodded in agreement.

'We've come this far, I'm not going to give in now,' Manny smiled grimly, pointing ahead with his good hand yelling, 'Charge.'

The two Kubelwagens accelerated towards the enemy. Rothman's face set in a grin as he pressed the trigger, yelling, 'As someone once said, it's a good day to die.'

Intense fire from the German half-track engulfed David's vehicle. Rothman and Sam fired back. The combination of both guns cocooned the advancing German's vehicle, which suddenly turned over and over, finally crashing into the wall.

Manny looked across at David. He was slumped against the steering wheel, his vehicle swaying from side to side out of control. Rothman lay across the front seat, he couldn't see Koning.

Isaac braked, letting the other vehicle move in front of him as it came to a gradual stop.

Ignoring his injuries, Manny leapt out, running across the road calling, 'David, David.' Reaching his friend, he gently pulled him away from the steering wheel.

But David was dead; blood flowed from multiple wounds to his chest, one just above the heart. Manny moved quickly to Rothman and Koning. They were dead, too.

Sam leaned over Bergman, checking his wounds and saying hoarsely, 'Manny, we'd better get going; Zach's lost a lot of blood and is in a bad way.'

Manny nodded. 'I hate to leave David, Koning and Rothman here, but they would want the Nazi scum to know it was Jews who caused them this much trouble. I'll say a prayer for them when we get back home.'

Isaac gasped in pain as he put the vehicle into gear. He gunned the engine and they drove onward, passing through Lermos where, between some high rocks, a flat meadow unfolded in front of them. They drove into the meadow. Manny and Sam looked up, as above the sound of the Kubelwagen's engine they heard that of an aeroplane, their faces anxiously looking for it. They smiled with relief as a JU52 transport plane came in to land, running along the field, swinging around at the other end, coming to a halt, its engines idling.

Isaac, his foot hard down on the accelerator, drove towards it, braking to a halt as the fuselage door opened.

Joshua stood by the open door, a huge grin on his face. 'You called for a tax—' The smile disappeared, his hazel eyes moved across the field searching, then down at them. 'Where are the others?'

Manny shook his head, answering grimly, 'They aren't coming.'

Two men appeared behind Joshua, jumping down from the aircraft and assisting them aboard.

'We'd better get out of here before someone comes to see why the aircraft landed.' Joshua said, looking around. 'I'm going to get ready for take-off. I'll speak to you later.'

Once everyone was aboard, Joshua pushed the throttles forward and the plane raced across the field, leaving the ground and disappearing into the clouds, while two crewmen attended to their passengers' wounds.

\*

Manny, his broken arm in a sling, blond hair protruding over the bandage around his head, said 'Thanks' to the crewman as he handed him a mug of tea.

Sadness, like he hadn't felt since his parents' passing, engulfed him as pictures of the men he'd left behind flashed across his mind. For the first time since Joan's death, uncontrollable tears streamed down his blackened face.

An arm went around his shoulder. He turned and it was Sam.

'I know how you feel. Remember Rubenstein? He thanked you for giving him the chance for revenge. That's what kept you going, that's why you do what you do. Isaac told me that you once told the men you wanted revenge for what the Nazis had done to our family, and others. You asked, did they want revenge? What was their reply?'

The tears stopped flowing. 'They wanted revenge too.'

'They got it; they killed a lot of Germans, destroyed planes and fuel that would be hard to replace. The communications centre should take the Germans weeks to repair, if at all. Manny, your men had played a big part in avenging their families and friends.'

Manny nodded, 'Did you hear what Koning said?'

A smile creased Sam's sweat and blackened face. 'This was fun,' they said in unison.

'Thanks, you're right.' He looked at Sam. 'My one regret is that I couldn't bring them back with me.' His mouth formed a tight line. 'I tell you now, Sam, I'll never leave any of my men behind again, even if it kills me.'

Sam patted him on the shoulder before returning to sit beside a white-faced Bergman.

Manny wondered what Rita was doing at this moment. An expression of love slowly relieved the grim mask on his face. Yes, he loved her, that dimpled smile and infectious laugh. He sighed, yes, she was right; they must find happiness whenever they could, and this last mission had taught him that. He snuggled down into the seat, stretched out his legs and in an instant was asleep.

As the plane landed, ambulances followed it until it came to a stop. Medics helped the four wounded men from the plane into the ambulances and whisked them off to hospital.

*

In November for the first time in five years, the lights went on in Piccadilly and a frustrated Manny waited impatiently for his wounds to heal, so he could get back into the action. The radio and newspapers headlines were filled with the German's offensive in the forests of the Ardennes.

The monastery at Regensburger, because of Manny's discovery, was quickly captured and the barrels of chemicals disposed of safely.

To get back to full fitness, the sergeant major they'd met before their last mission had been assigned their fitness instructor. His name was Ironsides and it suited him. Whatever he ordered them to do, he would do himself, but quicker, and beat them in running and other exercises, which included unarmed combat. They were up at five o'clock every morning for callisthenics, followed by a run around the grounds. As the days and weeks passed, their run was extended to include full battlekit.

As his wounds healed, Manny could feel that, with the help of the sergeant major, he was now fitter and stronger than ever before. The last week of their training was at the Paras' assault course.

# Chapter 4

*31 December 1944*

THE shrill sound of sirens echoed throughout London, but no one in Aunt Doris and Uncle Mark's house took a blind bit of notice. It was New Year's Eve and no one, not even Hitler and his rockets, was going to spoil it for them.

Everyone had chipped in with their ration cards, and Aunt Doris had also managed, as usual, to find that little extra-something to make a wonderful meal. Mr White and Mr Amber arrived with two bottles of champagne.

The carpet had been turned back. Couples danced to the music coming from the radio in the corner of the room, waiting in anticipation for midnight and a prayer for peace.

There was a loud bang as another V2 rocket exploded, but the chatter, laughter and music carried on.

The lights were out, the candles around the room flickering on the people dancing cheek-to-cheek to the tune of 'You'll Never Know'.

Manny moved his face away from Rita's; in his mind, he was singing along with the singer.

*'You'll never know just how much I love you,*
*You'll never know how just how much I care.'*

He kissed her cheek pulling her a little closer. She sensed his mood, snuggling her chin into his shoulder, body moulded into his, her hair soft against his cheek.

Someone tapped them on the shoulder. It was Mr White, with a tray of glasses.

'Champagne?'

They both nodded, taking a glass from the tray.

The music stopped and the announcer began to count down the minutes to end another year of war. As the last peal of the bell of Big Ben echoed through the radio, there was a united shout of 'Happy New Year', by everyone in the room, raising their glasses to drink the toast.

Manny took the glass from Rita, placing it on a table close by turning back to look into her emerald-green eyes, saying, 'I love you, Happy New Year.'

She smiled, that dimple smile, just managing to say, 'I love you too,' before their lips met. Sam and Sarah pulled them away from each other to wish them a Happy New Year, with a hug and kiss. Manny looked at Rita, shrugged his shoulders, as once again they were engulfed by other well-wishers.

*

By three in the morning all the guests had gone. The only people left were Manny, Rita, Sam and Sarah, who were dancing in the middle of the room.

Joshua left just after midnight, with the WAAF officer he'd brought to the party. Sarah and Rita had stayed, as they were going to share his room.

Sam whispered something to Sarah; she nodded, and they moved across to Manny and Rita.

'We're going to bed, see you in the morning,' said Sam.

'Oh, umm, OK,' Manny stuttered.

Sam took Sarah's hand and they left the room.

'It looks as though we're alone at last,' Manny said.

Rita didn't reply, just wrapped her arms around his neck, pulling his face towards hers, kissing him passionately, her hips swaying to the rhythm of the music, his body responded, sure she could feel his erection by the way she moved her pelvis hard up against him, her kisses more demanding.

Slowly taking her lips from his, she said huskily, 'Did you mean what you said before?'

'Yes, every word.'

'Turn off the music.'

*David Brown*

He did as she asked, blew out the candles returning to her side. She took his hand and they walked side by side up the stairs, entering his bedroom, standing for a moment by the closed door and kissed. Rita stepped back, looking into his eyes, slipping off her dress, pointing at Manny, who smiled understandingly and began to strip. Within seconds they were both naked.

'You are ... absolutely gorgeous,' He whispered huskily, moving slowly towards her. They kissed, a gentle, no hands, or body touching kiss.

Rita was the first to move; sliding her hands along his waist and around his back, pulling him closer till their bodies touched.

Manny slid his mouth from her lips to her throat, moving slowly downward until reaching her breast, then taking his mouth away lifted her up, carrying her to the bed lowering her gently onto it moving beside her.

'Manny,' she whispered. 'I've never done this before.'

He looked into her eyes and stroked her face. 'We don't have to do anything. We could wait, if that's what you want?'

'No, oh no, that's not what I want. I just wanted you to know, that's all.'

'I've been such a fool. I've loved you for so long but—'

She placed her fingers to his lips, stopping him from saying anything else, slipping her arm around his neck pulling him to her breast. 'Please carry on.'

He kissed her breast, moving up to her mouth, his hand caressing her body, moving slowly down to her inner thigh and gradually up. She gasped as his fingers touched the lips of her vagina, wet with desire, fingers caressing, seeking to please. Their kisses were soft and gentle, tongues adding to the pleasure they were finding from each other. He moved over her, she grasped his back, pulling him down; a moan of pleasure escaped her lips as he entered, gently and slowly, pushing deeper and deeper.

Their hands caressed each other, bodies moving slowly in a rhythm that gradually moved faster as their excitement mounted; kisses tender and loving, they were both reluctant to part, but they gradually did.

Rita lay in the crook of his arm, 'Manny, I have to tell you—'

'Is it that serious?' he interrupted her

'No, not really, it's just—'

'Sorry, but before you say anything, there's something I must do. Something I should have done and said some time ago.' He moved away, rolled off the bed, standing holding out his hand for her to take it.

'Please, sit on the edge of the bed.'

She moved across the bed, feet dangling on the floor, as he dropped to one knee, taking her hand smiling up at her.

'I've been a fool, and should have done this a long time ago. Rita Kray, I love your dimpled smile, the way you tilt your head back when you laugh. You're in my thoughts when I wake and when I go to sleep; I love you with all my heart. Will you please marry me?'

There were tears in her eyes as she nodded, for a second unable to speak, and then said, 'I love you too. There's nothing in this world I want more than to marry you.'

He moved closer. Just before their lips met he said, 'If you tell anyone I was naked when I proposed to you, I'll deny it.'

She giggled. 'Let's face it, it's a novel way to propose, it could catch on.'

They kissed, and the house shook. They both laughed, knowing it wasn't the kiss, but another of Hitler's 'V' rockets exploding.

*

They awoke in each other's arms. He kissed the tip of her nose. 'Unfortunately, my angel, we can't stay here all day, as much as I would like to. Let's have a bath and have some—' He looked at his watch, disbelief on his face. 'No, it can't be.'

'Can't be what?'

'It's nearly midday.'

She giggled. 'You have to be somewhere?'

'No.'

'OK then, let's have that bath, you can scrub my back.'

He smiled, 'Only your back?'

She didn't say anything, just touched his face and kissed him – a twinkle in her eyes.

They lay in the bath, Rita between his legs, head on his chest, he kissed her neck, one hand caressing a breast.

'Mmmm, that's nice.'

'You were going to tell me something last night. Is something worrying you?'

She leaned back, looking up at him. 'No, nothing's worrying me now.'

As they dressed Manny said, 'After we've told my family about our engagement, we must go and tell your parents.'

'I don't know where my parents are, or if they're alive or dead,' she replied softly.

He suddenly realised, with shame, that he knew nothing about Rita's family.

'What do you mean?'

'We lived in Berlin. Things were becoming so bad that my parents decided to send my brother and me to stay with my aunt and uncle in London, who came here in 1933. They rented a house in Stepney Green.'

Rita picked up her handbag, extracting a photo from it, handing it to Manny. 'This is the only photo I have of my parents, brother and myself.'

Manny stared at the photo in disbelief. He thought that the coincidence of meeting Grübber on the mountain was something you only read in novels, but this was something from a fairy tale.

Rita pointed to the man in the photo. 'This is my father, Da—'

'Daniel Krantz,' Manny said quietly, still staring at the photo, shaking his head in disbelief.

Rita looked at him, as if to say *how do you know that?*

'Your mother's name was Miriam, your name is Rivka and your brother is Wilem. Your father was a baker whose speciality was pastries.'

Her eyes widened in surprise. 'Who told you?' She caught her breath, frowning trying to recall who she'd spoken to about her parents, whispering, 'It couldn't have been Hannah, she doesn't know my parents' name, and you haven't met my brother, he'd changed his name to William and was in Palestine.'

Manny could see that she was perturbed by what he had said. He took her hand, saying quietly, 'There's nothing sinister by what I've said. Let's have some breakfast and I'll tell you all about it.'

*

They said good afternoon to Aunt Doris, Uncle Mark, Sam and Sarah who were in the lounge, playing cards. Then over tea and toast, Manny told Rita about Mauthausen and how her father helped him escape.

'But why didn't he go with you?'

'Your father felt he'd have a better chance of finding your mother if he stayed, and also by coming with me he would be a burden and jeopardise my chances of escaping. I tried to find out how he was through Joan, but she was unable to get near the place. I still can't believe this; it's bizarre, to say the least.'

Rita shook her head. 'It's *Bashert* – it's destiny. How could it be otherwise? Of all the people I could be friends with, it's your sister. Then we met and fell in love. It's like a story in a novel.'

'Daniel told me so much about you.' Manny stroked her cheek. 'Your father didn't exaggerate when he said you were beautiful.' He rose to his feet, moving across to Rita and knelt besides her taking her right hand. 'I loved your father like my own, and I'm sure that if he knew about us, he would be over the moon.'

Rita's eyes sparkled with pleasure at his words. She bent and kissed him. 'I feel happier in my heart that you met my father, and knew him the way I did.'

'I've always felt that Daniel would survive, and I'm convinced more than ever now. Come on, let's go tell the others that we're going to marry.'

'Hold on,' she smiled. 'When is this event going to take place?'

'Sorry, getting carried away. Which was a bit stupid as I've got to get permission from my CO, but more important than that, I've to ask your aunt and uncle if I can marry you in the absence of your parents. Mind you, when they see me they'll be only too pleased to get rid of you.'

Rita giggled, slapping him playfully on the shoulder. 'I'm sure that when my aunt and uncle meet you, they'll lock me in my room while they look for someone bet—' She couldn't contain herself any more, bursting into laughter. Her laugh was contagious and had Manny laughing too. The others burst into the kitchen to see what was going on.

Wiping the tears of laughter from his eyes, Manny got to his feet, moving close to Rita, placing an arm around her waist.

'I've asked Rita to marry me, and she's accepted.'

There were yells of joy, everyone hugging one other and dancing around the room. Hannah and Isaac entered to see what all the commotion was about.

'It's about time too,' his sister said, hugging both of them.

'What I want to know,' Sam asked, 'is when do you plan to get married?'

'We haven't really spoken about that yet' – Manny looked at Rita, she raised her eyebrows at him, a smile on her lips. He gave her a look as if to say, you tell them. She giggled, clasping his hand. 'We haven't actually decided on a date.'

'We don't want to wait,' Manny added, 'so it'll be as soon as possible.'

Isaac had an arm around Hannah. They looked at each other and nodded.

'After that fantastic news,' Hannah said. 'I've some more happy news to tell you. I'm pregnant.'

Aunt Doris gave a screech; hands going to her face, eyes shining with tears of happiness. Then Hannah was surrounded by the others congratulating her.

It was late afternoon when Manny and Rita took the diamond his mother had left him to Mr Spivac, who was going to make Rita's engagement ring.

\*

Two days after his proposal and the news of Hannah's pregnancy, Manny, Isaac, and Sam returned to Reading.

On arrival, Manny went to see the medical officer, requesting his discharges as medically fit for combat duty. He wanted to return to his unit to get permission from his CO to get married.

'As far as I'm concerned, you could return to your unit today,' the doctor told him. 'It isn't up to me now. I passed you and the others medically fit a couple of weeks ago.'

Manny couldn't believe what he'd heard. 'Who did you tell, sir?' he asked quietly.

'Mr White and Mr Amber, and the others,' he replied.

Manny was livid. He thanked the doctor, and went looking for the two men, assuming by 'the others' the doctor meant Bergman and probably Sam. He stopped in mid-stride, a frown knitting his forehead.

*Something's going on. They must have something up their sleeves, but what?* Ironsides had been pushing them pretty hard the last few weeks. He snapped his fingers.

*I bet it's another mission. They ought to know him by now, all they have to do is ask,* he said angrily to himself.

Manny stormed into the dining room and as expected found Mr White and Mr Amber with Bergman, who looked up as he entered. It seemed he'd interrupted a conversation.

'Ahmm, Manny, sit down and join us,' said Mr White.

'We had a wonderful time at the New Year's Eve party,' said Mr Amber. 'Please thank your aunt and uncle. I ... we ... haven't enjoyed ourselves so much for many a long year.'

Manny brushed the comments aside as he strode over to them, anger showing on his face, the words harsh between tight lips, 'Why didn't you tell me I'm medically fit for duty? What's going on here? Have you got some other mission planned? Does Isaac know about this?'

Before anyone could answer Isaac entered the room with Sam. 'What's this, an AGM?' Isaac commented light-heartedly.

'Did you know about this?' Manny demanded belligerently.

Isaac spread his hands, a puzzled look on his face, 'About what?'

'That we're medically fit for duty.'

Isaac looked at the men sitting at the dining table and then at Sam. 'Are we?'

Sam didn't look at them, moving across the room to sit beside Bergman, who had a slight smile on his lips, but stayed silent.

Mr Amber raised a bushy eyebrow. 'Ah, mmm, well.' He stroked his beard pulling at his right ear. 'We, ahm, want to congratulate you on your engagement and Isaac on his good news, but—'

Manny stepped towards Mr Amber. 'I would like to get married as soon as possible and need my CO's permission to do that, so I need to return—'

'You have our permission,' Mr White said quickly.

'What!' Manny looked at him, a surprised expression on his face, pointing a finger. 'You give me—'

'Yes,' Mr White interrupted.

'What about returning to my unit?'

'Not just yet,' Bergman joined in, not looking up from his plate, a piece of fish on the end of his fork.

Manny looked across at Sam. 'Did you know about this?'

Sam nodded, silently.

'Hey! What about me?' Isaac joined in.

'Same reply,' said Bergman.

'I'm already married' – Isaac commented cheerfully, moving closer to Bergman and the others, adding, 'OK, what's going on here?'

Bergman looked up at Manny. 'Will two weeks give you enough time to get married?'

'Yes why?'

Bergman ignored the question. 'OK, you have it. Be back here on the 24th. I'll have your passes ready in an hour. You can take Isaac with you and don't forget to send us our invitations.'

Manny knew he wasn't going to get his question answered today. He looked at Bergman and the others smiling. 'Do you mind if I have something to eat first?'

*

He couldn't sleep; hands behind his head, staring out of the bedroom window at the moon shining bright in the starlit night, going over in his mind the last ten hectic days since leaving Reading.

Sarah's parents arrived quite unexpectedly from Canada. They were told the day before the ship sailed that a berth had become available, giving them no time to notify Sarah they were coming.

With her parents now in London, Sarah persuaded Sam, without much resistance, that they should get married. With the help of Mr White and Mr Amber, they were to be married on the 21st. He sighed, thinking of his parents, and how happy they would have been to see him married. They would have loved Rita. Gradually, his eyes closed and he fell asleep smiling.

Manny stood under the canopy, looking back down the aisle as Rita walked slowly towards him on the arm of her Uncle Max. She grasped Manny's hand on reaching his side, both gazing at each other with love in their eyes.

Once again, Aunt Doris and Uncle Mark hired the Bouverie Rooms for the wedding, and with the help of some friends, who she said would remain nameless, put on a magnificent spread. Manny tried to get the information from her, saying, 'I would like to thank them personally.'

Smiling, Aunt Doris said, 'If I tell you, I'd have to kill you.'

The toastmaster smacked his gavel on the table. 'Ladies and gentlemen, your bride and bridegroom, Mr and Mrs Grenfeldt, will open the ball with the first dance.'

Manny led Rita onto the dance floor; taking her in his arms and, before the music could start, kissed her on the lips, to the cheers of the guests. The music began, the singer moving to the microphone started to sing:

*'You'll never know just how much I love you.'*

The newly-weds moved gracefully around the dance floor, their guests clapping.

'Ladies and gentlemen, please take your partners and join your bride and bridegroom on the dance floor.'

After a wonderful and unforgettable honeymoon in Scotland, Manny and Rita returned to London to help with the arrangements for Sarah and Sam's wedding.

# Chapter 5

S AM was waiting by the barrier when Manny and Isaac arrived on the last train into Reading, following him out of the station to a small truck parked in the shadows. 'Get in the back,' Sam ordered.

Manny gives him a strange look, wondering what Sam's up to now, but they do as ordered.

Once Isaac and Manny were aboard, Sam followed them in slapping the side of the truck, pulling down the tarpaulin cover as they moved off.

Manny knew better than to ask where they were going, but Isaac always felt they should be told something.

'Where are we going, Sam?' Isaac asked.

'You knew I couldn't tell you that, even if I wanted to.'

'Is it another one of those missions?'

Sam didn't reply, but had that smile of secrecy on his face.

Manny decided that it was useless, asking his cousin anything; it was a waste of breath to try. 'How's Sarah?' he asked, changing the subject.

Sam's face lit up. 'She's fine. Much happier now we're married and her parents are here. They rented a house in Stepney Green.'

'I know what you mean. Rita's the same; about being married I mean.'

Sam looked at Isaac. 'Hannah OK?'

Isaac smiled. 'Moaning about her figure, but loving all the attention Aunt Doris and Rita were giving her.'

The truck came to a stop and someone pulled up the tarpaulin. 'We're here, sir.'

'Thanks, Corporal.' Sam leapt from the vehicle, followed by Manny and Isaac, who were surprised to find they were in a dimly lit aircraft hangar, standing beside a light military aircraft.

Someone walked from behind the plane. 'Nice to see you all again,' Joshua greeted them, a smile on his face, hugging his brother and adding, 'Better get aboard. We need to be there before daybreak.'

'Where's that?' Isaac asked quickly, hoping to get Joshua off-guard.

Joshua looked in Sam's direction and shook his head.

'Sorry, no can tell.'

Within minutes they were airborne.

\*

Manny folded his arms, snuggled into his seat with a slight smile on his face and closed his eyes, an image of Rita immediately appearing in his thoughts, where they were going or what they were doing disappearing from his mind. He could still smell her perfume on his tunic. She hadn't cried when they parted, just held him close and whispered in his ear, 'I love you, and wherever you'll be, we'll be there too,' giving him a long lingering kiss.

The bump of the plane landing awakened him. He looked out of the window. Lights of the landing strip flashed by, and in the moonlight he could see – no, it couldn't be. He cupped his hands around his eyes, looking through the window and turning to his cousin. 'Where the fuck are we?'

Sam looked across at Manny, a smile on his lips, as if to say, it's for me to know and you to find out. The plane did an about-turn, coming to a stop.

Figures ran along the field, picking up portable landing lights as a lorry pulled up beside them. The fuselage door opened and a strongly accented voice ordered, 'Hurry please.'

\*

As Manny stepped from the plane, the cold hit him like a hammer, and he could now clearly see the sand piled up alongside the makeshift airstrip.

Armed men, their faces covered by *keffiyeh* headdresses climbed aboard the lorry. The man who told them to hurry grabbed Manny's arm pointing to the lorry. 'Hurry, please.'

No sooner had Manny and the others climbed aboard the lorry than it moved off. At the same time the aeroplane's engines roared and it sped along the ground, lifting into the air disappearing into the night sky.

One of the men pulled down the tarpaulin, encasing the rear of the lorry in darkness as it rocked from side on the rough road.

'It'll be a smoother ride very soon,' said Sam.

Manny, his eyes now adjusted to the dark, looked at Isaac sitting across from him, who shrugged his shoulders as if to say, 'All we can do is wait and see.'

Manny turned to look around the lorry at their companions. All he could see was their eyes above the *keffiyehs* covering their faces. Some had Sten-guns across their knees, while others held rifles, the butts resting on the floor.

He wondered where they were, looked at the luminous dial of his watch, trying to judge by the time how far they'd travelled, but knowing how devious Sam could be: they could be anywhere, even on the coast of England. Pulling up the collar of his coat, he wrapped his arms around his body trying to keep warm, looking across at Sam, who still had that silly grin of secrecy on his face. He could at least have supplied warm clothing. The lorry slowed down, almost coming to a stop, and then accelerated again.

'We'll soon be there,' Sam repeated.

'How long is soon?' Isaac asked.

The lorry ground to a halt. Manny could see Sam smiling in reply, teeth white against the darkness. One of the men lifted the tarpaulin cover and jumped to the ground.

Sam patted Manny and Isaac on the knee, gesturing for them to follow him.

*

They entered a two-storey building, walking along a short corridor. Sam opened the first door on the right walking into the room saying, 'We're here.'

Manny and Isaac followed Sam into the room. Both stood for a moment by the open door on seeing the two men sitting at a table with as usual, a plate of food in front of them.

Manny was the first to speak. 'Well, I can honestly say I'm not surprised to see you both, although I must confess I didn't expect it.'

'I second that,' Isaac agreed, standing beside Manny not realising that Sam had left.

'Would you both like something to eat?' Mr Amber asked, grey eyes twinkling with good humour.

Manny couldn't believe this was the Mr Amber he saw last week at Sam's wedding. His bushy hair was cut; beard and moustache trimmed Edwardian-style; the light-blue short-sleeved shirt was open at the neck.

Mr White stood pointing to two chairs in front of them. 'Manny, Isaac, please join us. I'm sure you're both hungry and thirsty after your long journey.'

'To put it bluntly, Mr White, what the hell is going on, and where are we?'

'Palestine,' Mr White said, nonchalantly balancing some peas onto the fork.

Manny looked at Isaac, then back at the two men in front of them. 'Say that again,' they chorused, surprise and disbelief in their voices.

'Palestine,' Mr White repeated, the fork halfway to his mouth.

Manny and Isaac, as one, moved to sit opposite them, and for a moment there was silence. It was then that Manny noticed that Sam was missing.

'Where's Sam?'

'Oh! He'll be back in a moment,' Mr Amber remarked offhandedly.

Isaac leaned back in his seat, toying with the knife in front of him. 'Well then, what has this joint got for a very hungry traveller?'

Before either of them could answer Manny remarked, 'And what have our two friends here got up their sleeves that we could offer them?'

Mr White avoided eye contact with Manny, but looked at Isaac. 'The chicken soup with matzo balls was very tasty.'

'Roast chicken, roast potatoes and vegetables, or a sandwich if you prefer,' added Mr Amber, looking at Manny, a slight smile on his lips.

'The chicken sounded nice,' said Isaac, turning to Manny. 'What about you?'

'Mmm, sounds good to me too. And maybe we'll—'

The door opened, interrupting what he was about to say. Bergman and Sam walked into the room. Manny half leapt to his feet as if to confront them but as in a game of statues, was suddenly completely still, mouth agape in surprise on seeing their uniforms.

Sam and Bergman wore British army khaki, but their shoulder flashes were blue and white with a gold Star of David in the middle. Written in an arc across the top where the sleeve met the shoulder, in Hebrew and English were the words, 'Jewish Infantry Brigade Group'. Bergman was a major and Sam a lieutenant.

'What's this all about? And why are we in Palestine?' Manny asked belligerently, angry at all the secrecy and tired from the flight.

'I thought you were the waiters bringing our chicken,' Isaac joked, a big grin on his face as he walked over to Bergman. 'Nice to see you again, Zach, how's Dominique?'

'Pregnant.'

'What – when was she – you know?'

'It seemed about the same time as Hannah.'

A bell rung in Manny's mind, suddenly wondering what Rita meant when she said, 'We'll be there, too.' No, she couldn't be. Not after such a short time. He suddenly remembered that he hadn't worn protection the first time they made love. He frowned. Come to think of it, he'd never worn protection, but...

He smiled, Rita had surprised him at the oddest moments. Like two days before he was leaving, everyone was out, except for them. He was in the kitchen reading the paper when she walked in and said, 'Will this do for dinner?' He looked at her; she was completely naked apart from an apron.

'I can recommend the breast, or if you like something more succulent, there's the thigh.'

He moved across the kitchen towards her, tasting the breast, gradually working down to the thigh, saying, 'This is nice, can I have both?' They made love there and then. At the end she said, 'Thank you.'

He jerked back to the present, thinking, *No, there isn't a*— He shook his head – no, she wouldn't have known so soon, but the word, 'We.' He shrugged his shoulders. If it was to be, so be it.

'Manny, you OK?' Sam asked.

'Yes.'

'You have a silly grin on your face.'

Manny ignored the remark turning to Mr Amber. 'Where's this food? I'm famished.'

'It'll be here in a moment.'

'Well, when it does, you can put Isaac and me in the picture and tell us who you really are.'

Manny toyed with a knife, wondering why they're in Palestine, glancing at Sam and the shoulder flash; sat upright in his chair pointing the knife towards Bergman, and was about to say something when the door opened and the food arrived.

Manny picked up his fork and with a piece of chicken on the end, placed it in his mouth, chewed for a moment, giving a slight smile, looked at Bergman, pointing the fork at him. 'You were going to tell Isaac and me why we're here?'

Bergman stared at him for a moment, pursed his lips as though he was thinking of what to say, pointing at Sam, Mr White and Mr Amber. 'We are members of the Haganah. I know you trained in Vienna with one of our groups.'

Manny nodded.

Before Bergman could continue, Mr Amber took over. 'Mr White and I are officials of the Jewish Agency.' He picked up the wineglass and took a sip. 'As you might be aware, in 1917 Britain was given control by the League of Nations of the Balfour Declaration Mandate over Palestine. Explicit documents gave Britain responsibility and power to establish a Jewish National Home.'

'Never going to happen,' commented Manny, not looking up as he shovelled a piece of chicken onto his fork.

Mr Amber gave Manny a cold stare and carried on, 'Initially Jewish immigration to Palestine met little opposition from the Arabs. The Agency bought land from them, even though they charged exorbitant prices for what was considered barren areas, and to their greed we paid them.'

Mr Amber sat back, looked at his empty plate then at the two men in front of him. 'As anti-Semitism in Europe grew, so Jewish immigration to Palestine began to markedly increase. Incitement by Muslim leaders led to violent attacks against the Jewish population.'

'What has—'

Mr White stood, holding up a hand, stopping Manny from asking any questions. 'We just want you to know these things, so you can make a decision on our proposal.'

'And that is?' Isaac asked.

'We'll come to that in due course,' Mr White replied. 'Please, may I continue?'

Manny, having finished all he could eat, sat back in his seat, folded his arms across his chest, face intent on what was being said.

'Unfortunately, or fortunately, whichever way you feel; in reply to the Arab terrorists, more militant Jewish groups like Irgun and the Stern gang were formed. They responded to Arab terrorists with their own campaign of terrorism.'

Mr White sat down, pouring water from a jug into a glass in front of him. Taking a long drink, he looked at Mr Amber, who nodded.

Manny stood, taking a few paces forward and turned suddenly. 'You still haven't—'

'Let the man finish,' Sam uttered harshly.

'We want you to understand the situation and the reason why you're here,' Bergman said. 'I know it sounds like a history lesson, but—'

'OK, OK, sorry.' Manny held up his hands in surrender.

Mr White twirled the glass in front of him between his hands. 'The killing of European Jews by the Nazis had a major effect on the situation in Palestine.'

Manny leaned forward in his chair. 'This is a bit long-winded, where's this leading to where Isaac and I are concerned? I always thought that you worked for British Intelligence.'

'Let's just say we're helping them out,' Mr White replied.

'I suppose Mr White and Mr Amber are not your real names.'

'No, you're right; our—'

Manny held up his hands. 'I don't want to know, it would only confuse me.'

'Yeah, me too,' Isaac agreed.

'I still haven't the foggiest idea what we're doing here.'

'Can I continue?' Mr White asked.

Manny looked at Isaac, who nodded.

'We at the Jewish Agency realised that once the war was over we would need a well-armed and trained fighting force able to fight a superior enemy, the Arab.' He stood wagging a finger. 'Make no mistake, once the Mandate is accepted by the world's nations, and the State of Israel becomes a fact, the Arabs, and I mean all the Arab nations, would attack us – their aim would be to throw us into the sea.'

'Again I ask: where do we fit into this plan of yours?' Manny gestured with his hands.

Isaac nodded in agreement once again, but stayed silent.

'The Jewish Agency has been trying for some time to get the British Government to agree to a Jewish fighting force. So far they had resisted us because they need Arab oil more than they need us. Pressure from allied Governments has now forced the British hand, especially with the horror of the Holocaust becoming known. In September last year, they agreed to form a Jewish Brigade within the auspices of the British Army.' He turned to Bergman. 'Zach, you can carry on from here.'

Bergman moved away from the wall he was leaning on, cheekily taking a cigarette from Manny's packet lying on the table, lit it, letting the smoke trickle through his nostrils. 'Our first recruits were mostly Palestinian Jews, with others coming from virtually every country in Europe; they don't speak English and very little Hebrew, but they all speak Yiddish, or their mother tongue. Many had already suffered tyranny under the Nazi rule and the nightmare of concentration camps, and their hatred for the Germans was intense. All they wanted to do was kill them.'

'As we do,' Manny muttered.

Bergman gave a slight smile, and continued, 'We, the Haganah, and the Agency, have our own agendas for the future, not only for the State of Israel, but the Jewish people. We realised that every man and woman in the British armed forces had received invaluable training, and in many cases combat experience. What our new recruits needed was leadership and understanding.'

Bergman pointed at Manny and Isaac. 'This is where both of you, with the number of languages you speak could be of valuable assistance. Orders had been given that the main language spoken in Jewish units would be Hebrew and we need your help in training these men who would, in the future defend our faith, and country.'

Manny pursed his lips looking across at Isaac.

'We don't speak Hebrew,' Isaac said.

'You do, but don't realise it yet,' Sam pointed out. 'We'd help you. Because of your linguistic skills you would have a head-start over the British NCOs who were frustrated with the recruits for not understanding their orders and another plus is you have combat experience.'

'We're not NCOs,' Manny pointed out, pouring himself a cup of tea.

'Ah! That's something we hadn't mentioned,' Sam remarked quickly adding. 'I'm afraid you'll have to take a demotion.'

Manny pointed at Sam and Bergman. 'You haven't done too badly, so why must we take a big drop in rank?' But he had already made up his mind, looking across at Isaac asking, 'What do you think?'

'It would give us a chance to learn Hebrew. By the way, where are we?'

'Tel Aviv,' the others chorused.

Manny rose to his feet. 'OK, when do we start, and … what rank am I?'

'Staff-Sergeant,' Sam answered.

'It will do for now.' He pointed at Sam's uniform. 'I'll need one of those.'

'What about me? Am I a staff-sergeant too?' Isaac asked.

'No,' Bergman and Sam replied in unison.

'That's not fair. I'm better looking than Manny.'

'Sergeant,' said Sam. 'That way you could stay together.'

# Chapter 6

*Italy, February 1945*

IT WAS just before Passover when Manny and his men moved up the line, taking up positions on the South bank of the Senio River in Italy. He found it ironic that the Brigade was in Italy, and that he was part of the first Jewish fighting force since the time of the Romans.

Manny and Isaac had learnt a lot where training was concerned from Staff Sergeant Ironsides, which they used to good effect in training their raw recruits. They endured the same hardships as their men in the bitterly cold and icy conditions of the Italian mountains. Not asking them to do anything they couldn't do themselves and forming a close bond with them at the same time.

They were now at the peak of fitness; lean, muscular, ready and rearing for a fight. They were like mad dogs on a leash, wanting to break free and have their revenge on the enemy opposite. It didn't worry them one bit that facing them across the river were the elite paratroopers of the Jaeger Division. Morale was sky-high.

*

Manny was pleasantly surprised when on the first night of Passover they were given matzos instead of bread and Haggadahs to recite the Exodus, as was customary at this time of the year. The Rothschild's vineyards in Palestine had sent kosher wine.

Manny and his men, with others of the Jewish Brigade, sometimes crossed the river in small-scale attacks to test the enemy's strength.

It was nearly dark as Manny and four of his German-speaking men, dressed in captured German uniforms, get ready for a patrol. Their aim was to walk about the German lines, obtaining as much information as they could of their defences and strengths.

Once across the river, they split into two groups. Manny and Schwartz, a boxer from Hamburg, walked nonchalantly through the Germans' defence emplacements. Schwartz was loudly relating to Manny about his last leave in Rome, leaving nothing to the imagination in describing his two nights with a rather buxom woman. At the same time the pair took a mental note of men, arms and unit insignia.

They were about to turn back and meet the others when they come across a lieutenant sitting with his back to a tree, smoking. Manny looked around to see if there was anyone nearby; they had the area to themselves. Manny pulled Schwartz behind a bush outlining his plan; Schwartz nodded eagerly in agreement a big smile on his face.

The two men split up converging on the lieutenant from both sides. Schwartz moved out into the open, extracting a cigarette from a pack. 'Excuse me, sir; could I have a light please?'

The lieutenant nodded, taking a lighter from his pocket. Schwartz bent, cupping his hands around the officers, distracting him as Manny crept up behind, smacking him over the head with the end of his pistol. Schwartz stopped the unconscious German falling sideways to the ground.

They stood the officer up against a tree, arranging his uniform, and then with his arms around their shoulders, carried him to their rendezvous. Anyone looking at the lieutenant with the top buttons of his tunic and shirt undone, tie awry, would think he was drunk. They joined up with the others crossing the river, returning undetected back to their own lines.

Manny kicked the officer in the thigh to wake him. He opened his eyes, blinked a couple of times, looking up at his captors; on seeing the flashes on their shoulders, he shook with fear. Manny drew his knife and began interrogating him. The German was clearly frightened of what they would do to him and gave Manny a great deal of useful information.

# Chapter 7

CARRYING his favourite Russian Tommy gun, Manny waited with his men, who'd fixed bayonets, for the signal to attack the German positions. They were like greyhounds waiting in the traps at the start of the race.

Although he looked relaxed, Manny had butterflies flying around inside his stomach; it was the same every time, but he knew once they began the attack that would disappear. He swallowed nervously, looked at Isaac standing beside him and winked. Isaac smiled, winking back, just as they were given the order to advance. Isaac set off, a pace in front of Manny, yelling, 'See you on the other side.'

Some of the men, eager to get at the enemy passed them were shouting in Hebrew whatever comes into their heads.

Manny had the expected adrenalin rush as he raced forward, yelling at the top of his voice, 'Watch out, scum, here I come,' as bullets pinged around him, others hissing as they hit, or skid across the water.

Some of the men yelled in German, 'Watch out, the Jews are coming.'

Reaching the other side, Manny yelled obscenities at the enemy; the Nazis dying with the usual anti-Semitic words on their lips.

A paratrooper, an oafish grin on his face, confronted Manny, pointing at the blue and white flash, dropping his rifle unsheathing his knife. 'Jew boy, son of a whore, you're about to have an unpleasant death.'

Manny's eyes narrowed at the insult to his mother, which, in the past, he'd been unable to do anything about – until now. He withdrew his knife from its scabbard. 'Buffoon, idiot, I bet you didn't have a mother, and if you did, she must have been an ugly old hag, and you came out of her backside.'

The German's face contorted, screaming with rage at the insult, lunged at Manny, who slid to the left, grabbing the German's arm, kicking him in the stomach. The enemy Para recovered, face red with anger, eyes full of hatred, and moved into a knife-fighter's crouch, switching the knife from right hand to left, advancing slowly towards Manny, who danced on the balls of his feet, body weaving left and right like a boxer.

The German's knife hand darted forward like a striking snake, but Manny easily avoided it, laughing at the man and goading him once more. 'Where did you learn that, ladies needlework class?' The angrier his opponent got the better.

They circled each other. Suddenly, forgetting all his training, the German lunged blindly forward. Manny swayed away from the wicked-looking blade, caught his foot on something, and for a moment was off-balance. Thinking he'd caught his opponent off-guard, the Nazis thrust the knife towards Manny's heart.

Manny recovered quickly, slid to his right, pushing the German's knife arm away with the flat of his hand. At the same time he swivelled his right hip, stepping forward, adding the full force of his body as the razor-sharp blade entered the German's body. The German Para stood swaying from side to side for a second, and then dropped to his knees, eyes staring with unblinking hatred as blood gushed from the open wound. He tried to stand, but couldn't. He drew back his arm to throw his knife, but fell onto his face and with his last breath said, '*Juden* bastard.'

Manny moved cautiously towards German; rolled him over with a booted foot – he was dead; wiping the blade of his knife on the man's tunic, he picked up the Tommy gun. It was then that the noise and smoke of battle, men shouting and cursing, wounded yelling for help hit him as Jew and German were in hand-to-hand combat.

He spotted Isaac to his right in difficulty and ran across to help; a German moved in front of him, bayonet aimed at his stomach. Without changing stride, Manny fired from the hip. The force of the bullets knocked the German off his feet; he leapt over the body, eyes only on Isaac's opponent about to plunge a bayonet into his brother-in-law, who's tripped over a body behind him and was lying helpless on the ground. Manny fired; the German looked down at the blood seeping from his chest and then keeled over.

Manny gave a fleeting smile as he helped Isaac to his feet, yelling above the noise of battle, 'This wasn't the time to have a rest.'

Isaac retrieved his weapon, turning a grim smile on his face, and parried a bayonet thrust from another enemy soldier. 'Thanks.' He stepped forward, smashing the butt of his rifle into the German's face. 'You caught me napping. Better put me on a charge,' he yelled, adding, 'Piss off' to another attacker. Blocking the blow, he glanced quickly at Manny. 'Can't it wait till later?'

Manny shot the German as he came back for another go at Isaac. 'OK, but be careful.'

The training and confidence of the brothers-in-law in their own abilities had now taken over from the initial adrenalin rush, making fun of the situation. Turning as one, they ran towards the enemy who were retreating under the onslaught of the Brigadiers.

Flying the Union Jack and the Blue and White flag with the Star of David in the centre, the Jewish Brigade advanced into the Italian valleys. High trees and hedgerows restricted cross-country mobility, providing excellent cover for the defending Germans, who had dug an intricate system of trenches, dugouts and machine-gun emplacements. Every inch of ground was fought for by some of the most battle-hardened German troops. They didn't like retreating, but they had never come up against Manny and his men, who fought with abandoned ferocity, revenge their motive.

Throughout the Brigade there were stories of heroism. A corporal fell on a grenade to save his comrades, while another, armed only with a rifle, attacked a machine-gun emplacement, killing its occupants and turning the machine-gun on the Germans, before he was killed.

Manny was tired, as were his men. They'd had little rest since the Senio River. The Germans defended each village street by street, house by house. Manny had lost five men killed and three badly wounded. Both he and Isaac had superficial wounds, as did most of their men, but all were determined to carry on fighting.

They had learnt by experience to be ever-vigilant, as the Germans booby-trapped many of the houses they vacate. Sometimes it was a simple trip wire at the entrance to the house or room; a dead soldier's body, a bottle of drink, a bayonet lying on the floor, even food on the table. Manny had lost three men this way.

During a very rare lull in the fighting Manny, his chair tilted back against the wall, was reading a letter from Rita. He let the chair fall forward, slapping the page with the back of his hand. 'I knew it.'

'Knew what?' Isaac sat next to him reading a letter from Hannah.

'Rita's pregnant.'

Isaac smiled, 'Congrats, but how did you know?

With a happy father-to-be smile on his face, Manny lifted the letter to his nose inhaling the fragrance of her perfume, and then kissed it. 'It's something Rita said to me the day we left.'

'What was that?'

Manny looked at Isaac. 'Nothing really; how's my sister?'

'Says she's getting bigger by the minute, and glad I can't see the weight she's put on.'

On 25 April 1945 German resistance ended and 2 May the Germans surrendered and the division moved north to mop up.

# PART II

# Chapter 8

THE war in Europe was over, Hitler dead and the mighty Reich in pieces. Surrendering German soldiers preferred to be captured by the British or Americans than by the Russians.

In July, the Brigade moved to Tavisio on the borders of Italy, Austria and Yugoslavia. It was here that Manny came face to face with his skeletal brethren, the survivors of the Holocaust.

Allied Command, in its ignorance, was intent on returning refugees to their former countries where new and violent anti-Semitism had already claimed many lives. Refugees returning to reclaim their property found their new owner would not give them up. Some were beaten, others killed. If the refugees stayed, they lived under constant hostility and resentment. So in the end they were forced to go somewhere else.

Jews from other allied army units gave food and equipment to the refugees, also vehicles to carry the children, the old and the sick, directing these unwanted people who didn't believe there was a Jewish fighting force, towards the Brigade. When they saw the blue and white shoulder flashes with the Star of David, they touched them in awe, in many cases kissing them with tears in their eyes.

The arrival of so many refugees threw the Brigade into relief work. Manny had never seen so many people in such a pitiable condition. They came in ones and twos; sometimes in small groups. Other times they were escorted by armed young men and women, who'd witnessed and escaped death. The refugees received medical treatment, clothes and a hot meal; and for the first time in many years slept in a bed knowing they were safe.

With the refugees speaking a number of different languages, Manny and Isaac's linguistic skills were put to the test. They and other translators registered the names of the survivors, sending copies to all the units with Holocaust victims, where they were eagerly scrutinised by the survivors looking for loved ones.

The Brigade commandeers a hall in Tavisio to hold concerts. It was here the refugees could relax, dance, smile, and repair their minds and bodies.

The head of the Jewish agency, and the Haganah leadership within the Brigade, had devised a plan of their own. To rescue as many Jewish survivors as they could, and take them to shelters set up by the Brigade. Here, they would be mentally and physically rehabilitated. No one wanted them, except the Jewish community in Palestine, and somehow the agency was determined to get them there.

There was also concern and awareness by Haganah leaders of the lack of weapons available to effectively fight a war against the Arabs, if and when the British left Palestine.

With the war scarcely over, and with inspired zeal, men from the Brigade set out in small armed convoys to find and rescue as many of their fellow Jews as they could by stealing trucks, forging papers and documents, and bribing border guards to bring survivors to Tavisio, and at the same time appropriate arms and ammunition from ordinance depots throughout Europe, smuggling them to be hidden in farms and kibbutzim throughout Palestine.

*

As the months went by, it was here at Tavisio that Manny at last knew what he was going to do with the rest of his life. The days when Jews were easy targets were over, and would never return. Not if he had anything to do with it. Manny and Isaac took young fit male refugees into the

Italian mountains for weapon and field training, which included Hebrew lessons.

By the light of the campfire, Manny sat cross-legged on a groundsheet cleaning his weapon. Stopping for a moment, looked up at the clear starlit night sky, a smile on his lips as the words of his friend, Saul Steinberg, entered his head. *Come to Palestine with me; are you scared of becoming a Zionist?*

Manny's reply had been, *'I'm not a Zionist, I don't want to dig ditches and farm the land.'* Now his features changed to one of sorrow, remembering the way Saul had died and his last words to him Manny:

*'Plant a tree for me.'*

He nodded. 'Yes, Saul,' he whispered. 'I'll plant a dozen trees in your name, I promise.' He might not toil the soil, but he wanted to help build a better tomorrow, a country where Jews could lift their heads with pride and never again be afraid.

Deep in thought, Manny lit a cigarette reflecting that Jews had walked the Earth for hundreds of years before the time of Christianity, Islam, Hinduism, and other religions. Throughout the centuries, since the times of the Egyptians and Romans, Jews had been persecuted, murdered, and herded liked cattle to be slaughtered by those, like Hitler, who had tried to eradicate them from the world.

Hitler slaughtered six million Jews. Now he was dead. And like a phoenix rising from the flames, the survivors of the Holocaust would be reborn, with a country of their own, without pogroms or prejudice; and, if need arose, defend it and win.

*

Manny had written a long letter to Rita, telling her of his plans for the future, asking how she felt about it and to be truthful in her reply, as there would be hardships along the way.

He received a very quick and short reply. *I love you with all my heart and soul. Wherever you go, I will go. Whatever you decide, I will abide by your decision as long as we're together. Hugs, and kisses, from us all, Rita.*

On 22 August, to Hannah and Isaac a son was born. They named him Barry after Isaac's father. Two days later Dominique also had a little boy whom they called Harry – her father's name. On 22 September Rita gave birth to a son, naming him David, after Manny's father.

\*

Manny sat close to the campfire, writing another letter to Rita. His thoughts were interrupted by a voice he knew well.

'Move over and let someone else get some heat; it's cold up here.'

Placing the half-written letter into a folder, Manny stood to greet Bergman, saying with a smile on his face, 'You're getting old. Too many officer privileges, makes you soft. How are Dominique and the baby?'

'They're well, thank you. Have you heard from Rita?'

'Yes, she's very happy, and young David, it seems, is going to be an opera singer.' The two men hugged as Sam came into view with Isaac in tow. The two cousins greeted each other with a hug.

'You've lost a bit of weight,' Sam said.

Manny patted his cousin's stomach. 'A few weeks up here would do you the world of good,' he hesitated, and then asked, 'OK, where are we going?'

Bergman smiled, eyes sparkling in the firelight. 'What made you think—'

'Come off it, Zach,' Isaac interrupted, 'we know when you two appear out of the blue it isn't a social call.'

'How do you feel about getting away from here for a while?' Sam asked.

'Are we going on holiday? I could do with a break,' Manny remarked, a slight smile on his face, knowing where his cousin and friend were concerned there's no such word as holiday.

Bergman wasn't smiling now. 'Austria, Vienna to be exact. I think you might know the place.'

'The reason is?' Manny queried.

'Let's go somewhere where we could talk in private,' muttered Sam, nodding towards the trainees.

Manny grabbed his Tommy gun. 'OK, follow me.' They followed him along a path that becomes steeper yard by yard; he suddenly moved off into some rocks, coming to a stop in a small clearing. Cradling the Tommy gun in his arms he leaned his back against a rock, while Isaac moved beside him, lowering himself to sit cross-legged on the ground, his weapon across his knees.

Bergman started by saying, 'I know you're aware that anti-Semitism is stronger than ever in most European countries.'

Manny and Isaac nodded.

'Refugees returning to claim back their property are being met by hostility, not only by the new occupants, but by neighbours and officials. Austria is a prime example. The synagogue in Graz has once again been desecrated after being cleaned up by returning members. There is a public meeting in Salzburg against Jews, who are not allowed to rebuild their business. The Austrian Government doesn't want the returnees back. There's no future for—'

'Where do we come into this?' Manny interrupted.

'A refugee told us that there's a group of returnees in Vienna, who were being hounded, beaten, and refused accommodation and food. They've been to the British authorities, who sent soldiers to intervene, but as soon as the soldiers were out of sight, the returnee were beaten and thrown out onto the street again.'

Sam stepped forward, saying angrily. 'These refugees have been through a living hell, and now, when all they want to do is return home, they can't do that. The man asked us, if we could help these people.' He gestured towards them, 'We're going to Vienna, rescue them, and if necessary use force.'

'It's a tall order with just the four of us,' said Manny.

'We can do it,' Sam retorted quickly.

'What about my trainees?' Manny asked.

'Your replacement is arriving as we speak,' Bergman replied.

\*

The open-topped Mercedes staff car, which once belonged to General Rhinehart, passed through the Russian checkpoint and into British-controlled Vienna. The four heavily armed occupants, wearing British uniforms, took no notice of the people who stopped and stared as they passed, spitting, yelling, or making rude gestures when noticing the front wings and pennant with the blue and white markings and a gold Star of David in the centre.

Manny, who was driving, stopped the car outside a derelict building with boarded-up windows and doors, Swastikas and obscene graffiti painted all over them. Half the roof was missing. Weeds grew wild through cracks in the concrete steps and around the building that was once a synagogue. Above the oak doors, the jagged edges of a broken window here and there had gold Hebrew letters that once shone brightly but were now black with dried faeces.

All four men got out of the car. Manny and Isaac, the safety-catches of their weapons off, walked towards the front doors, while Bergman stood by the rear of the car, eyes searching the street, and Sam leaned against the front wing, looking in the other direction.

The streets were empty of people and vehicles. A curtain stirred. Bergman lifted his weapon, pointing it in that direction. The curtain fell back in place, as did others as he swept his Sten-gun along the row of houses that were once owned by Jews.

Manny walked up the synagogue steps, remembering happier times, especially Joshua and his barmitzvah. He recalled standing proudly between his father and the rabbi after saying his portion of the Torah, making him a man, while his mother, tears in her eyes with the other women, threw sweets from the gallery,

The right-hand door moved slowly on creaking hinges as he pushed it open. Cautiously, taking no chances, Tommy-gun ready, he entered, moved to the right and swung the weapon in a slow arc around the synagogue as Isaac stepped to the left doing the same.

Light from the broken roof flooded into the synagogue; the benches where once men sat and prayed were broken. The ark that held the holy scrolls was open, one of its doors missing. Graffiti was everywhere, on walls, doors and floor. Bare electric wires hung from what was left of the ceiling.

'This is the Jewish Brigade, anyone here?' Manny called loudly.

A door to the rabbi's robing room, just to the right of the bema, opened, and a skeletal man stood in the doorway, his face thin, skin tight against protruding cheekbones, haunting eyes gleamed in sunken sockets. He gave a toothless smile, and then looked back into the room, whispering, 'They're here.'

He moved towards Manny and Isaac, eyes riveted on their flashes. Others followed him out of the room into the synagogue; their ragged clothes hung loose on their emaciated bodies. The first man gently touched Manny's flash, and then leaned forward to kiss the words 'Jewish Infantry Brigade Group' on his shoulder.

Manny and Isaac stood still, surrounded by about twenty people, all wanting to touch them. One man, unable to get near Isaac, crawled along the floor to kiss his boot.

Manny and Isaac, with tears in their eyes, patted each in turn on the back, or stroked their heads, saying in their native tongue, 'You're safe now.'

One man hung back from the others, eyes riveted on Manny, who suddenly noticed him and stepped towards him, stopping in mid-stride, body bent slightly forward, disbelief on his face and in his voice. 'Daniel.' Still a little unsure, he took another step forward. The man opened his mouth to speak, but couldn't get the words out.

'Daniel...' Manny's voice choked with emotion as the man nodded holding out his arms. Manny moved quickly to Daniel and gently, scared of breaking his protruding bones, hugged him close, kissing him, not caring about the smell of his unwashed body.

'We have to tell the others, we need transport to get these people out of here,' said Isaac, adding, 'You know that man?'

Manny pulled away from Daniel, a smile on his face, wiping away the tears. 'Yes, I know him. I'll tell you all about it later. Go tell Bergman and Sam.'

Leaving Manny with the refugees, Isaac ran outside to tell Sam what they needed.

'OK, you stay here with Manny, Zach and I will get the transport. Be ready for trouble. There've been a few curtains moving.'

'Nosey, aren't they. Don't worry they'll get more than they bargained for if they start something. Could you get some food and drink?'

'No problem,' said Sam, getting behind the wheel of the Mercedes as Bergman climbed onto the rear seat, weapon ready.

*

As they drove away Isaac searched the street for watching eyes, and then entered the synagogue striding quickly over to Manny.

'I think we'd better barricade the entrance. Sam said there are some prying eyes, he's right; I saw a few curtains moving. The locals might want to try something now they've seen the car drive away.'

Manny, an arm round Daniel's shoulder, said to his father-in-law, 'We'll talk later. I have a lot to tell you.' He moved away from Daniel turning to Isaac saying, 'We'll open both doors, it would give us a clear view of the street.' He pointed to the benches. 'We'll use the benches as a barricade.'

'Good idea.'

The brothers-in-law quickly set about their task. Manny turned to the refugees, 'This was just a precaution while we wait for our friends to arrive with transport to get you out of here.' He walked over to the barricade in front of the synagogue to stand beside Isaac, Tommy gun in the crook of his folded arms.

'How do you know that man? Was he a neighbour?' Isaac asked,

Manny's eyes moved slowly along the street. 'He's Rita's father.'

'What! My God, that is unbelievable, what are the chances—'

Manny placed a hand on Isaac's shoulder, interrupting what he was about to say as someone emerged from one of the houses. His body stiffened in recognition. 'Sergeant Eisenbrüchmann,' Manny whispered. Other men and women emerged from the houses following the sergeant, who was not in uniform, towards the synagogue.

There was a click as Isaac took off the safety catch of his weapon. 'I count twenty at the moment. It seems you know everyone.'

'No, not everyone—'

'Juden bastards,' Eisenbrüchmann yelled, walking towards them. 'Pieces of shit.' He stopped where there once stood a gate leading up to the synagogue. Waving his arms he shouted, 'Fuck off out of here, Jew, you're not wanted.'

A crowd of people, some armed, joined him and started the usual chant.

Manny walked around the barricade.

'Manny, are you mad? Get back here!' Isaac yelled loudly, but he ignored his brother-in-law. Manny had had enough, and was very angry, not only at the ex-policeman, but the ignorance of these bigoted people who chanted the same old thing over and over again, thinking that the Jews would as usual shuffle away when seeing the baying crowd. But they didn't know him, and even those that did were in for a shock. His eyes moved from one to the other as he walked along the path, stopping in front of the policeman who was at least three inches taller than him.

The ex-sergeant reeked of beer, and was unshaven, the fat belly hung over the top of his trousers, held up by a pair of dirty braces, the sleeves of his shirt rolled up above the elbows, buttons undone around his bull neck, showing a mat of dark hair.

In contrast, Manny's trousers were pressed with knife-edged creases. The uniform fit his broad shoulders and slim waist perfectly. The Nazi glanced at the red beret with the Pegasus badge folded through the epaulette with the blue and white flash.

'Are you speaking to me, you brainless fool?' Manny said quietly, but loud enough for all to hear, adding, 'Can't you people ever think of something original to say? You're like a broken record.'

'Listen, you son of a—' He got no further as Manny stepped forward and slapped him once, very hard. The man reeled back, stunned and silent, his face bright red, lips turned back in a snarl. He took a pace towards Manny, right arm drawn back, fists clenched, but suddenly doubled over as Manny without warning kicked him in the groin.

'What were you going to say about my mother? Who, incidentally, you knew.'

The Nazi held his testicles with both hands, looking up in pain, and then his eyes showed recognition. A shot rang out. Manny looked round at Isaac, whose Sten gun was pointing at a man lying on the ground, holding his leg, with a pistol by his side as he yelled and swore at them.

Isaac shrugged his shoulders. 'He was about to shoot you.' He fired again, this time at the ground in front of the yelling man. 'If you don't shut up, I'll shut you up permanently.' There was immediate silence. Someone went to the wounded man's aid.

'Leave him,' yelled Manny.

The man, in faded army shirt, blond hair long and uncombed, hesitated on seeing Manny's weapon pointing at him.

Manny turned and smiled at Isaac, then back to face the big police sergeant who lumbered towards him, swearing.

Calmly, Manny sidestepped him and stuck out a leg. Eisenbrüchmann fell heavily to the ground. Manny followed him down, dropping onto the Nazi's rib cage. There was a crack and the fat policeman yelled in pain. Manny got to his feet, a look of contempt on his face.

'You big fat oaf. You speak like a woman and waddle around like a pregnant one. How could you hate Jews, you brainless idiot, when you worship a Jew? Jesus was a Jew, in fact a Pharisee. You ignorant pig, you probably don't know what that is.'

He stared silently at the groaning man on the floor, prodding him with a foot. 'What I can tell you,' he hesitated and looked up at the crowd of people that had now doubled in size after hearing the shot.

'In fact,' he raised his voice so they could all hear him, taking a few steps towards them. 'I can tell you all now, the days when we Jews were used as whipping blocks, and an excuse for your incompetence, stupidity and ignorance, are over. Never again will you excuses for human beings see a Jew cow down. You've tried to exterminate us.'

He moved towards them, arms outstretched, chest out. 'We're still here, and now we're strong,' he pointed to his weapon, 'and we're armed.' He beckoned them to him, a slight smile on his lips. 'Please, please try. I would like nothing better than the excuse to kill you.'

There was a yell behind him. Manny turned just in time to jump to his left as Eisenbrüchmann was about to thrust a knife into his back. The policeman turned, to charge again. Manny fired a short burst from his Tommy gun. For a second, there's a stunned expression on the policeman's face and then he fell forward onto the ground with a thud, a pool of blood flowing from under his body towards the crowd who looked at him and then at Manny with expressions of disbelief on their faces. Suddenly, they let out a roar of anger and begin to move forward.

Manny fired in the air then swung his Tommy gun in their direction, moving it slowly left to right and then back again face white with anger, wanting them to attack so he could kill them all, as a feeling of loathing and hatred engulfed him, but instead of pulling the trigger said harshly, 'Anyone else want to die?'

There was silence, their eyes and faces showing their fear and hatred. 'Thought not,' Manny sneered.

Just then a truck and the Mercedes pulled up. Bergman leapt out of the Mercedes moving quickly beside Manny, gun ready, 'Everything OK?'

Manny smiled, nodding towards Isaac. 'Nothing we couldn't handle.'

Turning back to the crowd, who were staring at the front wings of the Mercedes, a man ran towards the offside wing a knife in his hand. Manny shot him; turning quickly back to the crowd, face hard, voice filled with contempt. 'You don't know how much pleasure it would give me to shoot all of you. Please, please, I beg you, someone try again.' He smiled sinisterly, taking a step forward, face still showing his mood. 'Charge you cowards so I can snuff you out like I would a bug,' He spat each word out like slivers of ice.

The crowd stepped a couple of paces back, faces showing their fear of Manny after his tirade.

Sam turned to Manny, 'Trouble?'

'No, they're pussy cats.'

'Where are the refugees?'

'In the synagogue,' Manny replied.

Sam moved towards the entrance. 'I've brought some food and drink.'

'Well done,' Isaac said, moving to stand beside Manny.

'I think it best we get out of here,' said Bergman. 'They could eat on the way.'

'I have to go into the American sector before we leave,' Manny declared, adding, 'I must see some old friends of mine and make sure they're safe.'

Bergman nodded understandingly and walked towards the entrance of the synagogue. 'Make sure those vermin stay quiet. I'll get Sam; we'd better quickly load up and be on our way before they get up enough courage to charge.'

With Manny, Isaac and Bergman standing guard, Sam helped the refugees into the truck. Once they were all on board he slid onto the driving seat.

'Manny, you and Isaac get into the Mercedes,' Bergman said, 'I'll cover you and Isaac over me as I get into the truck. Manny, take the lead as you know where you're going.'

The truck and Mercedes pulled away from the kerbside. The crowd becomes braver, and hurled stones, yelling and swearing. Someone fired a hopeful shot at them.

Manny pulled to the side, allowing the lorry to pass, shouting angrily back at the crowd that was running towards them, and was reminded by their shouts and distorted faces of all that had happened to his parents and many of his brethren here in Vienna. As the pictures of the past filtered through his mind, he fired a full magazine into the crowd, seeing with satisfaction many of them drop to the ground. He reloaded before driving away.

Isaac glanced back, but couldn't see anything as the lorry had moved in behind them, blocking his view. He turned to look at Manny. 'You're one bad, mad Jew.'

*David Brown*

Manny looked at him for a second, and then back to the front. 'I'm fed up with those scum thinking they could get away with treating us the way they do. It's payback time.'

# Chapter 9

T HEY passed through the French controlled sector stopping at the American checkpoint. While one guard checked their papers, another looked at the wings of their car and strolled over to Manny.

'Gee, am I glad to see you guys.' He held out his hand, 'Joseph Marks, Brooklyn.' He then said in Yiddish, 'There are about thirty refugees housed in a school in the old Jewish quarter of Währing. There are three other Jewish guys in my unit. Unfortunately we couldn't be there to protect them from the anti-Semitic Nazi bastards all the time as we're on duty. Is there any chance of you taking them with you?'

'We have some business to attend to first,' Manny said. 'I know the school. As soon as we've finished with what we have to do, we'll pick them up.'

The GI sighed. 'Thanks. I heard about you guys. I never believed it, but now...' his voice trailed off as the other guard handed them back their papers.

Manny held out his hand. The GI grasps it. 'Thanks, Joseph,' Manny let go the American's hand, put the car in gear and moved off, Isaac giving a mock salute as they passed through the barrier.

Fifteen minutes later, Manny braked outside his old apartment in *Klostergrasse* and got out of the vehicle. 'I won't be long.'

'I'm coming with you,' Isaac declared.

Bergman ran quickly over to Manny. 'Where are you going?'

Manny pointed. 'In there. I won't be long, Isaac's coming with me.'

Bergman nodded. 'OK, keep it as short as you can.'

Manny patted Bergman on the arm, turned and entered the building. He stood by the door to the apartment for a second and then knocked.

'Who's there?' a trembling voice called from the other side of the door.

'Helga, is that you?' Manny asked.

The door opened slightly, held by a chain. An eye peeped from behind it. There was a shrill cry of 'Manny!' The chain was quickly taken off, the door flung open and Helga leapt at him, arms around his neck, hugging him to her. He gently pulled her from him, holding her at arm's length, noticing the drawn features and black rings under her eyes; she held her cardigan tightly around her body.

'Helga, what's the matter?' he whispered. 'What are you scared of?'

She tried to say something, but cried instead, tears steaming down her face.

'Helga, there's nothing to worry about,' he insisted, pulling her to him. 'We were close by and I wanted to see how you're getting on. How are your mother and your son? Is there any news of Hans?'

She stopped crying, wiped her nose with a hankie, taking his hand, and then looked at Isaac.

'It's OK,' Manny said. 'This is my brother-in-law, Isaac.'

Helga sniffed saying tearfully, 'Pleased to meet you.'

'Likewise,' Isaac wondered what this was all about.

Helga led Manny into the apartment, noticing most of his mother's ornaments were missing. Helga saw him looking around. 'I'm sorry, but we had to eat.'

He patted her arm. 'I understand.'

She led him into the dining room. 'Manny, sit,' she ordered.

He smiled. 'I see you're as bossy as ever.'

She knelt in front of him taking his hand. 'Mama is dead. She was killed when a bomb landed on our old house.' Her mouth quivered, distorted with anguish, and tears filled her eyes once more. 'My son was with her.'

Manny stood, and gently lifted her to her feet, wrapping his arms around her. 'Oh! Helga, I'm so, so sorry. I loved your mother as my own. What about your husband?'

'Dead.' Her voice choked as she added. 'He was conscripted and sent to the Russian front.' She pulled away, taking the hankie from her apron pocket wiping her eyes. 'Hans,' she hesitated looking into his eyes, 'Hans, he—'

Manny nodded, waiting for a second for her to continue. 'What about him?'

'He's hiding.'

'Where, from who?'

She pointed outside. 'Everyone. Our lives were a living hell because you gave me this apartment. We're spat at and called Juden lovers. I'm forever scrubbing off graffiti.'

'But Hans was in the army, I can't understand—'

She cut in, 'He tried to help a Jewish couple who returned to claim their property, and was beaten for it.'

'Where is he now?'

She pointed to the door of his old bedroom.

Manny moved towards it.

'Wait, he has a gun.' Helga moved in front of Manny and knocked twice on the door. 'Hans, it's Helga, Manny's here, please open the door.'

There was a click as the door was unlocked and opened. Hans stood in the doorway, a Luger in his hand. 'I... I heard voices, but wasn't sure who was in the room, we have to be careful, nowadays.' He dropped his arm to his side, moving quickly across the room and the two friends embraced.

Manny pulled away from Hans, introducing him to Isaac.

The two men shook hands. Isaac pointed to a black eye and lacerations on his face. 'Did your neighbours do that?'

Helga moved to her brother's side, lifting his shirt, showing a bandage around his ribs. 'They kicked him when he was on the ground; broke two of his ribs and...' she turned him around, showing red welts on his back from waist to shoulder '...and whipped him.'

Hans looked at Manny, at the same time placing a protective arm around his sister's shoulders. 'They... they...' his voice faltered. 'Manny, they raped her,' he whispered.

There was shock and disgust on both Manny and Isaac's faces. 'Who raped you, do you know who they are?' he asked softly.

She didn't say anything, just looked down at the floor, but Hans nodded.

'Who?' Manny asked angrily, adding between clenched teeth, 'Show me.'

'Manny, please, we have to live here.'

'No, you don't; you can come with us.'

'What about the apartment? It belonged to your parents,' said Helga.

'That was another time, another life. Who raped you?

'What are you going to do?' Her eyes widened in panic.

'Who raped you?' Manny repeated icily; a feeling of anger, loathing and hatred for the men who raped his friend.

She didn't answer. Manny turned to Hans. 'Do you know?'

'Yes, there were three of them. I went to see them.' He pointed to his eye. 'They did this.'

'OK, Helga, pack a few things for you and Hans; nothing too heavy, only essentials. Don't forget any heirlooms from your parents,' Manny ordered, turning back to Hans. 'Take me to these men. Isaac, stay here in case someone comes looking for Helga. They can see the car and know we're here. When she's packed, take her downstairs.'

Isaac nodded. 'What about Bergman and Sam?'

'I'll handle them. Come on, Hans.'

Manny quickly explained to Bergman that there's something he must attend to. 'I won't be long.' He followed Hans into the next street, stopping outside a house that

Manny knew once belonged to a family called Schlitz, who was a shoemaker. Manny placed the sling of his Tommy gun across his shoulders, letting it hang by his side, and strode purposefully up to the front door and knocked loudly.

A man, the same height as Manny opened the door; shirt unbuttoned to the waist, showing chest and stomach muscles, blond hair cropped close to his skull. 'What do you want?' he demanded belligerently, looking Manny up and down, eyes coming to rest on the shoulder flashes. The unshaven face twisted with hatred as he took a stride towards Manny. 'Piss off, Jew, before I skin you alive.'

Without warning Manny smashed the palm of his hand into the man's nose, breaking it instantly. 'Hans, what's his name?'

'Klingsmann.'

Manny pushed Klingsmann back into the house.

'You fucking Jew-bastard, you broke my nose.' He shouted, voice hoarse, and lunged at Manny, who did his favourite move, kicking him in the groin. The rapist doubled over, not knowing whether to hold his nose or testicles.

Just then two men appeared in the hallway. One pointed a gun at Manny, who fired his Tommy gun at the man's legs. He screamed curses as he fell to the ground.

The other man held his hands up in surrender, but Manny ignored this and also shot him in the legs. The two men lay writhing on the ground, yelling in pain.

Manny knelt beside them, grabbed the chin of the one nearest to him between thumb and fingers, forcing him to look at Hans. 'This is my best friend,' he said icily. 'You raped his sister, also a friend of mine. They're Austrian, just like you. He fought for you and his country. Look at him, because he's the last thing you'll ever see.'

Manny stood, taking his pistol from its holster and shot him in the head, and quickly turned to the second man, who was trying to crawl away, babbling with fright as Manny grabbed his bleeding legs ignoring the screams of pain, and dragged him back, saying like a court judge, 'I charge you with rape and sentence you to death.' He fired again.

Manny turned to Hans nodding towards Klingsman, 'If you want, you can attend to that bit of slime.'

Hans smiled grimly. 'Could I borrow your knife?'

Manny bowed. 'My pleasure,' handing it to him.

Hans took the offered knife walking the few paces to Klingsmann, who was shaking with fear. 'I would love to torture you, the way you tortured my sister.' Hans slammed the blade into the rapist's stomach. 'Have you ever seen a gut wound?'

Klingsmann screamed, eyes wide with fear, and then shrieked in agony as Hans pulled the blade across. Blood spurted from the open wound onto the ground.

'You're going to die a very slow and painful death.' Relishing every word, Hans continued with a slight smile on his face. 'It may take an hour or two; hopefully longer, but while you lay here, think, was it worth it?'

'We'd better get going as my friends will wonder what's keeping us,' said Manny.

'Where are we going?'

'Italy. I'll explain as we go.'

*

Manny and Hans returned to the two vehicles. Isaac started the engine as soon as he spotted them saying, 'About time too.'

Manny slid onto the seat beside him, with Hans settled in the back beside his sister. The Mercedes and lorry pulled quickly away from the kerb. Manny directed Isaac to what was once the Jewish school where they pick up another twenty-four refugees.

At the checkpoint, an American corporal asked if they had room for any more.

'We'll need another lorry,' Manny replied.

The American smiled and slapped the side of the car. 'No problem.'

While they waited Manny explained to Bergman and Sam about Rita's father. He's going to tell him about their marriage when they get to Tavisio.

'What about your two friends?' Bergman asked.

'They're not Jewish, but they're my dearest friends.' He placed a hand on Bergman's arm. 'Please, Zach, it's become very dangerous for them to stay as they've helped me in the past, and Jews returning to their properties. Helga was raped because of it.'

'OK,' Bergman said, looking across at Helga and Hans, 'They're your responsibility.'

'Thanks.'

The lorry arrived, all its markings obliterated. Even the number plate had been changed around so it couldn't be traced. 'There's some food and blankets in the back,' said the corporal. He winked, 'and some bourbon.'

They thanked him and Manny got behind the wheel of the Mercedes. Wth Isaac driving their latest acquisition, the convoy of three vehicles headed back to Tavisio.

*

On the way, Manny described to Helga and Hans all that had happened to him since they last met, including marriage to Rita.

Hans quietly told Manny about his war. 'My last battle was in the Ardennes. I was lucky, all I received was a shoulder wound, but the rest of my crew were killed when my tank was hit. It's the third time I've been wounded. Instead of being sent home I was posted to Italy, but just before the retreat to the Senio River I was sent home to recuperate from my wounds. Luckily for Helga and me we were in the American sector when the war ended. What are you going to do once you're released from the army?'

'I'm going to live in Israel. It won't be long before we're given statehood. The new state would need people to help defend it against the Arabs.' He turned, glanced at the road in front of them, and then back to Hans. 'I've seen men do terrible things to their fellow man, especially Jews, and I've vowed that it would never happen again.'

'Where's that fun-loving, caring person I once knew?' Helga asked, smiling at him.

Manny smiled back. 'Helga, my darling, he's still here, just a little older, and maybe a little wiser, but I can assure you, he's still here.'

Manny was worried at what would happen to his two friends once they reached Tavisio. He glanced in the rearview mirror at Helga. Since leaving Vienna she had changed. It was as though a heavy weight had lifted from her, and the further away from Vienna they travelled the more she became the old Helga, smiling eyes shining mischievously.

She suddenly leaned forward, placing her arms around Manny's shoulders. 'Thank you.' She kissed the side of his face, and then mischievously stuck her tongue in his ear.

There was laughter in his voice as he said, 'Hey, your brother's watching, and I'm a happily married man.'

The answer was a loud happy laugh, as she stood taking the clips holding up her hair, shook her head and light brown hair tumbled down streaming out behind her. She turned, waving happily at Sam and Bergman in the truck behind them, who waved back.

# Chapter 10

THE Jewish Brigade's camp could be called orderly chaos, as people came and went day and night. All new arrivals were registered, and whenever possible family members, of which there were very few, were kept together, while behind the scenes, Haganah leaders organise ships to take the refugees south to Palestine, and salvation.

It had been a week since Manny returned to camp. He had spoken to Bergman and Sam about Hans and Helga to see what could be done for them, but he needn't have worried. Hans had settled very quickly, finding a niche in the motor pool helping repair German military vehicles, and Helga's smiling face and bubbly personality soon rubbed off on helping new arrivals to settle down.

At last, Manny, who with the others returned once again to Austria rescuing other Jews escaping from an anti-Semitic society, was able to meet up with Daniel, who had filled out a little and looking a lot brighter since their first meeting. The two men hugged, both smiling with the joy of seeing each other again. Taking a small flask from his pocket, Manny handed it to Daniel.

'What's this?'

'It's to make a toast and drink the health of...' He tried to say the right words '... I've some good news, something I think, well... I hope would make you happy... I'm married.'

Daniel looked at Manny, a beaming smile on his face. 'You married that girl, what was her name? Ah! I remember, Joan, you made an honest woman at last.'

Manny's face changed to one of sadness. 'No, Joan was killed.'

'Oh, I'm so sorry.'

'It took time, but time heals. I thought I would never love another, but I met this girl... woman. She's a nurse and

121

my sister's best friend. I didn't realise I loved her at first. Lucky for me,' he smiled, 'She loved me and waited until I realised my feelings. I adore her.'

Taking two small glasses from his pocket, he set one down in front of Daniel. 'I wanted to ask her father if I could marry her, but, well, let's say, I couldn't at the time.'

'I'm sure that when he meets you, he would approve immediately.'

'You would?'

'I would what?'

'Approve of me marrying your daughter?'

'What—' Daniel stared at Manny, who was smiling as he poured whisky into the two glasses. 'You…' He pointed at Manny '… and my…' pointing to himself; while Manny nodded his head up and down, a silly grin on his face handing Daniel a glass.

Tears of happiness ran down Daniels cheeks. They clink glasses. 'The bride and groom,' said Daniel, and downed the whisky in one go.

Manny said, 'The other day I was putting up a list of names on the notice board when a man next to me turned from the list and muttered dejectedly, "Miracles are for fairies, not for Jews." I think he was wrong, what do you think, Papa?'

'I agree with you, son. We're living proof.'

'Oh, and by the way,' said Manny, 'you're also a grandfather; his name is David. I know this is a lot to take in at the moment, but…' He was silent, seeing the big smile on his father-in-law's face.

'I never ever thought that I would be this happy, and laugh again. I think it called for a toast.' Daniel held out his glass. 'Let's drink to family, both past and present, *L'chaim.*'

Manny told Daniel about his escape and internment on the Isle of Mann, and how he had met Rita. It was then, probably because of the good news he received and perhaps the drink, that Daniel related to Manny what had happened at the camp when they found Böhll dead.

'We were ordered into the square; the entire contingent of SS-soldiers was there, and as we filed in, they randomly grabbed a prisoner, dragged him away and beat him mercilessly; I was lucky. Within days, Conning was relieved of his post and sent to the Russian front.'

'What about the dog?'

Daniel's face lit up with a big smile. 'Someone killed it, and it was unknowingly eaten by the guards.'

Manny stared at Daniel, eyes wide in amazement, a silly grin on his face, and pointed to his father-in-law. 'You didn't.'

Daniel nodded, 'Not just me, but the whole bakery. The new officer in charge asked about the colour of the bread. I told him it was a new type of rye bread.' Manny roared with laughter at the demise of the vicious dog and its fitting ending.

*

The last few months had gone by in a flash. The Brigade was busier than ever in rescuing fellow Jews escape Central and Southern Europe who were now pouring into Italy, in what was being called The Flight.

Orders were received that in May the Brigade would be disbanded at five hundred men a month, and be demobilised in Palestine. Manny, Isaac and Sam were told to report to Bergman. Manny was worried about getting Daniel to London. His father-in-law had been assisting the bakers in Tavisio and he still hadn't told Rita about Daniel who agreed with his decision, as they both wanted to surprise her.

Bergman yelled, 'Enter.' He smiled at them, got to his feet and walked around a desk piled high with forms, at the same time picking up some envelopes from the desk and said, 'You've two days to pack your things. Here are your travel documents and release papers.' He handed each an envelope. 'You'll be officially demobilised in London. We've been in some hairy situations together.' He looked at each in turn. 'And I'm sure they won't be the last.' He picked up another envelope from the desk, handing it to Manny. 'Daniel's papers, a gesture from Mr White and Amber.'

'Thank them for me. I've been wondering how I was going to get him to England. Why aren't we being demobilised in Palestine?'

Bergman sighed and moved back behind his desk, gesturing to some chairs. 'Sit.'

Once they were seated, his face and voice became serious. 'The new Jewish enemy is Ernest Bevin. He made no bones about his determination to crush the Zionist movement, having said at a recent meeting that it's *them or us*. The British support the Arabs, and it's become apparent that they had no intention of changing their policies in spite of the Holocaust.'

Bergman picked up a jug of water, poured some into a glass, taking a sip and continued, 'I'm also receiving reports that Arabs were raiding kibbutzim and ambushing convoys taking supplies to outlying settlements. As you know, we, the Haganah, adopted a policy of restraint. But now, Ben-Gurion favours a large-scale cooperative effort, hoping that it would win the sympathy of world opinion.

'How do you intend to do that?' Manny asked.

'We've established a Jewish Resistance Movement with the aim of unifying the three organisations, us, Irgun and the Stern Gang.' He paused taking a cigarette from a pack on the table, offering them around. Isaac handed back the pack; Bergman looked inside: it was empty. He screwed it up and threw it expertly into the waste bin, then lit his cigarette, blowing a smoke ring across the room.

'The leaders of the three organisations consented to form a committee with the name of X, to enforce discipline amongst the three organisations and approve military operations.'

Manny leaned forward. 'Zach, I spoke to you a while ago about my intention of helping to establish a Jewish state, so why are you sending me back to England when I want to be part of this?'

For a second Bergman was silent toying with his pen and then looked at Manny. 'I can assure you that you'll have your chance to help, but it isn't now. I had this same conversation with Sam yesterday.' He looked in Sam's direction, who nodded.

'You have a wife whom you've hardly seen since you were married, and a son you've never seen. They're your priority.' Bergman handed each of them a piece of paper. 'Remember this phone number and address. If you need me, this is where you'll find me. When you've remembered them, place the papers in the ashtray.' Two minutes later Bergman set them alight.

The following day, Manny and the others said their goodbyes to Helga and Hans, who had made plans to settle in Palestine.

# Chapter 11

*Waterloo Station, 8 May 1946*

THE train from Southampton pulled slowly into Waterloo Station. Eager faces, brows creased in concentration, looked for loved ones they hadn't seen for many years. Worried eyes moved from one carriage to the next, hands held against their mouths worried in case they had missed their husband, son, or father. Children cried, laughed, or stood silent, holding their mothers' hands, waiting for the fathers they had never seen except in photos.

Suddenly one of the women screamed, grabbing her son, lifting him onto her shoulder with one hand, while waving with the other shouting, 'There's your father.' The child tried to see where his mother was pointing but couldn't, his little head bobbing up and down as she ran alongside the train, until it eventually came to a stop. A soldier leapt from an open door, hugged his wife, kissed her, and then looked at the son he'd never seen, taking him from her. 'Hello son; my, you're a big boy.' He hugged the boy, tears in his eyes; a scene repeated the length of the platform.

Rita, Hannah and Sarah looked anxiously along the train as it came to a stop. They were too scared to move in case they missed their husbands in the crowd. The two children, Barry and David, lay sleeping in their mothers' arms.

Sarah was the first to spot them. 'There they are.' She pointed, not daring to look round unless she lost sight of them in the crowd. She moved slowly at first, eyes fixed firmly on the three men who strode side by side along the platform. Her pace quickened until she was running, leaping into Sam's arms.

Hannah, who was just behind her, stood for a second in front of Isaac. He stepped forward, placing an arm around her waist, and gently pulled her towards him and they kissed; careful not to squash their son lying snugly in the crook of his mother's arm. They parted and Sarah lifted the baby upright so Isaac could for the first time see his son.

Rita was a few feet away from Manny when he turned to someone behind and then moved to one side, allowing Daniel to walk beside him. Rita stopped in mid-stride, the knuckles of her hand in her mouth in disbelief. The two men stopped in front of her. Manny bent to kiss his wife and gently took their son, allowing Rita to embrace Daniel, at the same time looking at the son he had never seen and kissing his closed eyes.

After a few seconds Rita and Daniel moved apart, tenderly touching each other's face, both crying with happiness, and then they're in each other's arms once again.

Aunt Doris and Uncle Mark borrowed tables and chairs from their neighbours to accommodate their extended family when that evening they sat down to dinner.

Aunt Doris looked around the table at the smiling faces. She knew that very soon, these gatherings would soon be a thing of the past. Apart from Isaac, who was about to start medical school, the others, including her son, had their sights set firmly on returning to Palestine.

*

Manny and Rita rented a three-bedroom house in Stamford Hill, North London. It was the nearest place to the East End they could find. Bergman was right about spending time with his family. Manny bought a car, and whenever there was a sunny day they took a picnic and drove to Southend. Most Sundays they visited Aunt Doris and Uncle Mark, as did the rest of the family, including Sam's in-laws and Daniel.

These were always happy occasions. Manny still thought about Palestine, and knew that when it was time Bergman would get in touch with Sam and him, but in the meantime they were enjoying family life.

Whenever the cousins met, their conversation inevitably turned to Palestine and the Jewish Resistance Movement. Radio and newspaper reports were full of its activities; rescuing immigrants from internment camps, blowing up railway lines, bringing rail traffic to a complete halt, and trying to rescue men and women held in detention centres.

The resistance's most daring operation, called the 'Night of the Bridges', took place on 17 June. Its objective was to destroy the bridges connecting Palestine with neighbouring territories. The operation was a complete success. Ten bridges out of eleven were destroyed.

\*

On Sunday, 30 June, the family were as usual at Aunt Doris and Uncle Mark's house, when the music on the radio was interrupted by the voice of the BBC news announcer.

'This is a special report from Palestine. Yesterday, 29 June, twelve days after Jewish resistance fighters destroyed ten bridges; 17,000 British soldiers and policemen carried out the most extensive operation to date against Jewish terrorists. The operation took place at dawn and lasted the entire day. The Commander of the British forces told our reporter that the operation's objective was to destroy the Hagana, and its strike force, the Palmach.

'Two thousand seven hundred people have been arrested, including Jewish Agency leaders with connections to the Haganah, and members of the Zionist movement. The Army and police also conducted a weapons search on 27 settlements throughout the country. This operation was also successful. A curfew was imposed on Jewish towns and settlements. This is the end of the special announcement.'

\*

29 June 1946 had been named Black Sabbath by the Jewish community in Palestine.

Sarah was visiting her parents, who lived nearby, to tell them she was pregnant, giving Sam the opportunity to see Manny and discuss the latest events in Palestine.

'We received a message at the Haganah office,' said Sam, 'from Chaim Weizmann. He said that because of the risk of war between us and the British, all military operations against them must cease.'

'Is there any news about Dominique, the baby and Zach?' Manny asked.

'Nothing concrete; but I do know that Mr White and Amber have been imprisoned. I've telephoned the number Zach gave us, but—'

'You didn't use your home phone?' Manny said quickly.

'No, I'm not an idiot. I used a public phone a couple of miles away.'

'Sorry, I didn't mean—' The ringing of the doorbell interrupted Manny. He headed for the door, looking over his shoulder at Sam. 'I tried the number yesterday and like you got no reply.'

As Manny opened the front door, his mouth dropped open in surprise on seeing the man in front of him. He was wearing a camel-haired coat, a light brown fedora hat, the brim slightly down over his forehead, a silver-topped walking stick in his right hand, and briefcase in the other.

'Manny Grenfeldt, you're a hard man to find,' he said, a big smile on his face.

'Joseph, Joseph Rosenblatt.' Manny stared at Rosenblatt and for the first time in many years was lost for words.

Rosenblatt took off his hat. 'Can I come in, or shall we talk out here?'

'No, no, sorry, please come in. I'm – to say the least – flabbergasted to see you after all this time. How are you?' Manny stepped aside to allow Rosenblatt to enter.

'I'm well, thank you,' was the smiled reply. He walked with a slight limp into the hallway, using the stick for support.

Manny closed the door. 'Follow me.' He led Rosenblatt into the dining room.

Sam stood as they entered. 'Joseph, may I introduce my cousin Sam.' The two men shook hands.

Manny pointed to an armchair. 'Have a seat. Would you like a drink, tea, coffee, or something stronger?'

'Tea would do nicely, thank you.' Rosenblatt shrugged off his camel-haired coat, and was about to place it over the back of a chair when Manny said, 'I'll hang it up.' Taking the coat from Rosenblatt he asked Sam, 'Tea?'

'No thanks. I'd better get going. I've left Sarah for far too long as it is.' He turned to Joseph. 'Nice to have met you; something tells me we'll meet again.'

'I'm sure we will,' Joseph replied, shaking the outstretched hand.

'I'll see you out,' Manny said, adding once they were in the hallway. 'Let me know if you get any information on Zach.'

'As soon as I hear anything, so will you.'

'OK, see you soon.' The two men hugged.

Manny returned to the dining room with two cups, a pot of tea and a plate of biscuits on a tray, laying it on the table, 'What happened to your leg?'

'Bullet; I wouldn't mind if it was a German one, but in truth, it was just bad luck. We were on a training exercise, a bullet ricocheted off something.' Rosenblatt gives a throaty laugh. 'That bullet did me a favour, and in a way so did you.'

'Me?' Manny poured the tea, giving a sideways glance at Rosenblatt, 'How?'

Rosenblatt leaned forward to take the offered cup. 'Don't tell me you've forgotten about your investments?'

Manny offered the biscuit. 'Invest... oh, yes. Do you know I'm ashamed to say I had? So much has happened since we last saw each other.' Manny sat on the armchair opposite Rosenblatt, who took a sip of his tea.

'Nice cuppa.' He said placing the cup on the small coffee table beside him and pointed to the dining table at the other end of the room. 'Could we sit over there?'

'Sure, why not?'

The two men moved to the table. Manny waited for Rosenblatt to continue their conversation, but he just picked up the briefcase, opened it, pulling out a folder laying it squarely on the table, placing the briefcase by his right leg. Taking a bite of the biscuit and a sip of tea with deliberate movements, Rosenblatt pulled a spectacles case from the inside pocket of his brown double-breasted jacket and extracted a pair of wire glasses, placing the case precisely above and in the middle of the folder which he opened.

Manny watched in fascination and amusement at each precise movement as Rosenblatt took a hanky from his top pocket, carefully removed his glasses, wiped the lenses and looked through them before putting them on. He gave a slight businesslike cough and then looked down at the folder, and then at Manny over the top of his glasses.

'Firstly, I've changed my name to Joe Rosen. Mainly for business reasons and it sounds better than Rosenblatt.' Manny was about to interrupt, but Rosen held up his hand, stopping him. 'Please let me finish; questions later.'

'While I was in the army, under our agreement...' He showed white teeth, giving a brisk smile '... and with your money I bought some shares which may I say have done very well.' He leaned towards Manny. 'More than that really, I should have said exceptionally well. With my percentage, and profits from those shares, I expanded our transactions.' Rosen picked up his cup, and drank the rest of the tea and then asked, 'Could I have another, please?'

As Manny poured him another cup, Rosen continued. 'With my injury, the army released me and I decided to open my own stockbroker's business. The bombing, apart from doodlebugs, was over so I rented an office in Coleman

David Brown

Street in the city, and as I said changed my name. That was just over a year ago.' He took a sip of tea.

'What about teaching? You're a professor.'

'Professor shmessa. I told you on the Isle of Man that I did this before the war, and had a very lucrative business. The Nazis took it all away, every penny, and for good measure killed my parents and two sisters...' There were tears in Rosen's eyes. 'If I hadn't signed everything over to that...' he hesitated for a moment, staring into space and whispered '... that mumser, Major Hoffmiester was his name. At least he kept his promise and let me go. I sometimes wonder if it was through the guilt of killing my family, or because I helped him with homework after school; we were in the same class.' He wiped his eyes with a handkerchief and blew his nose.

They were both silent for a second, staring at each other, as for a moment they remembered their families. The spell was broken by the front door opening and Rita calling.

'Manny could you give me hand with the shopping?'

Manny grinned. 'I won't be a moment.'

A few seconds later, Rita carrying David walked into the room. 'Hallo, I'm Rita, Manny's wife; sorry for any inconvenience, but Manny won't be a moment.' She tilted the baby, who was asleep in her arms so Rosen could see his face. 'This is our son, David. Do you have any children?'

'He's very handsome, no, I'm not married yet. I'm engaged, we hope to get married in September.'

'Congratulations, what's your fiancée's name?'

'Marlene.'

Manny walked into the room, placing an arm around Rita's waist. 'It seems you two have introduced yourselves.'

'I'm very sorry, here am I rattling on about the baby, and I never asked your name.'

132

Rosen stood, holding out his hand. 'Joe Rosen. It's a pleasure to meet you,' he stroked David's cheek, 'and your son.'

Rita smiled at Rosen. 'I'll leave you two gentlemen to your … well, whatever. I have dinner to prepare.' She turned to go and then looked back. 'Mr Rosen, would you like to join us for dinner?'

'I would love to, thank you.'

While Rita disappeared into the kitchen, Manny and Rosen returned to their seats. Joe took a sheath of paper from the folder, sliding it across the table to Manny and turning it the right way for him to read.

'Although we had a verbal contract of two per cent – and as far as I'm concerned it's still binding – I… we… have to ensure everything is now in writing. One reason is for tax purposes and the other…' he shrugged his shoulders '…just so everything is kosher. I hear that you want to live in Palestine, which I'm sure you know is at the moment a very volatile place to be. I'm positive, knowing you the way I do, you've made a will. If anything were to happen to you, God forbid, then your shares will be part of your estate. Please read the contract very carefully. If there's anything you don't agree with, or want changed, tell me now before you sign it.

Manny nodded, and began reading the contract. At the same time Rosen extracted a cheque book from his briefcase, opened it and wrote a cheque, signing it with a flourish, tore it from the book and then took another sip of tea

Manny looked up. 'Joe, have you got a pen?'

Rosen smiled, handing the pen to Manny, who signed the contract sliding it back across the table to Rosen who glanced at it, placing it neatly into the folder and handed Manny the cheque. 'This is yours.'

Manny took the cheque, looked at it, and whistled. 'This is a lot of money, are you sure—?'

Rosen nodded his head, smiling. 'Yes, I'm sure. You've not received anything since we first started. I couldn't find you. In fact I didn't know whether you were alive or dead. I was in the synagogue last Shabbat. I went to Egerton Road; and was talking to a new congregant, a Mr Faulkner. As was usual with us Jews, within half an hour I knew everything about him, his family and who his daughter was married to. As soon as he said Grenfeldt, I asked if he knew you. So here I am, a very happy man.'

Rosen took another sip of tea and leaned forward pointing a finger. 'If it hadn't been for you, I would never have started up again – and to be honest, to be in the position I am today—'

Rita entered the room with the baby in one hand and a bottle in the other. 'Sorry to interrupt again, but David wanted his daddy to feed him.' She handed the baby and the bottle to Manny. 'Dinner won't be long, and then you can tell me what you two have been talking about.'

\*

That night, Manny and Rita lay contentedly in each other's arms, the perspiration of their lovemaking still on their bodies. He turned slightly to kiss her left nipple. 'I think we should have a holiday, somewhere in the sun. I've spoken to Sam and Isaac. They think it's a good idea.' He moved onto his elbow stroking a curl away from her forehead, 'What do you think?'

She smiled. 'I'm all for it.' Pushing him onto his back, straddling him. 'Where are we going?' She bent to kiss him. While their lips were glued together he answered, but it was just drivel. He tickled her and she pulled away laughing, 'Where?'

'Nice, on the French Riviera. There's a lovely hotel right on the beach. Your father, Aunt Doris and Uncle Mark could come as well. They haven't had a holiday since...' he paused, stared at the ceiling and then at his wife '...since my barmitzvah. We'll get everyone together, and plan for the beginning of next year.'

Rita ran a finger down his nose and across his lips. 'I saw Dr Cohen yesterday.'

'Is everything all right?' Alarm showed on his face and in his voice.

She gave a dimpled grin. 'Everything's fine, we're going to have another baby.'

His eyes lit up. 'How long have you—'

'Two months.'

'We'd better stop.'

'Stop what?'

'You know.'

She laughed. 'Don't be silly, it won't harm the baby. In fact we could do it as many times as we like. If you're up to it, now would be a good time.'

# Chapter 12

*Nice, February 1947*

**M**ANNY leapt out of the pool and ran to where Rita was sunbathing, shook his head, showering her with water. She let out a yell, and in one movement was on her feet chasing him. He dived into the pool, with Rita close behind. Manny surfaced behind another swimmer. Rita looked around, ducked under the water, but still couldn't see him.

Smiling, he swam just under the surface towards where she was treading water, placing one hand on her left breast, the other on her pregnant belly. Rita turned quickly around as he surfaced; her arms going around his neck giving him a peck on the lips. 'I love you, Manny Grenfeldt.'

*

That evening, the family, all with healthy tans, sat happily chatting at the dinner table. The children, David and Barry, were asleep in their rooms being looked after by the hotel's babysitter.

All the family were there, even Joshua, who had managed to get two weeks' leave from the RAF with his girlfriend Freda, who was talking to Manny.

Aunt Doris was very happy. Her daughter-in-law Sarah was pregnant, as were her two nieces, Hannah and Rita.

The atmosphere was one of relaxed happiness as Joshua stood and clinked a glass for attention. Everyone stopped talking, turning towards him. For a second he looked around the table and then at Freda, dropping to one knee at the same time taking a velvet box from his pocket. 'Freda, my darling, I love you with all my heart, and...' he swallowed nervously '... will you please marry me?'

There was a second's silence as the family looked on. Some nodded at Freda, although she couldn't see them as she was looking down at the kneeling Joshua, tears in her eyes, and a happy smile on her face as she whispered, 'Yes.'

'I didn't hear your reply,' Manny said, a mischievous grin on his face.

Some of the others joined in. 'Neither did we.'

'Perhaps a little louder then,' laughed Manny, ducking as Rita hit him playfully with her napkin.

Freda turned, saying loudly, 'I said yes,' adding with a giggle in her voice. 'I think you should all see a doctor about your hearing.' She turned back to Joshua, who was placing a ring he had made from one of the diamonds his mother bequeathed him onto her finger to the cheers of the family.

'Oh! Joshua, it's beautiful.' She bent to kiss him – a long lingering kiss – to the whistles and clapping from those around the table, while other diners looked on in amusement.

*

Three days after Joshua's proposal, Manny, Joshua, Isaac, and Daniel were playing cards. The women were shopping. 'Anyone know where Sam is?' Manny asked.

The others shook their heads, except Joshua. 'I saw him leave the hotel just after breakfast. I called to him, but he didn't hear me, seemed to be in a hurry.'

The women returned from their shopping spree, carrying a multitude of bags. Manny asked Sarah if she knew where Sam was.

'No, I thought he was with you.'

Manny could see she was lying, but didn't want to press it. He'd find out in due course.

The women decided to change and meet the men for a snack by the pool.

Manny watched Sarah, Rita and Hannah playing with the children in the baby pool, his eyes wandering around the pool area as Isaac said, 'I'm seriously thinking of becoming a surgeon.'

'That's great—' Manny stopped in mid-sentence, climbing slowly to his feet, and in barely a whisper said, 'Bergman.'

Isaac turned in the direction Manny was looking, 'Where? So it is; and there's Sam.' He rose to his feet as the two men walked towards them.

Bergman stood silent for a moment in front of them as if wondering what to say, but Manny moved quickly forward, giving him a hug. 'I've been worried sick about you, baby Harry and Dominique. I'm very happy to see you.'

The two men parted, then Isaac gave Bergman a hug. 'You look fine, how's Harry and Dominique?'

'She's pretty good, considering she's four months pregnant.'

'Where are they now?' Manny asked.

'The hotel, they're resting. The pregnancy and what she had been through these last few months have taken their toll.'

'How did you know we were here?' Manny queried, looking in Sam's direction.

Bergman could see that Manny was a little peeved at Sam. 'I've managed to get a babysitter for Harry while Dominique is resting. Don't blame Sam, I told him not to tell you, I—'

Manny ignored Bergman, turning angrily on Sam, he was hurt that Sam didn't trust him enough to tell him that Bergman and the others were safe, and wasn't really listening to what Bergman was saying. 'Sam, you know I've been worried sick about Zach and the others, and yet you keep me in the dark.' He stabbed a finger at Sam, 'You knew this, and you still didn't tell me they were safe.'

'I didn't know my—'

Bergman moved between the two cousins, facing Manny. 'Don't blame Sam. If you're going to have a go at someone have a go at me. I told him not to tell you; anyway, he's only known for two days.'

Manny's voice was unsteady with emotion, 'After all we've been through, Zach, it seems you don't trust me.'

Bergman moved towards Manny, placing a hand on his shoulder, looking seriously into his friend's eyes. 'Manny, I trust you with my life. I needed to contact certain people, and Sam knew how I could do that. I assure you there's no big secret, and if there were, you would be one of the first to know.' He smiled. 'Now lighten up, we don't want to worry the ladies do we?'

Manny face relaxed, realising with shame that he'd been acting like a spoilt jealous child. 'I'm sorry, Zach, and you're right. What would you have to drink?'

'A large scotch would do nicely, thank you.'

Manny nodded, turning to Sam. 'If I ever act like that again, you have permission to punch me on the chin.'

Sam laughed. 'You might regret you said that.'

\*

At the pool, Sarah said something to the others, pointing in their husbands' direction. Leaving the children with the nanny, the women walked quickly over to surround Bergman, giving hugs and kisses, saying how happy they were to see him.

'Where are Dominique and Harry?' Rita asked. 'Is she OK?'

'She's fine,' Bergman replied. 'Resting at the hotel.'

Manny could see that Bergman wanted to talk to them about something, but couldn't with the women around.

'Where are you staying?' Manny asked.

'Scalia Hotel.'

'How long are you in Nice for?' Isaac enquired, lifting a glass of Bacardi to his lips.

'I'm not sure, four, five days.'

'Why don't you move into this hotel? That way we could all be together and Dominique would have the girls to talk to. Harry can join David and Barry' Manny said.

Bergman looked down, twiddling his glass between his fingers. 'Not possible.'

'Why?' Rita asked.

Bergman kept his head down, ringing his glass with the tip of his index finger, as he said quietly, 'I'm embarrassed to say that it's financial. I can't get to my account.'

'Is that all?' Manny quickly rose to his fee,. 'Come on, Zach, we'll book you in right away.'

Bergman shook his head, 'I can't accept it—'

'I … we, will not take no for an answer,' said Manny emphatically, taking the glass from Bergman's hands, placing it on the table; grabbing his friend's arm and lifting him from the seat, with the others voicing their agreement.

*

Having booked Bergman into a room, Manny hired a taxi to take them to the Scalia Hotel.

Manny told the driver to wait for them.

'Why don't you wait in the taxi?' Bergman said.

Manny placed a hand on Bergman's shoulder. 'While you get packed and fetch Dominique and Harry, I'll pay the bill.'

'Manny, I can't—'

'Look, Zach.' Manny only called Bergman by his first name when it was something personal between them. 'I'm not going to take any argument from you, just go and get Dominique and Harry.'

Bergman said softly, 'Thanks, I'll—'

'Yes, I know. Hurry up, the meter's ticking.'

Manny greeted Dominique, who looked pale, with a hug and a kiss on both cheeks, looking down at her belly, 'Congratulations.' He could see by their luggage that they had left Palestine in a hurry, and he was determined to help his friends get over their ordeal.

Dominique was overwhelmed by the greetings she received, hugging everyone, with tears in her eyes.

Taking Rita aside, Manny said, 'I want to take Dominique and Zach shopping. They're too proud to tell us, but by the look of things they escaped with just the bare necessities.'

'Manny Grenfeldt, you're a big softy, that's one of the things I love about you.'

\*

The following day, with the children being looked after, Rita and Manny took their friends shopping. At first they protested, but in the end gave in gracefully as their protests fell on deaf ears.

The afternoon sun was high in a clear blue sky as the women left their menfolk at the hotel to have their hair done and be pampered.

Manny, Isaac, Sam and Bergman sat under a huge umbrella around a circular table with an assortment of drinks in front of them, to do what men do better than women – talk.

Manny sipped his drink, the ice clinking in the glass, looked at Bergman and said quietly. 'We telephoned the number you gave us, but…' his voice trailed off.

'How did you escape the British?' asked Isaac, following Manny's gaze.

Bergman poured himself a glass of whisky from the bottle on the table, took a sip, and then held the glass between his hands, elbows on the table, playing with it for a second, and then looked at the men around the table. 'On the 29th – Black Sabbath – Dominique, Harry and I were visiting friends in Tel Aviv. Luckily for us, we stayed the night because of the Shabbat. The following morning as we were leaving the synagogue, one of my men, who'd managed to escape the British, came to warn me not to go home, or anywhere near Haganah HQ.'

Bergman took a drink; the others silently waiting for him to continue. Looking over the rim of the glass he continued, 'I always had a contingency plan, just in case...' He shook his head. 'The British Intelligence Service knew more than we gave them credit for. Most of our safe houses were compromised. I managed to get Dominique and Harry to my in-laws, and then, with some of my men, commandeered a ship, which was about to leave Tel Aviv. We hugged the coast to avoid the British Navy till we reached Tunisia.'

He pulled a pack of cigarettes from his pocket, offering them around, then lit his, blew the smoke into the air, twirling the lighter between his fingers, while they waited patiently for him to carry on. 'We then crossed the Mediterranean to Italy, beached the ship and made our way to Tavisio, where we still had friends.' Bergman's eyes moved around the pool, coming to a stop at the entrance, his lips moving in a smile.

Manny followed Bergman's gaze, but couldn't see anything out of the ordinary and didn't say anything, wondering if Bergman was making sure there weren't any British agents around.

'How did you know we were here?' Isaac asked.

'Sam notified the Jewish Agency in London that if there were any messages for him, they could contact him here. I telephoned the other day and we—'

'So that's where you went,' Manny interrupted, looking at Sam.

Sam nodded.

Manny turned back to Bergman. 'So, what now? What are your plans?'

Bergman didn't answer right away, but looked down at the glass, twisting it round and around, then up at Manny, who knew through Bergman's intense, brown-eyed look that he had something in mind for them.

'Now that all the people arrested on Black Sabbath, have been released, I must get back to Pal—' Bergman's face broke into a smile, half rising from his chair.

'It's nice to see you all again,' a voice behind Manny said.

Knowing the voice, Manny turned, and at first didn't recognise Mr White, who had lost a lot of weight. Standing beside him was Mr Amber, whose usual shaggy beard was neatly trimmed into a small goatee; the once unruly grey hair now cut, as was his usually bushy eyebrows. Manny and the others got quickly to their feet, happily greeting the men with handshakes and hugs.

'Could we offer you a drink, and may I say,' Manny patted Mr White's stomach, 'prison seems to have agreed with you.'

'Prison was not renowned for its cuisine,' Mr White replied smiling.

'A large scotch, for me,' said Mr Amber.

'Me too,' Mr White joined in, adding, 'A few nibbles wont go amiss.'

Manny called the waiter over and ordered the drinks while Sam and Isaac brought over two extra chairs.

'OK, who's going to tell us what's going on?' Manny asked quietly, looking from one to the other.

Mr White coughed, as though about to say something, but it was Bergman who spoke with a grin, 'You know us too well,' he took a swig of his drink, face now serious. 'The Palmach was the strike force of the Haganah, and us, me—'

'Zach, we know from past experience, that when you three appear you have something in mind for us, so don't beat around the bush – what do you want?' Manny raised his sunglasses onto his forehead.

Before Bergman could answer, Mr White said, 'We, the Agency, have tried to make peace with the Arabs, but it's become clear the two communities cannot be reconciled, especially the Arabs. A UN special committee is visiting

Palestine in April. I would assure you now they'll recommend partition between Arab and Jew, and on—' The waiter brought their drinks interrupting him.

When the waiter had walked away, Mr Amber took a sip of his drink and leaned forward, taking over from Mr White. 'When that happens, all hell will break loose, and the Arabs will lose no time in attacking us.'

Sam leaned forward in his chair, adding his thoughts to the conversation. 'Especially with the Grand Mufti Hajj Amin al-Husseini crying out to murder the Jews, saying kill them all.'

'The Grand Mufti isn't the only one,' Mr Amber added angrily. 'There are many others who have this hatred for the Jew. Why, I cannot tell you, as I don't know.'

'You still haven't told us why you're here,' Isaac said, lifting his glass of Bacardi and coke. '*L'chaim*,' he toasted. They all raised their glass repeating the toast.

Manny looked at Sam, lifting his eyebrows shrugging his shoulders, as if asking him, if something sinister was going on? Sam shook his head, mouthing the word 'No'.

Taking a handful of nuts from the dish in front of him, Bergman pointed a finger at no one in particular saying, 'We need your help, or should I say your expertise once again.' Holding up his right hand to fend off any questions.

'It's inevitable,' Mr Amber interjected, 'that there's going to be a State of Israel and we're going to need a trained army to defend ourselves, and that's where you come in.' Like Bergman he pointed a finger at no one in particular. 'After peace was declared, you wanted to go to Palestine. We asked you to wait awhile and spend time with your families, but now – it's time, and we need your help.'

There was a moment's silence finally broken by Mr White, who asked, 'Anyone like another drink?' Holding up his hands as they all replied at once, 'Whoa back, hang on,' Lifting his arm and yelling, 'Waiter!'

Once the waiter has taken their order, the atmosphere around the table relaxed.

'OK, Zach, what do you need us to do?' Manny asked, pulling his sunglasses over his eyes.

'We have placed a platoon of Palmach in most kibbutzim throughout Palestine. The kibbutz supplies the troops with food, homes and resources; in return they help with the land and defence of the kibbutz. What most of them lack is training, the sort of training we—' he pointed to himself, Sam and Manny '—have as well as the skills needed. We would spend four weeks at a Kibbutz, and then move off to another.'

'And me, what about me?' Isaac asked.

'I think I'm right in saying, you must finish med-school. We're going to need trained doctors.'

Isaac nodded in reply.

Manny's thoughts turned to Rita. 'What about our wives? I can't see Rita letting me go without her, especially now she's pregnant. I missed David's birth. I can assure you she won't want me to miss this one.'

'I would like the women to stay in London until it's safe for them to join us,' Bergman replied.

'Does that include Dominique and Harry?' Sam queried, adding, 'And when do you envisage it would be safe for our wives to join us?'

'As far as Dominique and Harry are concerned, I was hoping they could stay with you, well not with you exactly, nearby, I'll rent a place. I'll feel a lot happier knowing that they were away from any danger, so I'll be able to concentrate on what had to be done, and not have to worry about their safety.'

'What about the baby, don't you want to be around for its birth?' Sam asked.

Bergman's face softened. 'Sam, you know me better than that. Of course I'd like to be around for the birth. Dominique understands that I'm fighting for a better tomorrow and a homeland where we could raise our children free from persecution or anti-Semitism. If that happened, then it would be worth the sacrifice.'

'In that case,' Manny said, 'you can tell Rita.'

'And Sarah,' Sam raised his glass, 'Good luck with that.'

'Where are you both staying?' Manny asked the two Agency men.

Mr Amber smiled, 'Here of course.'

'I'll book a table in the restaurant for this evening,' Mr White said, rising from his chair. Taking a couple of steps, and then turned back. 'Will eight o'clock be convenient? Umm, and how many of us are there?'

'Table for fifteen,' Manny answered. They all agreed the time.

*

Rita was singing happily as they dressed for dinner. Manny sat on the edge of the bed staring down at the floor. He'd been trying to think of a way to tell her about Bergman's offer, but decided to put it off until tomorrow, not wanting to spoil her evening. He looked up, and was as always, stunned by her beauty.

She smiled. 'Come on, slowcoach, otherwise we'll be late. Talk about women keeping the men waiting.'

'Stop yakking, woman, I guarantee I'll be ready before you.'

Rita went to pass him to get a dress hanging in the cupboard, but he placed an arm around her waist, leaning forward to kiss her. She moved her head away giving a throaty laugh. 'Not now, big boy, you'll smudge my lipstick. But, if you're good—' she ran her hand along the inside of his thigh, a mischievous grin on her face '—who knows what could happen later.' He gave her a peck on the cheek taking his arm from around her waist.

*

There was light-hearted banter around the table, from friends who hadn't seen each other for some time. No one mentioned Palestine, but there was a lot of talk amongst the women about babies. Aunt Doris and Sarah's mother gave versions of their labours, which had the table in tears of laughter at the expense of their husbands.

Manny looked across at Bergman, their eyes met, Manny raised an eyebrow. Bergman knew what it meant, and his tight-lipped grimace, and little gesture with his head, told him that Zach hadn't said anything to his wife. He looked at his friend giving a little wag of his forefinger.

With a slight smile on his face Bergman shrugged his shoulders spreading his hands.

As they said goodnight, Bergman whispered to Manny, 'Dominique and I will meet you in the morning, say ten o'clock, after breakfast. I've already arranged it with Sam and Isaac.'

*

The following morning, as they headed towards the coffee lounge, Rita said for the umpteenth time, 'What's going on? Why can't you tell me what this meeting's about? We need to spend time with David, which we haven't done for the last couple of days.'

Manny gave an inward sigh, knowing she was right, turning his head to look at her. 'I promise that we'll spend the rest of the day with David.'

She came to an abrupt halt, pulling him back, stopping them from going any further, not uttering a word as she stepped in front of him, staring into his eyes, which he turned from her gaze. Her face and voice showed she was aggravated. 'Manny Grenfeldt, something's going on here and I'm sure I'm not going to like it.'

He didn't answer.

She stamped her foot in anger. 'You're infuriating when you're like this.'

Feigning ignorance and trying hard to keep a straight face, as she looked so pretty when she was angry, she said, 'Like what?'

'Secretive.' Not letting go his hand, she turned, moving abruptly forward, dragging him onward, saying between clenched teeth, 'Come on, so I can find out from someone else what my coward of a husband cannot tell me.'

\*

When they arrived, the others were already there. Armchairs and two settees surrounded a circular table with jugs of iced water and glasses in the centre. Rita hugged the women, and the men stood to greet them.

Rita said, 'This looks like a meeting of the board,' and moved to the armchair next to Dominique. 'Have you any idea what this is about?'

'No, and Zach won't tell me.'

She turned to Sarah. 'What about you, anything?'

Sarah shook her head, as did Hannah.

Bergman coughed to clear his throat. 'Ladies, you are...' He looked at them, placing a hand to his forehead rubbing it, a worried look on his face. Manny had never seen him so indecisive; perhaps scared would probably be the right word.

'What Zach is trying to say,' Mr Amber spoke in a quiet, unassuming voice, 'is that we've asked Manny and Sam to help us with training recruits in Palestine for a battle that's inevitable. The problem your husbands are having is it means that you, their wives, are staying in England.'

He held up his hands to fend off the tirade coming from the women. 'Please, ladies, let me finish, and then you can throw the tomatoes. We know you're pregnant, and want your husbands to be at the birth and to tell you the truth, I would if...' his eyes watered, looking down at the table, then up at those around it who waited for him to continue.

Bergman was the only person there who knew that Mr Amber's family – wife, son and two daughters – were killed by Arabs while he was in England. He stood moving towards Mr Amber, placing an arm around his shoulders, whispering, 'I'll take over.'

'The thing is…' Bergman said, moving back to his seat '… it's too dangerous for you to come with us. We would worry about your safety.' He sat down. 'We're sure that by next year there'll be a Jewish state. But before that can happen there are many hurdles to cross.' He looked at his wife, as if asking for reassurance, but she and the other women stared impassively back at him.

'When that happened, the whole of the Arab world will rise up against us.' Taking a cigarette from the packet in front of him, he lit it, exhaling the smoke through his nostrils and continued. 'We need an army to defend ourselves. What happened in the Holocaust must never happen again. I know there are other trained men to help, but we still haven't enough. I haven't told Dominique about staying in England, and to tell you the truth I was dreading it.'

'It's not fair on us,' Rita said bitterly between tight lips, looking quickly at the men in turn as she added quietly, 'Manny wasn't there when David was born.' She blinked her eyes as if holding back tears. 'I hoped that he would be there,' she added, rubbing her belly, 'when this one's born.'

'I feel the same way,' Sarah spoke, a tear running down her cheek at the thought of Sam not being there at the birth of their first child.

Dominique turned, her face showing the anger of what she has just heard from her husband, and was about to say something when Manny said sharply, 'Wait.'

There was silence, all eyes on him. 'Let's look at this sensibly. We would all like to be there for the births, but at the same time we also want to help in Palestine. If I'm correct, Sarah and Rita, all being well, are expecting in June; Dominique in July. Isaac's staying in London to finish becoming a doctor, so in Hannah's case it's irrelevant. What if Zach, Sam and myself get started in Palestine and return to London in late May for the births.' He looked from one to the other. 'We'll be happy that you're safe in London, and we promise to return in May. Would you agree to that?' His brow creased. The eyes had that hangdog look, as if pleading for them to say yes.

'Give us a few moments to talk it over,' Rita said.

'Would you like us to leave?' Bergman asked.

'No,' the women said as one, going into a huddle.

Five minutes later they moved apart and Rita, who seemed to be the spokeswoman, said, 'We agree.'

# Chapter 13

*Palestine, April 1947*

MANNY was pleased with the news they had received from England. Ernest Bevin's stubbornness had succeeding in turning the British press, as well as public and world opinion, against his sledgehammer policies in Palestine. Manny shook his head as he read the speech Bevin made in the House of Commons. He turned to Sam, 'Did you read the speech by Bevin?'

'No.'

'He's one belligerent so and so. Bevin said that he had come to the conclusion that the only course now open to Britain, was to submit the Palestine problem to the judgement of the United Nations to recommend a settlement.'

Sam laughed, 'Bevin was convinced that the United Nations would not touch such a diplomatic hot potato, and would just throw it back to Britain, giving him complete freedom to impose a solution favourable to his beliefs regarding the Middle East; he's in for a big shock.'

'I would love to be a fly on the wall when he learnt the UN would take over, as they were very unhappy at the way the British were handling the refugee problem.'

\*

Manny knew that Sam was right. The British Navy and army tried stopping refugee ships from unloading their human cargos on the beaches of Palestine, where they dispersed to various kibbutzim. In that confrontation the British had superior manpower and equipment. The refugees had nothing but their stubbornness, and the will to sacrifice themselves by smashing through the British blockade in crumbling unseaworthy vessels.

Meanwhile Manny and Sam, both lieutenants, and Bergman a captain, were busy training the Palmach. They knew that by combining British para and commando training, their Strike Force would be like no other.

Today, like in other kibbutzim, they had marked out a two-mile circuit. Manny, Sam and Bergman gather the men in a semi-circle in front of them.

'Smoke if you want,' said Bergman, lighting his cigarette, and from habit cupping the flame against the slight breeze, blowing out the smoke and pointing, 'That two-mile circuit must be completed in full battle order in seventeen minutes and everything else you do must be done at the double. We,' he pointed at Sam and Manny, 'are going to be your instructors.'

Manny stepped forward. 'We would demand from you a very high standard of fitness.' He smiled his eyes sweeping the men in front. 'There's no better time to start than now, so I'm going to make it easy for you today. Stub out your cigarettes, strip to the waist and follow me.' He waited until everyone was ready and then set off at an easy jog, with Bergman and Sam taking up the rear, urging on any stragglers.

*

As the days went by, the men realised that their three instructors don't demand anything from them that they would not do themselves. The three friends were always sorry to say goodbye to their new recruits, but knew that they had done a good job, and they would truly live up to the meaning of Palmach.

Manny's missing Rita and David, writing to her as often as he could and she in turn wrote to him. He was reading her latest letter.

*David is growing, and every day he's doing something new. I'm
getting bigger and waddling around like a duck. Aunt Doris and
Sarah's mother Ruth have taken us under their wing and look
after the children so we can have a lie down in the afternoon.*

*Aunt Doris says that I'm having a girl, Sarah and
Dominique boys. It seems that from what she said, she's never
wrong.*

As usual Rita reminded him:

*Please don't forget your promise and be home by the first of May.*

Although Manny enjoyed what he was doing, wild
horses wouldn't keep him away for the birth. Today was 1
May; and as promised, he, Sam and Bergman were packed
and waiting for their transport.

There was a knock at the door, and a familiar voice said,
'Your chariot awaits thee.'

'Hans,' Manny yelled. The two men met each other in
the middle of the room, and bearhugged, and then, 'What
about me?'

Manny couldn't believe his eyes, moving away from
Hans, holding out his arms to enfold Helga, who kissed him
on both cheeks.

'How did you?' He looked across at Bergman, who had
that, 'Yep, it was me' look on his face. 'You knew where
they were all along and didn't tell me.'

'We were busy, and you had other things on your mind.'
Bergman picked up his gear. 'I think we should be on our
way.'

Sitting between Helga and Hans, who was driving,
Helga told Manny all that had happened to them since
arriving in Palestine.

'Firstly, Hans and I converted to Judaism. I've been
married for two months to Yitzak Friedman, he's German.
I've told him the truth about us, except you-know-what.'
She touched his lips, stopping him from saying anything.

'We have a very short journey and I want to tell you everything.'

'Hey, I can speak for myself.' Hans turned to glance at them, and then back to the road. 'I'm now Hans Meyer,' he laughed happily, 'I've been married for two weeks and three days to Yitzak's sister, Mulka.'

Manny turned to Bergman. 'Why didn't you tell me?'

Bergman shrugged his shoulders but didn't reply.

'We told him not to say anything as you've enough on your plate at the moment, and anyway, you're coming back and then we could get together. You can meet our other halves, as they say. We are in the Haganah and live on a kibbutz, Mishmar Haemek, it's just west of the Esdraelon Valley. Oh! We're here already.'

Manny looked through the windscreen, surprise on his face and in his voice as they stopped at the end of a field. 'This is a—'

Hans turned to Manny, a big smile on his face. 'Special transport.' He looked up at the sky as they heard the faint noise of an aeroplane. 'There he is.' Hans pointed towards the hedgehopping plane that came in to land. Hans gunned the car's engine following the plane that pulled up at the end of the field, turning a full circle, facing back down the field, its propellers turning lazily. Hans braked beside the plane. Bergman stepped from the car with Sam, as a side door opened and a goggled figure leapt down.

'Come on, you three, I haven't got all day. I've just borrowed this for a joyride,' Joshua yelled against the noise from the aeroplane's engine and the cars.

Manny grabbed his gear, gave Helga a kiss on both cheeks, and shook hands with Hans. 'I'll be back and I'll see you both then.'

Brother and sister stood, arms around each other, waving goodbye as the plane sped along the grass and took off, vanishing into the distance.

# Chapter 14

THE waiting was over. On 8 May Hannah had another boy, naming him Jacob. Two days later, Sarah also had a boy, Michael; and arriving two weeks late, on 22 May 1947, Rita and Manny had a daughter, Miriam, after Rita's mother. All the grandparents were over the moon. Sam and Sarah's parents were already planning the circumcision ceremony. Aunt Doris kept her hundred per cent record in predicting the births when Dominique had another boy, Abraham, on 7 June.

Bergman had rented a house near Manny, and as a commander in Haganah received up-to-date news. While the three friends played happy fathers with their children, they met to obtain the latest news from Palestine.

Looking through the french door windows at their wives having tea in the garden, Bergman tried not to show his anger as he said to Manny and Sam. 'Things, as they say, were not going our way. Committee X approached the Irgun to defer plans to blow up the King David Hotel. The operation was planned before Weitzman ordered us to cease military action against the British.'

He slammed his fist on the table, rattling the cups and saucers. 'The Irgun rejected the appeal, 91 people killed, hundreds injured, including Jews and Arabs. I've been told, by a reliable source, they did telephone the hotel warning them to evacuate everyone, but the management didn't believe them.'

'I can't understand,' Manny commented, 'why the British kept stopping refugees from landing. It's no skin off their nose.'

'You're right, but they don't see it that way,' Sam agreed. 'We have vessels of all types, some carrying under a hundred refugees, others up to 7,000, leaving Europe for the shores of Palestine.'

'What happened to the Exodus is disgusting,' said Manny, taking a cigarette from Bergman's pack. 'The British knew the 4,500 people were extermination camp survivors, and some of the soldiers had seen at first hand what they had been through. The British should have escorted them in, instead of deporting them back to Germany. It's inhuman.'

*

It was a dull, dark, cloudy, late October day, as Manny and Bergman took their usual early morning run in Springfield Park. Manny's thoughts were as usual, on Palestine. With all that was happening there, he knew they would soon have to return. He and Bergman raced the last hundred yards, and as always Bergman won by an inch.

Manny, body bent, hands on his knees, gulping in a lungful of air, said breathlessly, 'I'll beat you if it kills me.'

Bergman laughed, and was about to respond when he spotted a black Bentley parked at the kerbside outside Manny's house. 'What's Rosen doing here?'

'There's only one way to find out, follow me.'

'I need a shower and change. Give me half an hour and I'll be over.'

'OK, see you soon.'

Manny's grateful, that his investments, thanks to Joe Rosen, had been very lucrative; not only for him, but for Sam, Bergman, Isaac and his brother Joshua. All had taken Rosen's advice and invested some of their savings, and were very happy with the ex-professor's shrewdness with their money.

Manny entered the house, finding Rosen playing with Miriam, while David sat quietly in his playpen.

'Is everything OK, where's Rita?' Manny asked.

Rosen smiled down at the baby, then at Manny. 'She's beautiful.'

'Rita.'

'No, you idiot, the baby… Oh, ah, Rita's beautiful too.'

Rita entered the room holding a tray on which stood two cups of tea and the baby's bottle. 'I'll make you a cup when you've showered and changed.'

'You had better make that two; Zach will be here in about thirty minutes.'

\*

Showered and dressed in grey slacks, white short-sleeve shirt open at the neck, Manny had just reached the bottom of the stairs when there was a knock at the door. 'I'll get it,' he yelled, knowing it was Bergman, and was pleasantly surprised on opening the door to see Dominique holding Abraham, with Harry perched on his father's broad shoulders.

'The boys asked if they could visit, especially Abraham who was in love with Miriam. Who am I to deny my sons?'

'If Abraham wants to marry my daughter, he'd better have a good job and lots of money.' Manny stepped aside to let them enter. 'They're in the dining room.'

Rita smiled on seeing Dominique and the boys. 'We'll leave you to it.' The two mothers, with their children, retired to another part of the house.

Manny looked across at Rosen who took a bite of his biscuit, left hand open under it to catch any crumbs. Bergman leaned across, taking a biscuit from the plate, raised an eyebrow in the stockbroker's direction, dunked the biscuit in his tea and took a bite.

Manny was the first to break the silence. 'How's the wife?'

'She's very well, thank you.'

'Nice car, Joe, expensive?' Bergman asked.

'Got it secondhand. The owner needed some cash on the quick, but you knew that.'

'OK, now that's out of the way,' laughed Manny, 'I know you don't come to see me unless there's a reason, so, are we to guess, or—'

Rosen's expression showed hurt. 'That's unfair; I do visit from time to time, but you're right, there's a very good reason for this one. You remember when we first met, and we talked about investing in all sorts of things, including armaments?'

Manny quickly glanced at Bergman who leaned forward, arms on the table, hands together, fingers entwined, staring at Rosen.

'Yeees,' replied Manny in a drawn-out way.

'I know where you can obtain two hundred Lee Enfield rifles with ammo.' Rosen hesitated for moment, looking at them for some sign of 'well done' on the faces of the two men in front of him, but they remained silent, knowing there was more to come.

Rosen stood and walked a few paces away from them, and spun back. 'I can also obtain two artillery pieces with shells, grenades; not too many of those, about two crates.' His two friends were still silent, but he could see they were interested.

Manny took a sip of tea, placing the cup with a deliberate motion onto the saucer, saying, 'How much?'

'You, nothing,' was the clipped reply.

Manny's face showed his astonishment, 'Nothing! But, but,' he stammered, 'who's paying for it?'

'Me,' Rosen replied.

'You?' the two men said in unison.

'But how could you afford such a large sum of money?' Manny asked.

'Well, not only me, but the members of the synagogue. Let me explain. I found out about the armaments by chance. It's – what shall I say? – from an old acquaintance who's a shady dealer. I approached the synagogue committee and they agreed that you should have them. We raised the money in a month, it's all paid for.'

The two men in front of him were speechless, a look of disbelief and wonder on their faces. Rosen continued. 'I knew that in a month or so, you would be returning to Palestine. I wanted you to ensure they got there.' He paused for a moment, took a sip of tea, and the continued, voice more intent. 'Look, I'm not a fighter, I'm a businessman. Like Jews throughout the world, I wanted us to have a homeland – a State of Israel – and if I could help in some small way by obtaining what you need to buy, land, arms, whatever, I'll do all I could to help you obtain them.'

Manny walked over to Rosen, too choked to say anything but hug him.

Bergman moved across the room to stand in front of Rosen. 'Thank you, when can you obtain the, er, cargo, and how would we get it to Palestine without it being confiscated by the British?'

'I can get it all by tomorrow, if you want. There's a ship, *The Isle of Man*, leaving Dover in November for Haifa with steel and machinery. I know the Captain, he's a Portuguese Jew, as is half his crew; we could hide the crates aboard her.'

Bergman turned to Manny, 'Can I use your phone? It's long distance.'

'Go ahead, you know where it is.'

'Have you a list of the equipment?' Bergman asked

Rosen took a piece of paper form his pocket handing it to Bergman.

As Bergman left the room Rosen sat down holding out his cup, 'Any chance of some more tea?'

Manny smiled, 'Of course.'

'What's it like?'

Manny stopped pouring to look at Rosen. 'What do mean?'

'Going into battle, how does it feel before an attack, or when you're actually fighting, aren't you scared? I'd probably mess my pants.'

Manny filled the cup, handing it to Rosen, and then sat facing him looking down at the carpet brow creased trying to think of a way to explain the question which he had often tried to analyse himself. He looked at Rosen, pursed his lips, and then said, 'The first time, and to be honest, most times you're scared of getting killed or badly injured; but once you start adrenalin takes over, you suddenly find yourself running towards the enemy.' He paused for a second as if remembering Italy, and smiled. 'While you charging towards the enemy you yell all sorts of silly things, and—'

'What about hand to hand, or killing someone?' Rosen interrupted.

Manny stared at the wall behind Rosen thinking, *yes, how do I feel about that?* His eyes returned to his friend and he answered slowly and deliberately, 'It's not an easy question to answer, but all the training you do before going into combat, well, once you're actually in that situation training takes over, it's second nature, and if you're philosophical about it, it's them or you, and it's better if it's them.'

He stood, taking a biscuit from the plate on the table, taking a bite and turning back to Rosen. 'To tell you the truth, Joe, I sometimes wonder if I have become the sort of person that... do you know, now that I come to think of it, when I'm fighting I'm a different person...'

He hesitated. 'I think it started in Italy – before that, when we were on Ochan I just wanted revenge.' Tears ran down his cheeks as he continued in barely a whisper. 'When I saw those people from the concentration camps, revenge turned to hatred.' He wiped the tears away with a hankie. Rosen stood and hugged him.

After a few seconds Manny pulled away. 'It was then, at Tavisio, that I decided I would fight to defend our people, those that cannot defend themselves; never again would we give up, never again would I allow these anti-Semitic people to run over us because we are Jews. If that made me into a cold-blooded killer then so be it. To answer your question, no, I'm now never scared; yes, I'm worried about leaving my family, but I wanted to bring my children up in a country—' He was interrupted by Bergman entering the room holding out the phone to Rosen. 'Joe, there's someone who wishes to speak to you.'

Ten minutes later, a look of pleasure on his face, Rosen came back into the room. 'I must go now and make all the arrangements. I'll be in touch.'

Manny knew it was time to return to Palestine. He arranged for the families to meet at the weekend to discuss this inevitable move.

*

November arrived very quickly. Rosen waved goodbye to the three men standing by the rail that waved back as the cargo ship, *The Isle of Man,* left Dover Docks on its journey to Haifa. Onboard, safely hidden, was an abundance of armaments that were badly needed to defend a Jewish homeland.

As the ship disappeared from view, an outburst of public opinion against Britain's handling of the Palestinian problem pushed Bevin over the edge in his resolve that Britain would never give up its Mandate, but the General Assembly of the UN, recommended partition in Palestine.

In January 1948, 'Mickey' Marcus, an ex-American army colonel, arrived in Tel Aviv under the alias of *Michael Stone,* to act as a military advisor to Israel. He was confronted with a near-impossible situation, with widely spread Jewish settlements surrounded by hostile Arabs. There was no air power, except a couple of old by-planes, a few tanks, no artillery apart for a few ancient pieces, and hardly any arms or ammunition. He must be mad to take on what seemed an impossible task. The one thing he did have was a people willing to fight for freedom.

# Chapter 15

*Palestine, February 1948*

SINCE his arrival in Palestine Manny had hardly had a respite from the fighting. The Arabs, enraged over the UN ruling, concentrated their efforts on cutting off roads to Jewish towns, and outlying isolated settlements, especially those along the Tel Aviv–Jerusalem road.

Bergman, stripped to his underwear, was cleaning his weapon, eyes squinting slightly from the smoke rising from the cigarette dangling at the corner of his mouth. Manny, his uniform sweat-stained, dropped down onto a chair opposite. Bergman stopped what he was doing, taking a last drag before stubbing it out in the full ashtray on top of his locker.

'Seemed like you've had a bad day?'

Manny wiped his blackened brow with the edge of his kuffiyeh, took a squashed packet of cigarettes from his pocket and shook one out. It was wet from his sweat. 'It was bad, we lost half the convoy,' he said bitterly. 'Got a dry cigarette?'

Bergman tossed him a packet which Manny caught one handed.

'Thanks.' He lit it and continued. 'We lost twenty men and three women. With those Arab villages having the advantage of the high ground from Bab-el-Wad right up to the outskirts of Jerusalem, we don't stand a chance of supplying the beleaguered people with food and badly needed medical supplies. That fucking village—' Manny inhaled angrily blowing out a cloud of smoke '—you know the one, Kastal,' his face showed his frustration, 'has a 360 degree view of the whole area.'

Manny stood, stubbed out the half-smoked cigarette, and began to strip off. 'We need to have a go at capturing that fucking place.' He picked up a towel and soap from his locker, heading for the shower as Bergman, who had sat quietly listening to his friend's bitter comments, said in a matter-of-fact tone. 'We are.'

Manny turned. 'We are what?'

'Going to attack Kastal.'

Manny moved back, leaning towards him, 'When?'

Bergman worked the mechanism of his weapon, answering in a matter-of-fact tone, 'A month or so.'

'We have to take all this shit for another month or more?'

'No, we're cutting back the amount of lorries we send on each convoy.' Bergman stood, pointing his weapon at the floor, saying as he pulled the trigger, 'Be sensible, if we suddenly stopped sending convoys, the Arabs would know something's going on.'

Manny shrugged his shoulders. 'I understand, but at the moment we're losing the battle and people are dying.' He turned and headed once more to the shower.

'Hey, how about returning my cigarettes?' yelled Bergman as Manny disappeared into the shower.

*

On 2 April Manny, with other officers and senior non-commissioned officers, was seated in front of their commanding officer, who held a pointing stick in his hand.

'OK, settle down, you can smoke.'

He waited for the men to light up, and then stepped back to stand beside a large-scale map pinned to a board and slapped the pointing stick against it. 'The objective of Operation Nachshon is to open the road from Tel Aviv to Jerusalem by seizing and holding the tactical heights above it.'

He looked round at the men in front of him. 'Our forces will consist of two units of the Palmach, and two battalions of Field Army.' He tapped the pointer on the map. 'While one group attacks from the east,' he moved the pointer across the map, 'the other will attack here, from the west.' He turned back to face the men, 'Any questions?'

The room was silent as Manny lit another cigarette. He knew it was going to be a hard and bloody battle, with the Arabs having the upper hand. The commanding office slapped the stick against his boot and said, 'Good luck everyone.'

*

Manny, shirt soaked with sweat, urged the men onward as they attacked Kastal. Time and time again they were pushed back. The yelling of scared and wounded men could be heard above that of shells landing, throwing up mounds of earth and bodies; bullets whizzed through the air, some finding their target, killing or maiming.

The smell of smoke, burnt wood and cordite drifted across the battlefield, as gradually, yard by yard, the Jewish forces with grim determination and guts moved upward, until at last, whooping with triumph, they stood victorious in the captured village, but there was little respite, with just time to tend the wounded, grab a drink and something to eat, before the Arabs counter-attacked.

Manny, his face black, uniform torn and bloody was disappointed and frustrated. Outnumbered he and his men were driven back.

Manny radioed his CO, 'Sir, I need reinforcements. I've ten men killed, six wounded two seriously.'

'I'll do what I can, but everyone is in the same boat,' was the reply.

'Whatever can be spared would be of great help, sir,' Manny knew the Arabs had lost a lot more men than he, but they still outnumbered them.

Manny sat with his men sipping hot soup when the radio operator walked over to him, holding out the receiver. 'Excuse me, sir, CO's on the line.'

Manny took the receiver, placing it against his ear. 'Grenfeldt here, sir.'

'I'm sorry, Captain, but you must attack Kastal again. There will be a five-minute artillery barrage in ten minutes time.'

Manny looked at his watch and enquired, 'What about my reinforcements, sir?'

'I'm afraid you'll have to manage with what you have, sorry.' There was a click and the line went dead.

Manny gathered the men around him. 'I know you're tired, but we've been ordered to attack once again. It's up to us to relieve Jerusalem of this strangle hold the enemy have on it.' He looked at the tired, blackened faces around him. 'What do you say, let's give those Arabs hell?' There was a weary, 'Yes, sir.'

This time they were successful, but within minutes were defending themselves against a fierce counter-attack. After running out of ammunition Manny and his men were in hand-to-hand combat. Five hours of harsh, no-quarter-given fighting, the Arabs were driven off and Kastel was at last in Jewish hands.

Manny watched them go with relief. He lifted his sweat and blooded shirt to look at the gash from front to back, the Arab that did it wasn't so lucky; it wasn't too bad, just hurt a little. Wiping the sweat from his eyes, he walked over to the medic. 'Hey, Corporal, just patch me up. I need to get back into action.'

After Kastel other victories followed, the Arabs fleeing to the cheers of their conquerors, as the high ground was taken.

Manny stood beside Bergman looking down at a convoy of 170 vehicles passing in front of them. 'This time,' said Manny, 'they should arrive safely in Jerusalem.'

But there was no respite for Manny and the ragtag Jewish army as they continued the assault, capturing village after village. Operation Nachshon came to a halt, and another convoy of 290 vehicles entered Jerusalem.

Manny, looking like a scarecrow, walked wearily towards the mess area, eyes sore and heavy. What he needed badly was a bath and a good night's sleep.

He looked at Sam walking beside him and smiled, teeth white against the grime. 'If I look as bad as you, I think I'll request a transfer.'

Sam laughed. 'I didn't want to say anything before, but now you've brought up the subject, you look like shit.'

The two cousins were tucking into their first hot meal for days, when Bergman appeared. Face red with anger, he threw his plate onto the table, spilling some of its contents, and dropped heavily onto his seat.

Manny hadn't seen him that angry for a very long time. 'What's the matter, what's happened?'

Bergman shook his head as he whispered, 'They threw their bodies down a well; the entire village at Deir Yassin massacred, men, women and children.'

'Who?' Manny asked, his fork halfway to his mouth.

Bergman looked from one to the other. 'The Irgun and Stern group were given the task of attacking the village, but came up against very heavy opposition and requested reinforcements, which was sent, and the village captured. Once that was over the reinforcements left.'

Manny and Sam stared at Bergman, mouths open in astonishment. 'Who gave the order?' Manny whispered.

'It wasn't the Haganah,' was the hoarse reply.

It left a sour taste in Manny's mouth that any Jew, for whatever reason, resorted to killing innocent people; especially after what had happened in the Holocaust.

\*

Five days later the Arabs ambushed a Jewish medical convoy, killing 77 people, mostly doctors and nurses. The Jewish Agency protested that the convoy was a humane and harmless one; the reply was, 'Tell that to the people of Deir Yassin.'

Manny, Sam and Bergman sat by a half-track having a meal and a cigarette, while reading their  commander, David Marcus's manual.

Manny curled up the manual saying, 'The hit and run tactics stated here,' he slapped the manual, 'are a brilliant idea. It brings to mind how a small motorised unit like the WW2 Long Range Desert group caused havoc behind enemy lines to Rommel's troops and supplies; we should form such a group.'

'That's a great idea,' said Bergman, 'but before we can take it any further, we need to know the sort of equipment we'll need.'

Manny frowned in thought and then commented, 'It would have to be vehicles that could take a hammering over a long period of time, easy to repair, carry heavy armaments and equipment.'

'We need expert opinion,' Bergman stated.

Sam, who's stayed silent up to now, said quietly, 'I know someone who was in the Long Range Desert Group. Give me half an hour.'

True to his word, half an hour later Sam returned with a tall, thin, wiry-looking man with brown, bulging eyes and sandy-coloured hair thinning into baldness, who stood to attention and saluted.

'This is Staff Sergeant Ivan Kraven,' said Sam.

'Sam told me that you want some information on the Long Range Desert Group.' Kraven spoke with a heavy smoker's rasping voice, the use of Sam's first name by the staff-sergeant not bothering the other two. 'What do you need to know?'

'How many men do you need on a patrol?' Bergman asked.

'Usually about forty. Do you mind if I smoke?'

The three men shook their heads. Kraven lit up, inhaling with the sigh of someone who'd being dying for one, letting the smoke trickle through his nostrils while leaving the cigarette dangling from the corner of his mouth.

'I'm more interested in the equipment,' Manny said eagerly.

Squinting his eyes against the smoke from his cigarette, Kraven replied, 'We were pretty well equipped; Lewis machine guns, Bren guns, and Thompson sub-machine guns.' He hesitated for a moment, took a drag from the cigarette and from habit cupped it in the palm of his hand. 'We also had anti-tank rifles. Those beauties got us out of a couple of hot scraps.'

'You must have had some sturdy transport,' Manny pointed out, pencil poised over his notepad.

'Yes sir, Chevrolet 30-hundredweight trucks. They've a range of about 1,100 miles.' Kraven smiled, brown eyes taking on that faraway, remembering look as he inhaled again, 'We modified the vehicles to suit our needs. Took off the cabin roof, used large sand tyres and mounted the guns front and rear. There was a radio truck, and a medical truck, fitted with stretchers and medical supplies.'

'What about, petrol, ammunition, spares, etcetera?' Manny asked.

Taking a last drag, Kraven looked for an ashtray; unable to find one dropped the butt onto the sand and stepped on it, then looked up at Manny.

'We carried three weeks' supplies of food and water; with petrol cans strapped to the sides of the vehicle, or anywhere we could stow them. Apart from the Chevys we had jeeps; they're light and fast vehicles, with a front-mounted machine gun.'

'What about protection?' Bergman asked, looking at Kraven in astonishment.

'The only vehicles with any cover were the radio and medical trucks,' was the crisp reply. 'We needed to strip the vehicles of all unnecessary items for more important equipment such as water, food, petrol and ammo. Speed and surprise was our armour. If we managed to obtain extra supplies during the three weeks we were out, then we stayed out longer.'

Manny looked across at Bergman, raising a questioning eyebrow.

Bergman smiled, giving a slight nod in reply.

'Staff … we need to form such a group … and were wondering if you'd like to be part of it? Help us choose the men and equipment we need. There's a promotion with the job to company sergeant major.'

Kraven adopted the stance of a man deep in thought, taking a cigarette pack from his pocket, offering it around, finding himself minus three cigarettes, prolonging the moment by offering them a light, which they accepted.

Manny blew a smoke ring into the air, a slight knowing smile on his face; Kraven was milking the moment.

'Sir, I accept the offer. When do we start?'

'Right now,' Bergman said.

*

For the next five hours, the four men got down to planning what they needed in men and equipment, the latter being the hardest to obtain. A phone call to Mr White and Amber had a promise of two Chevy 30 cwt trucks and six jeeps.

'I'll try and obtain the armaments you need, but can't promise,' Mr Amber said.

'We're going to need more trucks and jeeps than you're offering. Is there any chance of getting some from the Americans?'

'As I said, we'll do what we can.' The reply was a little curt.

Manny decided to telephone Rosen, hoping that with his contacts they might get what they needed. 'Joe, was there any chance of you getting hold of some Chevy trucks and jeeps?'

'How many?'

'Six of each and spares would do very nicely, thanks.'

Joe laughed. 'Anything else?'

'Well, come of think of it, some—'

'OK, I get the picture, I'll be in touch.'

The line went dead. Manny replaced the receiver, a smile on his lips.

'What did he say?' Isaac asked.

'He would see what he could do.'

\*

Gradually, with the blessing of their CO, the vehicles and equipment they needed arrived secretly at various places along the coastline.

The men they had chosen for their attack force were all ex-Jewish Brigadiers, who had been in combat against Germany's elite, and won. With the help of Company Sergeant Major Kraven, they stripped the vehicles, making them ready for combat.

Manny decided that every man, including the officers, would learn how to maintain and repair the vehicles and radio equipment, plus basic medical skills. He wouldn't take any chances; if a mechanic or radio operator was wounded or killed, another man could take over his duties.

Manny and Sam put the men and themselves through a hard, gruelling physical-fitness regime, including vehicle manoeuvres and the use of all the weaponry they'd been able to obtain. Just under two months after their meeting with Kraven, they were ready and given the code sign of *Z* Company attached to the Negev Brigade.

In the south of the Negev, strung out over a wide area, were several Jewish settlements; giving the Haganah High Command cause for anxiety, as the semi-nomadic Bedouins of the Negev, had, since late 1947, commenced raiding the settlements, ambushing convoys and damaging water pipes. The Jewish High Command moved in more men to help with the defence of these settlements while at the same time the scheme for a fast-moving, go-anywhere force came into its own and was highly successful.

As Jewish forces advanced, an unusual feature occurred; the complete and voluntary evacuation of Arabs from Haifa, Jaffa, Tiberius and Safad, including villages large and small, adding to the hatred by Arabs for the Jews, blaming them for everything.

*

Manny stood beside his vehicle with Company Sergeant Major Kraven offering him a cigarette as he said, 'This mass exodus benefits us, but for the Arabs it has been a complete disaster as it has shattered their plans for an underground movement. If the respectable citizens had stayed, their army irregulars could easily have merged into the background.'

The smoke trickled from the side of his mouth as he added, 'In a way they've only themselves to blame. It's their leaders that ordered those living on the edge of mixed areas to evacuate by telling them that when they've killed all the Jews, the evacuees would be able to return to their homes and be compensated for any discomfort by looting Jewish property. How naïve some people are. Mind you, thousands of Jews did that by walking into cattle trucks.'

*

Manny was cleaning his Tommy gun, while all around him there was a hum of activity and an air of excitement. Mechanics serviced their vehicles and weapons, replenishing them with petrol and ammunition. Music from radios echoed loudly around the compound. Manny worked the mechanism of the weapon, smiled with satisfaction, pulled the webbing belt to its longest; strapped it across his back, joining the men in preparing their vehicles for what they knew was the coming fight.

Suddenly, the music stopped. All heads turned expectantly towards the radio. There was a vacuum of silence. Manny had one foot in his vehicle, the other on the ground. It was as though suddenly there was no air, the birds had stopped singing, and for a millisecond the earth had stopped spinning, as the voice of David Ben-Gurion echoed around the compound. 'Today, May 14th 1948, I hereby declare the establishment of a Jewish state in Israel, to be known as the State of Israel.'

Within a blink of an eye, the vacuum of stillness and silence was broken as the compound erupted in a mighty roar of cheering and yelling. Hats, shirts and other bits of material were thrown into the air. Manny, tears of happiness streaming down his face, did a backward flip, landing on his feet and stood still for a moment thinking, *Bloody heck, how did I do that?* Before he could think any more about it, Hans grabbed him in a bear-hug, shouting something, but Manny couldn't hear him above the noise of yelling men, and hooters beeping, both leaping up and down like schoolboys who'd scored a goal.

They joined a group that had formed a moving circle, arms around each other, singing and dancing to songs handed down throughout the centuries. After two thousand years of dispersion, the Jews had their own country.

*

No sooner had David Ben-Gurion, the first Prime Minister of the New State, made the announcement, then five Arab countries, Lebanon, Syria, Jordan, Egypt and Iraq, met to plan its destruction. Even then, Jewish politicians tried to meet Arab leaders to find a solution other than war. The Arabs wouldn't talk or compromise.

At mobilisation centres throughout the new State of Israel, men between the ages of 17 and 25 were called up for registration and medicals.

In the Arab countries surrounding Israel, troops, armour and artillery moved towards its borders with the words of Azzan Pasha – 'This is a war of extermination and a momentous annihilation which will be spoken of like the Mongolian massacre of the Crusades' – ringing in their ears. In overwhelming numbers, well armed and confident of victory, the Arab forces from north, south and east attacked.

Manny thought, but did not say anything to anyone, that once the State of Israel was declared the Arab nations would accept it, and there would be peace. How could he be so stupidly naïve to think the Arabs wouldn't attack? The world held its breath at the expected annihilation of Israel. Manny's lips drew in a straight and determined line, knowing that like him, with the Holocaust still embedded in their souls, the Jews were ready for the fight.

*

News reached Manny and his men as they waited for orders, that the Egyptian's first target was Kfar Darom, which the Arabs considered easy prey. But they were unprepared for how well-trained the defenders were, or their determination: they fought with doggedness, rage and unyielding spirit that completely unnerved their opponents. The Jews had been taught well and the Arabs retreated.

After the loss of so many men and equipment the Egyptians by-passed two settlements and sped towards Yad Mordachai, where the outnumbered defenders, fought for eight days against armour, and artillery. The defenders of those three settlements cost the Egyptians three hundred dead but most important of all; it cost them time. Time that gave Israel breathing space to prepare its fortifications, and acquire badly needed armaments, including fighter planes.

On 26 May, with Manny wanting desperately to get into the fight, the Israeli Defence Force (IDF) was formed by combining Haganah, Palmach and Etzel into Brigades.

# Chapter 16

*Negev, 25 May 1948*

THE heat of the late afternoon sun shimmered on the desert sand that formed contours like waves on an ocean. The haze in the distance danced enticingly, beckoning the unwary traveller into its bosom. A spider scurried under a rock where a lizard sat motionless head turned to one side as if listening to the hidden sounds around him.

On the brow of a sand dune, Manny with Hans and Sergeant Major Kraven either side of him looked through binoculars at the Egyptian column below them of tanks, half-tracks and trucks carrying troops and supplies.

Manny moved the binoculars along the column, a plan of attack forming in his mind thinking, *the biggest problem was the tanks flanking the convoy.* Taking the binoculars from his eyes he whispered, 'There's a solution, there's always an answer.'

'What did you say?' Hans asked.

Manny didn't reply, mulling over an attack in his mind, lifting the binoculars once more to his eyes, moving them left to right, face serious, brow knit in thought as he slowly lowered them to hang down on the strap around his neck. He patted the two men on the shoulder and crawled below the brow of the dune saying, 'I thought the tanks were going to be a problem...'

As he spoke he drew a line in the sand with Kraven and Hans looking on.

'...but halfway along the column there's a petrol-tanker with half a dozen vehicles ahead of it.' He drew some lines going downward and meeting the column. 'Then there's a gap as one of the trucks was having trouble keeping up...' he motioned with his hand in the direction of the column without looking up '... and another between the flanking tanks.'

He looked at the two men to see if they were paying attention, then back to the sand. 'This was the column...' He pointed at the line, and the ones going downward at either end, like a side view of a table. 'Hans, you take your men along here,' pointing to one of the lines.

'I'll take the rest of the troop along here, both lines abreast of each other. Schtick had an anti-tank gun in his vehicle, and Saunders the other. They'll take care of the armour. The tanker was a priority. I'll take care of that. Fifty yards from the column we'll swing into a line abreast of the column firing everything we have at them until we meet, and then turn and meet back here, swinging to the right. Once we're hidden from them and sure we aren't followed, we'll stop, camouflage the vehicles and wait.'

He looked up at the sky, and then his watch. 'It'll be dark soon; there's a wadi about three miles from here, I'm guessing they'll bivouac there for the night. Let's go.'

They slid backward another few feet, and then got to their feet returning to the men, where Manny quickly outlined the plan of attack.

*

Their engines muffled by those of the column, Manny and his men charged down at either end of the Arab convoy, turned towards each other, speeding alongside the convoy firing their mounted Lewis, Bren, and sub-machine guns at everything and anything that moved. Manny's driver, David Jacobs, an East Londoner with a broad Cockney accent, turned the jeep, foot down on the accelerator as they sped alongside the column, which was now in chaos; enemy vehicles swerved out of control, as their drivers were hit; some vehicles came to an abrupt stop, those behind trying to avoid crashing into them. Others turned over spilling equipment and men onto the sand that swirled into the air from the fast-moving Israeli vehicles. Egyptian soldiers leapt from burning upturned lorries and armoured personal carriers to be met by a hail of bullets from the Israelis.

The Lewis machine gun shuddered in Manny's hands firing a long burst at the tanker, raking it from right to left, then back again; petrol poured from numerous bullet holes in its side. The driver opened his door and was about to jump, but fell back into the cabin just as the tanker exploded into a moving ball of flame.

Above the noise of racing engines, machine guns and exploding ammunition could be heard the shouts of abuse by the Israeli gunners, the yelling of the wounded, and men fleeing in panic, some burrowing into the sand trying to escape the lethal fire power coming towards them.

The two Israeli groups met, turning quickly away, heading for the dunes without a shot being fired back at them. The quickness of the attack had taken the enemy completely by surprise. Once the Israelis were hidden from view, they turned right. Fifteen minutes later they bivouacked in a circle, covering their vehicles with camouflaged netting.

After setting a guard roster and ordering no smoking or lights, Manny walked amongst his men, making sure they were OK, and then moved to his jeep, hunching down beside it and running sand through his fingers. He looked disappointedly up at the night sky and shook his head. The moon was bright amongst a star-filled sky. He wanted to attack the enemy again, but now...

Sergeant Major Kraven hovered close by, as if sensing his commanding officer's thoughts. Manny turned to face him. 'Sergeant Major, please ask Lieutenant Meyer to join me.'

Kraven was about to salute.

'We aren't in barracks now. Manny doesn't want too much regimentation while they're on patrol.'

'Yes, sir, I'll get the lieutenant.'

*

Manny sat in the front seat of the jeep, his feet on the dashboard, eating a cheese sandwich, a faraway look in his eyes. He smiled as a picture of David playing the saxophone came to mind. That's when you saw the real David. Manny sighed, closing his eyes for a moment, hearing the music and began to hum the tune, moving his right hand to the rhythm.

The smile left his face and he stopped humming. David's sax was still in its case, in a cupboard at home. David's mother gave it to him, saying her son would have wanted him to have it. He should have brought David's body back, not left him like that. He nodded in agreement with his next thought. *When this is all over, I'll go back and see what happened to David's, and ... Rothman and Koning's bodies.* His thoughts were interrupted by Hans.

'You OK?' There was a worried look on his face.

Manny quickly wiped a tear from his eye before turning to Hans. 'Just remembering an old friend. I'll tell you about him some day. You would have liked him.'

'Sir, you wanted to see us?' Kraven said, urgency in his voice.

Manny stepped from the jeep, taking a map from his combat jacket pocket, spreading it on the bonnet. 'We're about here.' He moved his finger along the map, tapping it on a spot. 'I'd like to hit that column once more, which I'm sure would be just here, and then hightail it back to Tel Aviv as we're in need of supplies. The thing is that this time they'll be ready for another attack. Have either of you got any ideas?'

'It's a shame we haven't any mortars,' Kraven pointed out.

'It's no good wishing for something we haven't got, although I wouldn't mind getting hold of a tank,' Hans said with a wry smile.

Manny stared at Hans – a tank. In a split second his mind went into overdrive. He snapped his fingers. 'What if... no, it wouldn't work, it's too risky... and...' He turned to Kraven, 'Sergeant Major, do any of the men speak Arabic?'

'What? Mmm, yes, Goldberg and Freidman, I think.'

'Get them for me, please.'

Kraven nodded and moved across the circle.

'I see a glint of a challenge in your eyes, I know that look.' Hans stared into Manny's eyes. 'What are you planning?'

'It's just a wild idea; let's wait till the men get here.'

Manny squatted down, making shapes in the sand with a stick. It was a bold plan, if it worked. He stood as Kraven and the two men arrived.

Corporal Goldberg was short and stocky with a tanned, weather-beaten face and a permanent smile on his lips. Sergeant Freidman, why didn't he think of him? The man was educated. He had, at first, thought him too old for training; but looks could be deceiving: the guy spoke an abundance of different languages.

Manny drew a circle in the sand, looking at Freidman and Goldberg. 'How's your Arabic?'

'It's good,' Freidman replied.

'Mine too,' Goldberg said.

Manny looked at Hans. 'Could you muffle the sound of the vehicles somehow?'

Hans nodded. 'It could be done.'

'How long would it take you to do all the vehicles?'

'With help from two of the men, about twenty to thirty minutes, why?'

'You'll see why in a minute. I'm assuming that the column would be drawn up into a defensive circle, with armour on the outside. Knowing Arab mentality, it'll probably be spread out a bit. What I'd like to do is capture a tank and use it against its owners.'

'How are we going to do that?' asked Freidman, surprise in his voice, adding, 'sir.'

'We'll come in at the rear of the convoy. Hopefully, with the lieutenant's mufflers, they won't hear us. Do a quick recce to see what's what, and if possible infiltrate the defences and capture a tank. In case of any sticky situations, you and Goldberg would do the talking. The lieutenant, using the enemy's tank's gun, would fire at their armour, knocking out as many as he could.' Manny gave a tight-faced grin, 'and in the meantime the rest of us would deal with the other vehicles in the column. That's the plan, well, sort of plan; any questions?'

There was silence from the four men.

'OK, let's get going. Sergeant Major, order the men to refuel and re-arm their vehicles quickly and quietly.'

'Yes sir.'

\*

Forty-five minutes later they moved off with Manny's jeep in the lead, hoping that by coming up behind the Egyptians, if seen, they would be mistaken as friendly, which would give them time to get closer, abandon the original plan, hit them quickly and withdraw.

An hour later, parked in a line just below the brow of a dune, the men looked down at the enemy, who as Manny had predicted, were parked in a loose circle. In close proximity to the Israelis was a tank with two half-tracks parked beside it.

Manny swept his binocular slowly left to right and then back again; took them from his eyes turning to Hans. 'Apart from Freidman and Goldberg, we'll take Bernholtz, and Lishman, they are—'

'We, who's we?' Hans whispered in surprise.

Manny smiled, 'You don't think I'm going to stay behind while you have all the excitement?' He turned to

Kraven, on the other side of him. 'Sergeant Major, get Bernholtz and Lishman here.'

Without a word, just a slight nod of the head, Kraven snaked away, returning five minutes later with the two men. Manny told them his plan while pointing to the various armoured personnel below them. He ordered the men back to their vehicles, where he gathered them around him.

'I, with the Lieutenant, Freidman, Goldberg, Bernholtz and Lishman, are going to infiltrate the camp in the hope of getting into one of the tanks, and using it to knock out some of their armour. At the same time the rest of you will cause as much mayhem as you can. The tank nearest to us is just here.' He pointed to a section of the drawing he'd made in the sand. 'Either side of it were two half-tracks that I would like to...' he smiled at the men... 'add to our itinerary.'

'Freidman and Goldberg will do any talking that's necessary. The Lieutenant, Bernholtz, Lishman and I will take care of the guards and anyone around the tank and half-tracks. Freidman would help the Lieutenant, while Goldberg and Lishman take one half-track, Bernholtz and I the other. Sergeant Major Kraven and the rest of you will attack along this line through the encampment.' He pointed to the sketch in the sand. 'Once you're through we'd hopefully follow you in the half-tracks. If we are separated rendezvous at Nir Am.' He looked at the men around him, 'Any questions?'

There was silence.

Manny looked up at the sky, the moon still bright, casting shadows of the men and vehicles, thinking, *Not ideal conditions for a sneak attack, we could do with some cloud cover.*

He turned to Kraven. 'Give us thirty-minutes. If you hear any shooting before then come on in.'

'Yes, sir; be careful, don't take too many chances.'

Manny nodded, slapping Kraven on the shoulder. 'See you later.' As Manny strode away, the moon was covered by a cloud. He looked up saying, 'Thank you.'

A minute later he and the others, bent double, made their way cautiously towards the Egyptian camp, going to ground as a guard appeared from behind the half-track, opened his fly and with a sigh urinated into the sand.

Manny crawled towards him. The Arab turned, looking down and buttoning his fly as Manny rose up behind him. Manny clamped a hand over his mouth, and at the same time slid the sharp commando knife along his throat. He lowered the Arab to the ground and wiped the blade on his uniform before placing it back into its sheath, and then crawled forward, joining the others as they split into groups of two. Hans and Freidman crawled towards the tank, Manny and Berholtz the half-track on the right, the others to the one next to it.

Two men were asleep with their backs against the tank. They, like the others around the three vehicles, were quickly and silently taken care of. Manny looked across at the tank as Freidman placed one of the Arabs kuffiyeh on his head, looked inside the tank, saying something in Arabic, to which there was a muffled reply. Freidman quickly lowered himself into the tank; there was a cut-off cry. Manny waited with bated breath as a head appeared from the turret; it was Freidman who gave the thumbs up to him. Hans leapt expertly onto the tank, following Freidman as he ducked back inside.

Manny climbed aboard the half-track, checked to see if the machine gun was loaded, then checked his watch as Berholtz slid onto the driver's seat. The thirty minutes were nearly up. Gripping the handles of the machine gun, feet astride, Manny waited for Hans to fire the tank's gun, or Kraven to attack.

The turret of the tank moved slowly to the left and stopped. There was a sharp bang as a shell left the muzzle. A tank some fifty yards away erupted in flame. Manny smiled and began firing.

The Egyptians were quick to respond and returned fire, their bullets pinging off the tank's armoured plating.

Hans fired the tank's gun as quickly as Freidman could load, damaging two tanks and blew up two half-tracks.

Out of the corner of his eyes, Manny saw Kraven and his men driving through the Egyptian camp, causing havoc as enemy soldiers leapt for cover.

Some of the Egyptians seemed to have recovered from the surprise attack, now fired bravely back. A half-track on the other side of the camp moved forward its machine gun, firing a swathe of bullets at Kraven's men who emerged through the smoke of burning vehicles, racing clear of the enemy encampment bullets following close behind.

Manny ordered Berholtz to start up the engine and then leapt across to the tank, jumped up onto the turret, yelling, 'It's time to go.'

Goldberg, in the other half-track, reloaded the machine gun, turned on hearing Manny yelling at him above the sound of gunfire, making a start-up gesture. Goldberg nodded and tapped Lishman on the shoulder, and then suddenly fell back as he was hit. Manny ordered Freidman as he climbed off the tank's turret to take over from Goldberg, and then leapt down from the tank. Hans dropped two grenades through the turret and then jumped down on the run following Manny, both dodging bullets cutting up the sand behind them.

Hans yelled in pain as he was hit and Manny turned back, grabbed Hans webbing belt and in one movement lifted him off the ground and onto his shoulder, at the same time firing one-handed towards the enemy as he crossed the short distance to the half-track. He lowered Hans onto the floor, yelling at Berholtz to get going as he climbed aboard. They accelerated away.

Manny grabbed the half-track's machine gun, firing back at the Egyptians with Freidman in the other adding to their fire power. The two grenades blew up, setting off the tank's ammunition, its incendiaries lighting up the night sky, and then suddenly they were free with shells erupting all around them, throwing up showers of sand as they headed at full speed towards their rendezvous. Manny grunted, he was hit in the shoulder, the bullet exiting, it wasn't fatal.

*

They rendezvoused with Kraven and the rest of his troop. Two of his men were dead and five wounded none seriously. Manny's amazed at how calm he had been throughout the attack, and the buzz he got from it, and for a split second wondered if he'd become one of those men that enjoyed war and killing.

The medics patched up the wounded before the group set off for Yavneh, where they met up with Bergman and Sam, both wounded who had lost five men killed and three others wounded in an encounter with Egyptian forces near Beersheba.

While recovering from their wounds, David Marcus ordered the construction of a road, through the Judean hills to Jerusalem, naming it the Burma Road, after the one built by the Allies in WW2, from Burma to China. Soldiers and new immigrants worked night and day to finish it. The Arab siege on Jerusalem had been lifted and an Arab counter-attack repelled. Thousands of Arabs were fleeing to Lebanon from Galilee.

Throughout Israel, Jewish settlements and towns, outnumbered and outgunned, stopped the invading forces. Iraqi troops failed in their attack, and in the North the Syrian army came to a halt at Kibbutz Degania, The kibbuznics using Molotov cocktails to stop the enemy tanks.

The New State had withstood the Arab onslaught and their borders virtually intact. David Marcus's tactics had worked. In gratitude, David Ben-Gurion appointed him Lieutenant General of the Israeli army; the first Israeli General for two thousand years.

A truce had been negotiated by Count Folke Bernadotte, the UN mediator in Palestine, to begin at 6 am on 11 June until 9 July.

# PART III

# Chapter 17

MANNY, his arm in a sling, Sam on crutches and Bergman, whose cracked ribs were tightly bandaged, had been granted leave until 29 June. Hans, although still in hospital, was OK, and would be returning to his family within the next couple of days.

Manny didn't want to sit around twiddling his thumbs until the 29th. This was a good time to go home. Without telling the others, he telephoned Rosen, who apart from Mr White and Amber was the only person who might be able to arrange transport at a moment's notice.

'Hi, Joe, it's Manny.'

'Manny, how are you? Is everything OK?'

'We're a bit knocked about and in need of a little loving.'

'Oh! I see. How could I be of assistance?'

'Is there any possibility of hiring a plane to pick us up at Sde Dov, just north of Tel Aviv?'

There was silence at the other end. Manny, thinking they had been cut off, yelled down the receiver. 'Joe, Joe, you there?'

'I'm still here, just trying to think of a way to help. Could you ring me back in thirty minutes?'

'Yes, naturally we would naturally help with the expenses.'

'OK, I'll see what I'm able to do.' The line went dead.

Manny slowly replaced the receiver, looked at his watch deciding to hang around instead of going to the mess. Time passed slowly, and four cigarette butts later he phoned Rosen back.

'You better get packed, there's a transport plane arriving at Sde Dov at 1500 hrs with medical and other supplies, the pilot's expecting you. Joe, don't say anything to our wives, I'd like to surprise them.'

'No problem, see you later.'

Manny rounded up the other two, and with an air of excitement at surprising their wives, they headed to the airport.

\*

The transport plane landed on time, taxiing to a halt beside the dispersal hut where a group of men and women waited to unload its cargo.

Manny and the others moved slowly towards the plane where the pilot, after talking to the men refuelling the aircraft, walked towards them, taking off his flying helmet.

Manny smiled, he should have known; quickening his pace, he yelled at the top of his voice, '*Joshua!*'

The brothers hugged, Joshua careful not to press against his brother's injured shoulder. 'I'm happy to see you, but you better have a shave before seeing Rita.'

'They don't know we're coming, do they?'

'No, they've no idea.' Joshua turned to the others. 'You two been fighting again? I hate to think what the other guys looked—'

He was interrupted by one of the ground crew. 'Sir, you're refuelled and ready to go.'

'Thanks. I suppose we'd better get you three home.'

\*

It was raining when they landed at Northolt, where Rosen was waiting for them. They said goodbye to Joshua. 'I'll be over to see you in a couple of days,' he promised.

Rosen was as usual immaculately dressed, greeting them with a warm handshake and hugs, and then gestured for them to get into the Bentley. Manny slid onto the front seat, while Sam and Bergman, tried to minimise their pain, and got onto the back seat.

The guard opening the gate didn't look at the passengers as he leaned against the open window, expertly sliding money into his pocket before waving the car on. The Bentley purred through the open gate turning left onto the Northolt road, passing White City and through London's quiet Sunday streets. Manny frowned, when they turned off at Edgware Road, peering intently through the window, but didn't say anything until Rosen entered a narrow street by Little Venice canal.

'Where are you taking us? This isn't the way home,' Manny said sharply, which he hadn't intended to do, but his thoughts were full of Rita and the children, plus his shoulders were throbbing like mad.

Joe gave him a white-teeth smile, ignoring the tone of Manny's question. 'The three of you can't go home looking like scarecrows, just indulge me for a few moments, we're nearly there.' True to his word, two minutes later they pulled into the driveway of a small hotel.

'Joe, what's going on?' Sam demanded.

Rosen placed an arm around Manny's shoulder, turning to look at the two men on the back seat. 'Trust me, this won't take long.'

The four men entered the hotel with Rosen in the lead. A man in striped trousers and tailcoat, Brylcreemed hair sleeked back with a left-side parting, rubbing his hands together greeted them. 'All's ready for you, Mr Rosen; room ten.'

Rosen smiled and without stopping said, 'Thank you, Brian,' palming money into the man's hand.

Rosen opened the door of room ten, with Manny wondering what was going on. All he wanted to do was get home, as did the other two. They followed Rosen into the room to see four men by the far wall.

Rosen turned to them and with a sweeping gesture said, 'Gentlemen, these men are here to – mm, make you more presentable. I've some business to attend to, so I'll leave you in their capable hands.' He turned to face the men by the wall. 'I'll return in two hours.' Without saying another word he left the room.

*

In a whirlwind of two hours, Manny, Sam and Bergman were completely taken over by the four men.

Manny was led into a bathroom with a barber's chair by the sink. The moustached, waistcoated man with an unlit cigarette behind his right ear walked silently over to the chair, took the gown draped over the back, shook it, and gestured with a smile for Manny to sit. He was still in shock at what Joe had prepared for them, so painfully shrugging his shoulders placed himself into the capable hands of the barber whose name was Abe. Once Abe began cutting Manny's hair, he didn't stop telling jokes.

Feeling rejuvenated, Manny looked into the mirror as Abe showed him the back of his head. 'Thank you, Abe, that was the best haircut and shave I've ever had.'

An ex-army medic named Sam helped Manny bathe. He saw action in Europe, but didn't want to talk about it.

Manny wondered what other surprises Rosen had in store for them. He looked at Sam and Bergman and was about to say something when the door opened and Rosen walked in, followed by a hotel porter carrying two cases which he placed on the table in the centre of the room and then left.

'Gather around, gentlemen, and choose your clothes,' Rosen said, opening the cases.

After thanking the four men for their help, Manny stopped to look in the hallway mirror. A different person than the one that entered the hotel stared back; he smiled at the reflection saying, 'You're one handsome man.'

Before getting into the Bentley, Manny hugged Rosen, 'Joe, we'll never forget what you did for us today; there are no words to express our feelings, but to say, Thanks.'

With tears in his eyes Rosen was unable to say anything in reply except, 'My pleasure.'

*

Driving towards Clapton, Rosen said, 'I've managed to get the family together on the pretext of how we could raise more money by bringing a representative of the Israeli government with me.'

Manny smiled, Sam said, 'Very clever.'

Bergman tapped Joe on the shoulder. 'How did you get clearance for the transport plane to land?'

'Have you heard about the Berlin airlift?'

'No,' all three chorused.

'It seemed that the people of Berlin were starving, so Britain, feeling sorry for them, organised an airlift of food. I persuaded the powers to be that I had organised food and medical supplies for orphaned children in Israel. When they started to argue, I told them that they were doing the same thing for our late enemies; they never argued after that.'

Manny gave Rosen a funny look, 'If I believe that, I'd believe anything. How much did it cost you?'

Rosen patted Manny's knee. 'Don't worry about it. I managed to get some much needed medical supplies and other goodies to Israel and at the same time help my friends.'

They pulled up outside Manny's house. The four men got out of the car and as quietly as possible walked up the path to the front door. Rosen rang the bell, with Manny and the others standing with their backs flat against the wall.

Rita opened the door. 'Where have you been? You should have been here an hour ago, your wife was sick with worry. Where's the Israeli official?'

'I'm sorry, but something happened. He was waiting for an important message, and in the end apologised and—'

Rita didn't wait to hear any more, but turned and walked along the hallway and into the lounge, followed by Rosen and the others, hearing Rita saying angrily, 'It was Joe, but the man we're waiting for was unable to come.'

Rosen stood just inside the doorway of the lounge. 'Well, that was not exactly true,' and stepped aside. Manny, Sam and Bergman entered the room. For a moment there was silence, and then screams of delight as Rita, Sarah and Dominique leapt from their chairs, flinging themselves at their husbands, who endured the pain from their injuries on seeing their wives' happy faces Then as one, they turned and surrounded Rosen, engulfing him in their arms, kissing his cheeks and jumping up and down with excitement.

\*

That evening, Rita and Manny, arms around each other's waists, stood in the doorway of the nursery, looking at their sleeping children. She turned to face him, placing her arms around his neck, pulling his lips towards hers, at the same time crushing her body against his.

He whispered, 'Not in front of the children.'

Rita took his hand and led him towards their bedroom, where time stood still.

'That was wonderful.'

'I second that.' He was about to say something else when Miriam began to cry.

'I'll go,' he said, moving off the bed, giving Rita a quick kiss, and put on his dressing gown, entering the bathroom to wash before going into the nursery. He looked down at his daughter and smiled, but she cried louder, so he picked her up, slowly rocking her, singing a lullaby his mother sang to him, but Miriam would have none of it.

Thinking she was wet, or had a dirty nappy Manny laid her gently on the table and undid the safety-pin. While cleaning her and putting on a clean nappy, Miriam was quiet, but as soon as he picked her up, she started to cry so loudly that it woke David.

Rita, smiling, entered the nursery with a bottle taking Miriam from him, saying to their son, 'Daddy will help you back to bed.' No sooner did he lay David down than he was asleep.

Manny understood that he was a stranger to the children, as he hadn't seen them for over a year, except for photos that Rita had constantly shown them.

*

The following day, Rita placed Miriam in his arms to feed, but the baby took one look at him and began crying. Manny tried to put the bottle in her mouth, thinking she was hungry, but she wouldn't take it. Manny couldn't understand it, as he had also been having trouble with David, who would play with him but not sit on his lap, or even let Manny hold him.

Upset, he handed Miriam back to Rita, not understanding why the children seemed to shun him, and it showed on his face.

'Don't worry. Another couple of days and they'll be used to having you around,' Rita said, rocking Miriam, placing the bottle into the baby's mouth. Miriam grabbed Rita's finger with her tiny hands sucking contentedly at the teat.

Manny rubbed the back of his head in frustration, hoping Rita was right, but felt that it was something else making the children act that way. His eyes caught the photo Rita had shown the children of him; he stared at it for a moment, and then a smile creased his face as it dawned on him why. He looked in the mirror, and then at the photo, looking at Miriam, his mind saying, *No, she couldn't understand, not at that age.* But it was worth a try. He went to leave the room.

'Where are you going?' Rita asked.

'Won't be a moment, I have to do something.' He ran up the stairs to the bathroom, emerging five minutes later a smile on his face, minus the moustache.

Entering the dining room where Rita had just finished feeding the baby, Manny said, 'I'll change her.'

'She must be winded first.'

'I'll do that as well.'

'Fine, I can get on with making the dinner, but if she starts to cry, you can peel the potatoes.'

Manny smiled at Miriam, who looked at him in the I-know-you look that babies had, giving her a kiss and placing her on his shoulder, gently rubbing her back. She gave a burp and a little bit of milk dribbled down her chin and onto his back; he wiped it away from her chin, rubbing her back gently once more. 'Let's have another bit of wind,' he whispered, but this time Miriam let wind in a different place. Manny laughed, 'Just like your mum.'

Miriam gurgled, smiling up at him as he happily changed her nappy, and then picked her up, cuddling her to him. David entered the kitchen, looked at him for a second and then waddled towards him shouting, 'Daddy, Daddy.'

There were tears in Manny's eyes as he bent to pick David up in his other arm, wincing with the pain, having forgotten his wound which had nearly healed; but didn't care a damn as his son placed his arms around his neck and kissed him.

\*

It was a glorious sunny Sunday, and they were all gathered at Aunt Doris and Uncle Mark's house for the usual get-together and party. Everyone's brought a dish of food, including cakes and biscuits, and an area ringed off where the children could play safely.

Manny's wound was nearly healed, as were Sam's and Bergman's. But, even if they hadn't, nothing would stop them from participating once the truce with the Arabs was over and the fighting began again.

Rosen, a glass of wine in his hand, was talking to Manny. 'I've arranged transport back; it's on the evening of the 27th. How's the wound?'

Manny moved his arm in a circle. 'Good, just a little sore.'

'What are you two plotting now?' Joshua asked his arm around Freda's waist, a glass of brandy in his free hand.

'As a matter of fact, we were discussing how lucky I am to have such gorgeous daughters.'

'What are their names?' Freda asked.

'Adrianne and Anne, they're ten months old today, but who's counting.'

Manny smiled, 'You better save a lot of money. Two weddings to make and the clothes you'll have to buy.'

Manny and the other two burst into laughter at the look of dismay on Rosen's face. Manny slapped him on the back. 'Joe, it's a long way off; enjoy them, they'll grow up before you know it.'

Rosen smiled, 'You're right, and I better start now. I'll pop in and see you on Tuesday.' He turned, limping slightly as he walked over to his wife and children.

# Chapter 18

*27 June 1948*

IT WAS late afternoon when the Bentley came to a stop outside the house and Rosen pressed the horn. Manny, carrying the children in either arm, with Rita beside him carrying his suitcase, opened the front door. Rosen stood by the car; Sam and Bergman were already aboard. Manny gave Miriam a hug and a kiss and then handed her to Rita and knelt to lower David onto the floor, also giving him a hug and a kiss.

'Look after Mummy for me while I'm away?'

David nodded, placing his arms around his father's neck, holding him tightly. Manny gently and sadly took the boy's hands from his neck, and getting to his feet, slid an arm around Rita's waist, giving her a long lingering kiss that was interrupted by Rosen honking the horn.

'I'll write whenever I can.'

'Just be careful, don't do anything stupid.' He was about to kiss her again, but the shouts of, 'Hurry up!' from the three men stopped him and he reluctantly picked up the suitcase. 'I love you, don't forget that,' Manny whispered, and ran down the front steps. Just before entering the car he blew her a kiss and then slid onto the front seat.

Rosen pulled quickly away from the kerb, glanced at Manny and then the others in the rearview mirror. 'While we're together, he said.' I have a proposition for you,' hesitating as he glanced at Manny who turned to look at him.

'What sort of proposition?' Manny asked a little warily.

'I would like us to be partners.'

'What?' Sam remarked, astonishment in his voice.

'We don't know a thing about investments,' said Manny frowning.

'No, no not in – well, it's an investment in a way, but it's property.'

'I'm listening,' Manny said. The others made sounds of agreement.

'With all the bombing, houses and flats have to be built, and that's where the money is going to be. If we form a limited company, with us on the board so to speak, I think we could make a financial killing.'

They came to a stop at a red light. Rosen glanced at Manny, a quick look behind at Bergman and Sam, and then back to the road as the lights changed, and as they moved off asked, 'What do you think?'

Manny smiled, 'Joe, you haven't put us wrong yet. I'm game, but how will that affect us being in Israel?'

'Yes, how will that affect us?' Bergman and Sam repeated in unison.

'All you have to do is to put money into the venture.'

'How much?' It was an irrelevant question really as Manny knew he would agree to put in any amount Rosen asked for.

'Five hundred pounds each; that would give us an investment start of £2500, as I've already asked Isaac, who said he'd go with whatever decision you guys make.'

'Would it amalgamate with your broker company?' Manny asked, having twisted around to look at Joe.

'No, it would be a separate company under another name.'

'Well, I'm in. You've never given me any bad deals. Through you, I know that if anything should happen to me, Rita and the children would be financially sound.'

'Me too,' Bergman added.

'I'm in,' rejoined Sam.

'This partnership will have to have legal contracts to—'

'Naturally,' Rosen stated, a smile on his lips.

They were silent for a while as they neared Northolt.

'Joe, draw up the papers. Don't put in a lot of legal mumbo-jumbo. Make it straightforward and we'll sign them,' said Manny.

\*

Rosen was still smiling as they drove into the airport. The same sergeant asked for his papers, and once again didn't look at the passengers, expertly palming the money into his pocket and waving for the guard to lift the barrier.

Rosen pulled up beside a hangar, giving a toot on the horn, and the doors opened just wide enough for the car to enter, coming to stop beside a Dakota transport. 'That's your ride.'

'What? How did you get hold of that?' Bergman looked up in awe at the aircraft towering above them.

Rosen didn't reply, but said to Manny, 'When you arrive in Israel, give this to Mr White, or Mr Amber, they'll be waiting for you.' He handed Manny a large heavy buff envelope, the flap stapled down.

'Can you tell me what's—'

'Money,' Rosen said quietly, lots of money, so guard it well.'

The three men got out of the car. Rosen opened the boot for them to get their cases. While they're doing that, he pulled some folded papers from inside his jacket pocket.

'Before you go, could you please sign these?'

Manny smiled knowingly, 'You crafty devil.'

'I knew you would accept, well, Isaac said you would.' He handed Manny a pen.

The three men signed the document without reading it, knowing that Joe would never cheat them.

Rosen gave each a hug, the last being Manny. 'If there's anything you need, don't hesitate to call me.' He looked Manny in the eye, saying seriously; 'If you could, from time to time write to me; even if it's just to say hello, so I know you're safe.' He grabbed Manny and kissed him on both cheeks, and then moved away, tears in his eyes. 'Be careful, my friend.'

Before Manny could reply, Joe turned and without another word walked swiftly to the car, got in, giving a hoot and the hangar doors opened. He didn't look into his rearview mirror, otherwise he would have seen Manny waving goodbye.

\*

Manny watched the car disappear, the hangar doors closing quickly and silently. He vowed that he would write to his friend who had gone to such great trouble to allow him, Sam and Zach, to see their families. He sighed and joined the others. Joe's thoughtfulness with the hotel when they arrived, and not allowing them to go home looking like tramps, would never be forgotten.

He was not surprised to see Joshua attired in Israeli Air Force uniform. Joshua saluted Bergman. 'Lieutenant Grenfeldt reporting all's ready, sir, we take off at dusk.'

While a staff-sergeant took their cases, Bergman and Sam walked slowly around the transport, as men loaded equipment through the open doors. Manny pointed to his brother's epaulettes. 'When did you?'

'About a month ago; I would have resigned my commission from the RAF a lot sooner, but I wanted to get some experience with larger aircraft. When I finished the course, I asked if I could be discharged as I'd only signed-on for the duration of the war. They wanted me to reconsider and offered a promotion. I thanked them, well, my commanding officer really. We've been together from the time I joined up. In fact he taught me how to fly, knows I'm Jewish, so I told him the truth that I've already been offered a commission in the Israeli Air Force, such as it was at the moment.'

Joshua shrugged his shoulders. 'I asked him as a joke if I could take my aeroplane with me. If it were up to him, I could, but if I'm interested there's a Dakota doing nothing in a hangar at Northolt that landed there ten months ago the crew disappearing. No one seemed to know what to do with it. I got in touch with Rosen, and the rest, well here you are.'

'How are we going to get out of here without the whole world and his uncle knowing?' Manny enquired.

'Certain people have been given the day off, while others, if you get my meaning, take over. Our flight plan has been logged in and at a certain point in our flight I'll radio to control that we have a problem and have to descend. Then we'll wave-hop to Israel and, hey presto! We have a Dakota.' Joshua glanced at his watch, 'So let's get this show on the road.' The two brothers, arms around each other's shoulders, walked toward the aircraft.

The hangar doors opened, a tractor towed them to the dispersal area, unhooked and drove away. One by one the engines roar into life, the propellers spinning faster and faster, until they were a spinning blur. The aircraft shuddered as if rearing to be off into its element, the sky. They began to move, accelerating along the runway, leaving the ground and climbing into a starlit night sky.

# Chapter 19

*29 June 1948*

MANNY, Sam and Bergman reported back for duty to find they had been promoted; Bergman to major, Manny and Sam to captain. With other officers and men of his commando unit, Manny took an oath of allegiance to the State of Israel and its legitimate authority.

The next two days were a whirlwind of exercises and training. Manny realised very quickly that since they had been away structural changes to the newly formed Israeli Defence Force had been put into place.

With other field officers they joined an advanced training course, which, in Manny's opinion was far more extensive than he'd ever experienced before. Officers, no matter what their rank, had to take the initiative and be responsible for the actions and care of their men, and lead them into battle. No one, wounded, or dead, would be left behind.

There was a buoyant atmosphere amongst the officers racing through the assault course, yelling their new battle cry, '*Aharay!*' ('Follow me!').

Armaments of every description, with the help of Jews throughout the world, arrived at secret locations and were distributed to the newly formed Israeli Defence Force. As 9 July and the end of the truce drew closer, the little State of Israel was busy with its survival and plans for Israel to take the offensive.

Manny and other officers sat facing a stage where nailed to the wall was a huge map of Israel and its bordering countries. Cigarette smoke drifted towards the already nicotine-stained ceiling, and the noise of many voices filled the room.

A major from the newly formed Intelligence corps stood in front of them, a long pointing stick between his hands, suddenly raised a hand and there was immediate silence.

Looking for a moment at the faces in front of him, he said, 'We are going on the offensive; yes, we are going to take the fight to the Arabs.' He slapped the map with the stick, 'Operation Daniel was to be directed against the Arab Legion on the central front; our aim, to relieve Jerusalem and remove the threat to Tel Aviv.' He turned, tapping the map with the stick. 'We must capture and occupy the areas here at Lod and Ramle, and then capture Latrum and Ramallah.

'The operation was to be carried out by a task force comprising of two Palmach Brigades, the Yiftach Brigade, the newly formed 8th Armoured Brigade, made up of a tank battalion, and a commando battalion of jeeps and personal carriers.' This latter group was the one Manny was attached to. The speaker paused, lit a cigarette and then carried on. 'Surprise, timing and speed is essential.'

Manny had lost Hans to the only tank battalion, which he volunteered for. His skill with tanks was quickly recognised and he had been promoted to captain.

*

No sooner was the truce over than two Israeli forces struck in a pincer movement, one from the northwest to Lod, the other southwest to Ramale.

Manny, the excitement of battle on his dirty, sweat-streaked face, stood relaxed as his vehicle with a small group of armoured carriers, jeeps and tanks, detached itself from the main force and sped towards al-Safiriyya, which was quickly captured.

Bracing himself against the side of the vehicle, he took a drink from a water bottle, as the group moved rapidly on to Lod Airport. The battle was fierce, but after forty-five minutes of bitter fighting, Lod was in Israeli hands.

Manny, helmet in his hand, knelt beside a badly wounded Corporal Goldberg, while a medic injected him with a painkiller. Manny lit a cigarette, placing it in the wounded man's mouth, and looked at the medic, who shook his head. Goldberg coughed, blood trickled from the corner of his mouth. Manny gently took the cigarette and wiped the blood away with a piece of gauze.

'Thank you, sir,' the corporal whispered, coughing again, and in barely a whisper added, 'It's bad, isn't it, sir?'

Manny held back the tears of frustration in his helplessness, not wanting to lie to Goldberg, nor did he want the wounded man to give up hope, but before he could say anything the corporal said, 'Please, sir, tell me the truth.' He gave a weak smile. 'I'm a big boy now.'

Manny smiled back, placing a hand on the shoulder of a man who cracked a joke, even though he was dying. 'Yes, Corporal, it's bad.'

Goldberg grabbed his sleeve. 'Please, sir, don't leave me here.'

'I promise, it won't happen,' said Manny, but Goldberg didn't hear him.

A grim-faced Manny, goggles over his eyes, stood behind a double-barrelled machine gun. The dust from the speeding jeeps and other vehicles of the column swirled in the air, as they moved onto Latrum and Ramallah.

The attack was pushed back by the heavily defended police station, and the Israelis retreated, having sustained heavy casualties. A jeep burnt in front of the police station, while another lay on its side some fifty yards away.

Most of the unit's tyres were punctured, as were their radiators. Four men were missing, probably falling out of their jeeps when they turned quickly around in their haste to get away from the intense fire aimed at them.

As Manny, Freidman and Jacobs replaced two of their tyres, and bunged up holes in the radiator, Manny knew that compared to some they had been fortunate. Medics were caring for the wounded. Time was now precious as they had been ordered to retreat. He knew the longer they delayed the harder their withdrawal would be. He placed Lishman's body on the floor of his vehicle, wrapping him in a groundsheet. Having not seen Sam and Bergman since the attack, he went in search of them.

He found Sam tightening a wheelnut of a jeep. Manny knelt by his cousin asking, 'Have you seen Bergman?'

'No, I think his jeep was one of the first to be hit, but I was too busy trying to get out of there to notice.'

'Lost Lishman, three wounded, how about you?'

'Two dead and a couple slightly wounded, and a badly dented cigarette case.' He took it from his left breast pocket. 'Sarah's going to give me hell when I get back; it was her wedding present to me.'

Manny couldn't help but laugh at Sam's serious face. He was sure Sam didn't realise yet that the cigarette case saved his life. 'Now I know you're henpecked.'

Sam didn't reply, tightening the last bolt.

Bergman's driver, Schelling interrupted them. 'Excuse me sir, Major Bergman is still out there. He's trapped under our jeep. I was thrown clear and picked up.'

The cousins looked at each other, and as one jumped into Sam's jeep. Manny leapt from the vehicle and ran towards the corner of a building, peeking around the corner. He could see Bergman, who didn't seem badly hurt but couldn't move. Fortunately he couldn't be seen by the men in the police station. Manny ran back to the jeep trying to think of a way to rescue Zach without incurring any more casualties.

Manny stood by Sam, taking a pencil and pad from his pocket, quickly drawing an outline of the area and showing it to his cousin. 'If we make them think we're going to attack, using two half-track, one hiding the other as it dropped off three men who would try and get Zach out from under the jeep, the two vehicles would then retreat quickly back to cover. I'm sure that if they don't see us, they'll not be suspicious and won't expect another attack.'

Sam looked from the drawing to Manny. 'What do you mean another attack?'

'When I give the signal that we've got Zach, you come back doing exactly what we did before and pick us up. What do you think?'

Sam gave a grim, tight-lipped reply. 'It's as good a plan as any, and it would probably work. But who said you're going to pick up Bergman?'

'Sam, I can't ask the men to do something I'm not willing to do myself. You must agree with me on that point, and Zach's our friend.'

'You're right, as usual. OK, I'll tell my men what the plan is.'

The two vehicles, with every weapon firing at the police station, raced towards the jeep. At first there was no return fire, the men in the police station taken by surprise. Sam moved his vehicle beside Manny's, hiding him from the enemy.

Judging it perfectly, Manny leapt from the vehicle, Tommy gun strapped across his back and a spade in his right hand, landing behind the jeep, followed by two of his men.

'Hey, watch out,' spluttered Bergman, spitting sand out of his mouth.

'That's a nice way to greet the men who jeopardise life and limb to rescue you,' said Manny, smiling at his friend as bullets followed the two half-tracks retreating around the corner of a building.

'Well, if it isn't the big hero. Stop chattering away like a washerwoman and get me out of here.' Bergman's voice softened. 'Thanks for coming back for me. My arms are free, but this bugger's too heavy to lift on my own.'

While he was talking, Manny and the two men with him dug under the jeep and around Bergman. Making sure he couldn't be seen by those in the police station, Manny placed his back against the jeep, hands holding the edge, the two men grip Bergman under each arm, waiting for Manny's signal to haul him from underneath the jeep.

Manny said, 'One, two, three,' and straightened his legs and back. Sweat poured from his face as he lifted the jeep. Bergman screamed in pain as he was freed.

The scream alerted the men in the police station, who opened fire. Manny lowered the jeep, and while the two men with him returned fire, ripped open his friend's trousers with a commando knife. A bone protruded through the skin. Taking off the webbing from his Tommy gun and one of the rifles, he strapped Zack's legs together saying, 'Melv, give them the signal.'

Once again, the two vehicles dashed side by side, the intensity of their firepower keeping the Arabs' heads down. They stopped by the jeep. Manny and the two men lifted Bergman aboard the half-track as gently as they could. Giving a go, go sign, the two vehicles sped quickly away, followed once again by a line of bullets from the police station.

Manny and Sam were relieved that none of their men had been injured or killed in the rescue. The vehicles had sustained some damage, which necessitating a stop.

While making quick repairs, a medic tended to Bergman's leg. Manny helped Jacobs lay their dead comrades in the back of his half-track, covering them with ground-sheets.

After checking on his wounded men, Manny found Bergman, his back against the metal side of the half-track, Sten gun beside him; the broken leg with splints either side stretched out along the seat. Taking a pack of cigarettes from the top pocket of his fatigues, Manny offered one to his friend. 'Are you in pain?'

Bergman took the offered cigarette, bending slightly forward as Manny cupped the flame between his hands; inhaling, Bergman lay back, looking silently at Manny and slowly exhaled the smoke through his nostrils, saying solemnly, 'Thanks, I thought that was it. You didn't have to come back.'

Manny spreads his arm, gesturing at the men now boarding their vehicles. 'They volunteered, they knew the risks, and no thanks are necessary, as they, like me, knew that you would have done the same thing for us.' He patted his friend on the shoulder. 'See you later.'

Manny ran across to his vehicle; once aboard he gestured for the group to move off, heading for Ben-Shemen to rejoin the rest of the command.

\*

The impetus of the Israeli attack gave the Arabs a morale punch in the stomach and they withdrew in silence. On 12 July, Lod was in Israel's hands, and the following day so was Ramle.

The British demanded that the Security Council call an immediate ceasefire. Manny's commando unit was sent to the south to join the Givati Brigade. Their orders were to open the road to the Negev before the truce began. So as not to alert the Arabs to their true objective, diversionary night raids were planned before the main attack.

Manny and Sam waited by their vehicles, discussing the attack. 'What do you think? Will it work?' Manny asked.

'I don't see why not.'

'We're a bit low on manpower, and the vehicles need a complete overhaul, and—'

'What?' Sam interrupted. 'Am I hearing a moan from the positive-thinking, gung-ho, never-say-die Manny Grenfeldt?' It was said with a slight smile and mock surprise.

Manny looked at his cousin, holding up his hands in mock surrender a big grin on his tanned face. 'OK, I didn't mean it to sound like that; but the men are tired, they need to see their families, like us.'

'You're right, but we need to do this before the truce comes in, and then we might be able to get the vehicles serviced and receive new equipment, and men. And maybe...' his eyes took on a faraway look, '... we might get home for a week or two.'

'A letter would be nice. I haven't received one for three weeks,' Manny moaned.

'Me neither. I wonder how Bergman's getting on.'

'Probably giving the nurses hell, and badgering the doctors to take off the plaster.' The two cousins laughed at the thought.

The order was given to mount up. Hugging silently, they boarded their vehicles, having temporarily swapped their half-tracks for jeeps. Each commanded three jeeps and two half-tracks. Manny gave a mock salute to the others as the commandos split in different directions, with orders to harass the enemy wherever they could find them.

Manny ordered Corporal Chiam Spindler, an ex-American marine, to take up a position a mile in front of them in his jeep. An hour later, Spindler returned.

'There's a small convoy of trucks with an armoured escort ahead of us,' he told Manny.

'I'll go back with you and have a look.' Leaving Sergeant Freidman in charge, he slid onto the seat next to Spindler, and they accelerated away.

*

Lying on top of a hillock, Manny looked through night binoculars at the convoy of eight trucks, two armoured cars and two half-tracks as escort. He was not surprised to see there was a wide gap between each vehicle, with an armoured vehicle between every two trucks. He waited for them to pass, and then the two men ran back to their jeep and headed back to the unit, where Manny gathered the men around to outline the plan of attack in the sand.

'We'll charge down like a line of cavalry. As we reach the column, each of us will drive between every other two vehicles.' He pointed to Lance-Corporal Nathan Moritz. 'Nat, you'll attack the first two trucks; I'll take the two armoured vehicles.' He pointed to a private, 'Kurt, your next then, Mathew and—'

'So, I'm the last in line,' Joe Stern, an American from Brooklyn interrupted.

Manny gave a grim smile. 'I'm sorry, Joe, but you're the only other vehicle with an anti-tank gun, you get the armoured car in the rear.' He looked at the circle of men, 'Any questions?'

Mathew pointed to the sand drawing, 'Do we turn back and make a second attack?'

'No,' Manny said sternly. 'No one goes back, unless we have to.' They all knew the meaning to his words.

'Right, mount up.' He turned to Freidman saying in Arabic; 'Use the anti-tank gun on the first armoured vehicle you see.'

Freidman laughed.

Frank had been teaching him to speak Arabic. 'What did I say?' There was a look of dismay on his face as he moved behind the mounted Bofors gun, and then tapped Jacobs on the shoulder making a forward motion with his arm.

'You said, use the anti-tank gun on the first vehicle with one eye.' He then told Manny the correct translation.

In a line, guns blazing, they raced through the unsuspecting Arabs' convoy, leaving two armoured vehicles burning, and at least four trucks destroyed. Soldiers jumped from their vehicles, trying to avoid the bullets flying all around, returning fire as the darkness swallowed up the attacking Israelis.

*

Just before daybreak, Manny and his men returned jubilantly to their unit for a meal and to replenish their armaments before having a well-deserved sleep, knowing that tonight they would have to do it all over again.

Manny, his face dirt streaked, with white around his eyes where his goggles had covered them, smiled across the gap between his and Sam's jeep, but Sam didn't smile back.

'What's the matter? You OK.'

'Nathan Mortiz was killed in a freak accident. His driver tried to avoid an obstacle he thought was a mine, but it was a large piece of rock. The offside front wheel hit it with such force the jeep overturned. Moritz was thrown from the jeep, breaking his neck; the driver escaped with a few minor injuries.'

'Shit!' was all Manny could say.

*

At an officers' meeting they were told that the second truce was to begin at 1900 hrs on 18 July. The IDF had captured the whole of the Lower Galilee. The Egyptians' advance towards Tel Aviv had been stopped in its tracks at the bombed-out Ashdod Bridge, now known as Gesher Ad Halom. Manny thought it was a brilliant name, showing that the Egyptians had advanced 'Until Here'.

Manny and Sam were on their bunks reading a letter, one of the bundles they received from home, with photos of the children. 'What we need,' said Manny pulling a photo from the envelope, 'is to get home, even if it's for a couple of days.' He rolled off the bed a thoughtful look on his face. 'The only problem is how to get there.'

Sam kissed the photo in his hand. 'I can't see that happening. We're in the middle of rebuilding our units with fresh men and equipment that are arriving every day.'

Manny lit a cigarette offering one to Sam. 'Break over, we have to get back to work.' They picked up their letters, placing them in their lockers and walked out into the late morning sun.

Manny, stripped to the waist, was busy mounting twin machine guns onto his new half-track, when a voice said, 'Nice friend you are, not even a box of chocolates.'

Manny jumped in surprise, banging his head on the edge of one of the machine guns. 'Fuck it, Zach; you shouldn't creep up on someone like that.' He smiled down at Bergman, wiping the grease from his hands with a rag, stepping down from the half-track.

'You don't like chocolates, and it would have been a waste of good money as you would have given them to some nurse as a bribe to get you out of there. And, clever-dick, could you tell me where in the middle of Galilee I'm supposed to find chocolate?'

'Where's your initiative? Surely, one of those captured villages had a chocolate bar somewhere.'

'A drinks bar perhaps. I won't hug you, that uniform looks very clean. It's great to have you back.' Before Bergman could say anything, Manny yelled, 'Sam, look who's here.'

Sam poked his head around the half-track next to Manny's, looked at Bergman and then at Manny, a big grin on his face. 'Are you sure it's him and not a copy?'

Manny stepped back, stroking his chin in thought, then yelled in alarm, 'Sam, don't!' He was too late, and couldn't hold back the roar of laughter as his cousin ran across to embrace Bergman.

'Great to see you, Zach. How's the leg?' Sam moved away, with Bergman looking down at the black oil-stained hand-print on his clean uniform.

'The leg's fine, which you're going to find out in ten seconds when I boot you up the backside,' Bergman said a little angrily, taking off his shirt. 'You idiot, I can't report to the CO like this.'

'I tried to warn you,' Manny told his cousin, a big smile on his face, trying not to laugh again at the stain on the back of Bergman's shirt.

'Sorry, I'm so happy to see you, I... well,' He looked at Manny for help.

'I'm sure we could find you a clean shirt,' Manny said, unable to hold back the laughter any longer.

They found Bergman a shirt and he left to report to their CO, returning thirty minutes later, shaking his head.

'What's the matter?' Manny asked.

'I don't believe it.'

'Believe what?'

Bergman didn't reply. Manny leapt at him, wrestling him to the ground, trying to pin his arms down, but Bergman was too strong for him. 'Don't just stand there, give me a hand,' he yelled at Sam.

'Oh, umm, I thought you could handle him by yourself,' Sam remarked, trying not to laugh at the two of them rolling around in the sand.

Manny, with Bergman about to pin him onto his back, wriggled out of the hold and between huge gulps of air, said, 'Are you going to tell us what happened?'

For an answer, Bergman grabbed Manny, twisting behind him in a neck hold. Manny went limp, arms on the ground, body slightly bent, looking up at Sam, raising an eyebrow at his cousin standing in front of him with a foolish grin on his face.

'Oh, OK.' He stepped behind Bergman, and pinched the tip of his ears. Bergman yelled in surprise, letting go his hold on Manny who was instantly on top of him. Berman started to laugh as the cousins pinned him to the ground.

'OK, OK I give in. Get off me and I'll tell you.'

They got to their feet helping Bergman up, brushing the sand from their bodies. 'The CO said he's pleased to see me again. I have a week to get my vehicle ready, and then I can have two weeks' leave, starting on the 12th till the 27th.'

The cousins stared silently in open-mouthed disbelief.

Manny exploded. 'You've just had a bloody holiday, lying in bed.'

'Not even that,' Sam interrupted. 'Probably having a good time with the nurses.'

'We could make it very difficult for you, pal,' Manny joined in.

'Hey, what's going on here?' Bergman said in mock anger, a slight smile on his face. 'I didn't ask for the leave, he gave it to me.'

'Sorry, not good enough,' the cousins said together, with Manny adding, 'You could—'

'Anyway,' Bergman interrupted, taking something from his pocket, 'he gave me these.' He held up two pieces of paper.

'What are they?' Manny asked curiously.

'This one basically said, from the 12th to 27th July, Captain Manfred Grenfeldt is on leave.' He handed it to Manny saying, 'and this one, same date, Captain Samuel Grenfeldt is on—'

Both Manny and Sam leapt at Bergman, pulling him to the ground again. 'You could have told us that in the beginning,' laughed Manny.

'I second that,' Sam joined in.

'Hey, this isn't the way to treat your friend and superior officer; I could put you on a charge for the duration of your leave.' Bergman roared with laughter as his two friends pinned him to the ground, pouring sand down his trousers.

*

That evening, Manny was deep in thought as he cleaned his Tommy gun, when Sam walked over to him. 'What's the matter? You've been like this all evening.'

'It's great to have the leave, but it's impossible for us to get home. I'm dying to see Rita and the children. She hadn't had an easy ride with me since we married. I've been away most of the time. I'm sitting here trying to think of a way to get home, but short of stealing a plane, which I can't fly, I don't know what to do.' Manny worked the mechanism of his weapon. 'To tell you the truth, I might as well not have the leave.'

'I know what you're saying, and I feel the same way. I know we won't be able to do what we did last time; it's too dangerous, not only for us, but for Joe and those helping him. I'm sure something will crop up, it always does.'

'It'll take a miracle.' Manny face showed his frustration; he had always managed to think of something, but this time... He gave a deep sigh of resignation.

'Hey, it's not like you to be despondent like this, shake out of it.'

Manny didn't reply for a moment, and then gave a weak smile. 'OK, I'll try.'

Just then Bergman walked in. 'Why the glum faces?'

'Manny and I admit, and I'm sure you do, that this leave was a waste of time as we can't get home, and there's nothing much to do.'

'I'd rather stay here, so when the Arabs decide to start this war again, I'm going to be ready for them,' Manny said solemnly.

'What about Joshua? He sent us an invitation to go see him for a drink. Or we could go see Hans, and his sister – what's her name?'

'Helga,' Manny said in a monotone voice, adding, 'That'll take us about three days, four at the most.' He threw himself onto his bed. 'Anyway, Joshua's not at the airfield, he's on some flying course.'

Sam shrugged his shoulders, picked up his Sten gun. 'I'm going to get something to eat.'

'I'll come with you,' Bergman said, looking down at Manny. 'Are you coming?'

'I'll stay here, I don't feel hungry.'

'OK, I'll see you later.' He turned to go, and then turned back. 'You knew this might happen, and we agreed the girls should stay in London, so we don't have to worry about their safety; would you prefer they were here?'

Manny was silent as Bergman turned and followed Sam, leaving Manny staring sullenly at the door as it closed. An overwhelming feeling of sadness engulfed him. He got off the bed, smacked the locker with an open hand, and then leaned against it, head bowed. After a couple of minutes he picked up his weapon and headed for the telephone kiosk to phone Rita, hoping that would cheer him up.

'I miss you and the children so much. It's frustrating, I've two weeks' leave and I can't get over to see you,' he told Rita.

'I miss you too, and the children are growing every day.' Her voice told him how she felt. 'I know you said that we should stay here because it's safer.' There was a pause for a moment. 'Does this mean you've changed your mind? Manny what—'

Suddenly, a voice in his head said, *What would you do if something happened to Rita or the children?* He interrupted her. 'No, no, I haven't changed my mind, it's... been such a long time, and... I just needed to hold you.'

She could hear the longing and sadness in his voice. 'I feel the same, and I know we're doing the right thing by us staying here so you can concentrate on staying alive.' Her voice went from being soft and loving to one of telling him to do what he felt was right.

'Remember what you told me about the survivors from the camps, and how you felt about it. You said that you would help to ensure it would never happen again.'

Tears rolled down Manny's cheeks, not from sadness, but pride. Another wife might have cried on the phone, begging for him to come home; but as much as she was missing him, Rita knew about his determination to help secure a Jewish homeland, and was willing to sacrifice their being together so that he could help make it happen. He wiped the tears from his eyes. 'I love you, Rita Grenfeldt, more and more each day, you're a wise and clever woman.'

'Have a good rest; relax, read a book, go for a swim; we're OK. I better go now, this must cost a fortune.'

He smiled. 'You're right; I'll phone again same time next week.' He blew a kiss down the phone and replaced the receiver.

# Chapter 20

*12 July 1948*

BERGMAN'S jeep led the convoy of trucks moving along the road, with armoured vehicles placed at intervals between them. Manny stood behind the Bofor guns, sunglasses shielding his eyes from the glare of the sun; a Kuffiyeh over his mouth against the sand and dust flying through the air from the tyres of the four trucks ahead. He turned, looking back, and could just make out Sam's half-track three vehicles behind.

Even though there was a truce, they were taking no chances as they headed for Haifa to pick up spares, food and ammunition.

Leaving the vehicles at the dock's carpool, the three friends took a taxi to the Grande, an old Colonial hotel on the outskirts of the city overlooking the sea. A porter took their cases from the boot of the taxi. 'Gentlemen, your luggage will be in your rooms when you get there.'

They walked through swinging doors into a large foyer, the mosaic-tiled floor half covered by a Persian carpet. Large urns with Paradise palms, yuccas, and aspidistras stood against arched marble pillars. Hanging here and there were baskets of ivy and pink flowering bougainvillea. Vases with exotic flowers stood on glass-topped wicker tables beside high-backed chairs, tan leather armchairs and sofas. Mock Waterford crystal chandeliers and slow-turning fans hang from the ceiling.

At the marble-topped check-in-desk, Manny, who was still unhappy about not being able to see Rita and the children, signed the register and was handed a key by a tanned moustached man. 'I never ordered a suite,' he said in surprise, looking at the check-in clerk, and then at Bergman, who smiled at him.

'What's the matter? I booked each of us a suite so we could enjoy a bit of luxury; if you can't afford—'

Manny lifted both hands in surrender. 'No, please don't worry about it. You're right, a bit of pampering won't hurt.'

Bergman looked at his watch. 'Let's have a shower, get changed and meet at the restaurant at... nine o'clock. I could do with a decent meal.'

'Good idea,' Sam took his key from the clerk, glanced at the number and moved towards the lift, turning to Manny, whose eyes were on Bergman. 'Coming?'

'Umm, oh, yes OK.' Manny walked across the foyer to where the other two were standing by the lift. Bergman swayed backward and forward, humming quietly, a mischievous glint in his eyes and a smile on his lips as they entered the lift saying cheerfully to the bellboy. 'Fourth floor, please.'

The lift came to a halt, the bellboy opened the gates and they entered the plush carpeted hallway. Manny found the door to 401. Bergman was in the room next to him and Sam next to his. Bergman inserted the key into the lock, saying before opening the door, 'See you at nine.' Turning the key, he opened the door, but before entering, added, 'If you change your mind, you know where I am.' He disappeared into his room.

As he opened the door, Manny shrugged his shoulders, wondering for the umpteenth time why they couldn't share a room. Closing the door, he stood for a moment leaning against it. Looking up at the ceiling, he wished Rita could share this with him.

*What I need is a bath,* he said to himself, lowering his eyes to look around the room. Two soft-furnished armchairs faced each other, with a coffee table beside them and magazines on each. A table with vases of flowers stood beside a settee in front of french windows opening out onto a balcony with a wicker table and chairs overlooking the sea.

His eyes caught something bright on the plush fawn carpet. Rose petals made a line across the floor towards another room. Slowly and curiously he followed the petals into a bedroom, coming to a half-stride stop in the doorway, mouth open in surprise, and for a second couldn't believe his eyes.

'Hi,' Rita said softly, lying seductively in the middle of a four-poster king-sized bed, wearing a see-through negligee.

In a second they were in each other's arms, kissing and touching faces. He moved slightly away. 'I must have a shower, I smell like a camel.' Spotting a bottle of champagne in a bucket of ice, he said, 'Pour us one of those, I won't be long.'

He stripped off as he went, leaving a trail of clothes behind and stepped into the shower. *I can't believe it, Rita's here.* He smiled, *Bergman knew about this, the sly, no he made it happen, how? At this moment in time I don't care.*

Manny was back in the bedroom. Rita held out a glass of champagne, which he took from her. They clinked glasses, looking lovingly into each other's eyes, linking arms and taking a sip. Taking the glass from her, he placed it on the table beside the bed and turned back. Placing his arms around her, he moved closer and gently kissed her, a loving, long, yearning kiss, their hands caressing each other's bodies as they moved to the centre of the bed, stretching out beside each other. Both were thinking the same, not wanting to rush, exploring with hands, fingers and lips; then as if by consent and not wanting to wait any longer, moved together.

\*

Later, they lay silent and content in each other's arms. He kissed the top of her head and sighed happily. 'How did—'

She placed her fingers to his lips. 'Not now, I'll tell you later.' She picked up his arm to look at his watch, let it drop, smiled and straddled him, bending to kiss him, pulling her lips slightly away. 'We've an hour and a half before we have to get ready for dinner.'

It didn't surprise him that she knew about Bergman's suggestion that they meet for something to eat. What was it Bergman said before going into his room? *'If you change your mind let me know.'*

*I won't miss dinner tonight for all the tea in China*, was his last thought as passion took over.

Manny didn't mind being a little late, entering the dining room just after nine saying to the maître d', 'Mr Bergman's table, please.' They followed the man to a table by a picture window overlooking the sea and were the last to arrive.

Bergman, a big smile on his face, stood to greet them, kissing Rita as Manny bent to kiss a seated Dominique on the cheek.

'You look lovely, and it was great to see you.' Turning to stand in front of Bergman, 'Zach, I don't know how you did it, but I'll never forget this for as long as I live, thank you.' He hugged Bergman, and whispered, 'I owe you, big time.'

Bergman smiled back replying, 'No, you don't, and it's me that owed you. I'll not forget the kindness you showed us when we were in Nice. Now, don't get sentimental on me. Anyway, I was missing Dominique as much as you were missing Rita.' He looked across to where Rosen was talking to Sam. 'Joe helped. I told you, that man had so many contacts, it made you wonder if... forget it, let's sit down and enjoy a good meal, with beautiful women and family.'

The family and friends sat in a circle, chatting to each other as the wine waiter poured the wine – a white Franconia. For starters they were served hors d'oeuvres of pâté de fois gras with slivers of toasted bread, followed by lemon sorbet. The main course was chateaubriand cut into thick slices, surrounded by globes of artichokes filled with a béarnaise sauce, with mushrooms, baby carrots, celery and sauté potatoes.

Manny looked down at his dessert of pears soaked in Kirsch, and wondered for a second before spooning a piece of pear into his mouth how the hotel was able to obtain such a wonderful menu. He stood, and with a spoon clinked the wine glass for attention. All eyes turned on him, and for a second he looked around the table at the people he loved and said, 'I'm sure that I speak for everyone here, when I say thank you, Zach and Joe, for this fantastic surprise. There are members of our family that aren't here,' he smiled. 'They are, I pray, not having too difficult a time looking after our children, who we hope are behaving themselves.' Everyone around the table was smiling and nodding. 'So, ladies and gentlemen, I toast family and wonderful friends.'

Everyone repeated the toast.

*

The party retired to the lounge for coffee and biscuits, and, as usual, gradually split into two groups; women and men.

Manny, a brandy in one hand and cigar in the other, said to Bergman, 'What made you come up with this idea?'

'You did.'

'Me?'

'Basically, you said at the time if there were a way of seeing Rita, you would do it. I knew we couldn't get to England, but there might be a way of them coming here. Naturally, the question was the children: who would look after them, and how would the women get here?' He took a sip of brandy and continued.

'I spoke to Dominique, who said she would talk to the wives, and see what they could come up with. Two days later she contacted me to tell me that the grandparents would look after the children, with help from their friends. So that was solved. The next thing was transport. I spoke to

Mr White and Amber, but they were tied up with the truce, and couldn't be of assistance at this time. So I called Joe and he came up with the idea of the yacht.'

'He's a business man, and had in a short time become very rich, and may I add, so have we through him, plus he'd raised a lot of money for Israel,' Manny stated.

Bergman nodded his head in Marlene's direction. 'Do you know anything about his wife?'

'Not a lot. I know she comes from a wealthy family; their wedding was pretty lavish. You could see they love each other, and to me that's beyond wealth.'

'You might change your mind if you didn't have any money.'

'You might be right. Whose yacht was it? I dare not ask Rita, but do you know how long—'

'Four days, which I thought was bloody marvellous. I know Dominique's missing the children, as I am. It would have been nice if they could have brought them, but it wasn't practical. If anything should happen while they were here I'd never forgive myself; and for you're information, the yacht belongs to Marlene's father.'

'What! Are you sure?'

Bergman laughed, 'Positive.' He turned to face Manny. 'You know her second name, don't you? Think about it.'

Manny stared at Bergman, mouth open in surprise. 'To tell you the truth, I've never thought about it. Every time we've met, she's been...' He shrugged his shoulders, 'Marlene doesn't act...' He shook his head, 'Schulman shipping, I never put two and two together. It doesn't change anything. I like Marlene very much, and she's good for Joe. I haven't seen him so happy for years, and he's crazy about the twins. Four days, well it's better than nothing.' He patted Bergman on the shoulder. 'I'd better go and thank Joe.'

'Good idea. I need to have a chat with Joshua.'

Manny walked towards Rosen, who was in deep conversation with Sam. 'May I join you?'

'I'm about to circulate,' said Sam. 'He's all yours; see you later, Joe.'

'Thanks, Joe,' Manny said. 'I owe you once again.'

'Are you crazy? I could never repay you for what you've done for me; you've no idea … that because…' He looked at Manny's glass – it was empty. Rosen placed a hand on Manny's shoulder. 'Your glass is empty, and I need another drink.'

Manny hesitated, glancing across the room to where Rita was in deep conversation with Bergman, Marlene and Freda.

'She's OK,' said Rosen following Manny's gaze, 'and enjoying herself. She hadn't had a break from the children for months; come to think of it neither had Marlene. Let's get that drink.'

Manny knew Rosen was right. The two of them walked over to the bar, ordered double brandies, and with Rosen in the lead, walked through the open french doors onto a jetty with wicker tables and high-backed chairs.

Rosen stopped at an empty table and sat on one of the chairs. Taking a gold cigarette case from his pocket, he offered a cigarette to Manny, who smiled, 'Thanks.' He took a lighter from his pocket, flicked it alight, placing the cupped flame to Rosen's cigarette, and then his own. Blowing smoke up into the moonlit starry night, wondering why Joe kept saying he owed him. He hadn't done anything for Rosen, well not that… 'Joe, I don't understand, why do you owe me, I haven't done anything?'

Rosen leaned forward, elbows on the table, the glass of brandy held between his hands. 'You remembered in Ochan you asked me if I had any stocks or shares.'

Manny nodded, taking a drink of brandy as did Rosen.

'I was, at that time, for the want of a better word, suicidal.'

Manny was about to say something, but Rosen stopped him.

'Let me explain before you say anything. In Germany I was a very rich man,' he laughed. 'A very rich young man – in fact, by the time I was fifteen, I had 100,000 marks in my bank account.' He shrugged his shoulders. 'I had a talent with numbers. My junior schoolteacher called me a protégé. My parents, God rest their souls, took my advice in some business transactions and became very rich. With the money they opened a bank, and within three years, and by the time I was eighteen, we were millionaires.'

He twirled the brandy around in the glass, leaned back, taking a drag of his cigarette. 'I'm not a great-looking guy like you and the others, or a gung-ho type.' Rosen gave a wry smile. 'I'm a little short, losing my hair and have a slight belly. Too many dinner meetings, but I play tennis three times a week...' He hesitated, taking another drink.

'Sorry, I digress. When the Nazis came to power, well you know what happened to Jews. I lost everything, even my dignity. I gave everything I and my parents owned to save my life, while the rest of my family were being taken away to be gassed.'

There were tears in his eyes. Manny had a lump in his throat, and didn't know what to say. All he could do was be a good listener as this had been bottled up inside his friend for many years. Perhaps by talking about it, Joe could at last lay the ghosts to rest, as it seemed he was blaming himself for being alive. Manny placed a hand over his friend's, nodding for him to carry on.

'I escaped,' said Joe. 'I figured the major might change his mind, and I still had a little cash hidden away, which I used to get to England. I got a job at a college teaching economics, but then ended up like you on Ochan. To me, that was the end. In fact the day you met me I was going to kill myself. You saved me; your enthusiasm and grasp of what I told you made me decide to start all over again. Naturally I needed money, and as I once told you, with your percentage that's what I've done.'

'So, you took the percentage before you delivered anything to me,' said Manny. 'That doesn't mean you owe me anything. You shouldn't feel guilty for your family's death. If that were the case then thousands of Jews throughout the world would feel the same way. Believe it or not, it was – and is – your duty to stay alive so you don't break the chain. Look over there.' He gestured to the chattering, laughing women. 'You've a lovely wife, just think what you would have missed had you committed suicide. OK, you changed your name, but your parents still live on in your children and it's their blood that's flowing through their veins. Joe, you're a kind and generous man, you don't owe me anything, it's me that owes you. Because of you and that business brain I'm a wealthy man, and you are my dearest friend.' He smiled. 'That doesn't mean you have to raise your percentage.'

Rosen roared with laughter. 'I've never promised that, but for you, it will probably go up in half per cents.'

Manny could see that suddenly Rosen's a different man. The guilt he'd carried on his shoulders these last few years had disappeared. Manny picked up his glass. 'I'd like to make a toast.' The two men stood and clinked glasses as Manny said, 'To friends and family.' Rosen repeated the toast, and they drank.

*

It was hot, the midday sun bright in a clear blue sky. The luxury yacht tied up at the dock looked out of place amongst the dull, painted ships unloading their cargos under the watchful eyes of UN observers.

Manny and Rita walked arm in arm along the jetty, stopping at the gangway leading to the yacht. He was naturally sad to see her go, but happy at the same time. He stroked a hair away from her forehead and kissed her. Grudgingly they parted as a tall man in white uniform, with a weather-beaten face, walked up the gangway, saying in a

Liverpudlian accent; 'Ladies and gentlemen, it's time to board.' He touched the peak of his cap, turned and walked back onto the deck of the yacht where sailors ran to either end, standing by for the order to let go the lines.

'Thank everyone for looking after the children,' Manny said to Rita. They kissed once again. 'I love you,' he said, as everyone moved to the head of the gangway, each kissing the others goodbye.

Rosen hugged Manny. 'Joe, I don't know how to thank you and Marlene for these four days, except to say, thank you very much, it's been great.'

Rosen whispered in his ear; 'Marlene has had a great time as well, and made new friends. All I ask is that if you ever need anything, no matter what, all you have to do is ask.' He took Manny by surprise as he kissed him on the cheek.

*

Manny, Bergman and Sam watched the yacht disappear over the horizon before turning away, taking a taxi back to the hotel, heading straight for the bar. A bottle of brandy in the centre of the table, the three sat quietly drinking, thinking of their loved ones.

Manny was the first to break the silence, raising his glass towards Bergman. 'Our thanks once again for planning these last four days, Zach, I drink to you.'

'I second that,' Sam said.

'I didn't really do much, just spoke to Dominique and Joe, and hey-presto, it happened.'

Manny smiled, taking a sip of brandy and thinking of the last four whirlwind days. 'I tell you what,' he said, taking a pack of cigarettes from his pocket and offering them around, 'that has to be rated as the best four days I've ever had.' He lit his cigarette and blew out the smoke. Leaning back in the chair, legs outstretched, he gave a sigh of contentment.

'I second that,' said Sam quietly.

'There's nothing for us here, so why don't we go see Hans and his sister Helga,' Bergman suggested.

Manny sat bolt upright, 'What a bloody good idea, we'll go first thing in the morning, if that's OK with you.'

'I agree,' Sam nodded.

Laughing, Manny threw a napkin at him. 'Is that the only thing you can say?'

'I'm just agreeing with you.'

Manny went to reception. 'I'm very sorry,' he told the receptionist, 'but we'll be leaving in the morning after breakfast. I'd like to pay our bill.'

'Your bill had already been paid, sir. We would naturally remit the rest of the money to you.'

Manny wasn't surprised, although he hadn't expected it. 'Did Mr Rosen pay the bill?'

'Yes, sir,' was the fixed-smiled reply.

Manny took a piece of notepaper from the desk, writing down Rosen's address and handing it to the receptionist saying, 'Could you please send the balance to Mr Rosen at this address? Naturally, take ten per cent for the inconvenience.'

'That wouldn't be necessary, sir. Mr Rosen was very generous when he left.'

The three of them told their men what they intended to do. They agreed to go too as they'd had enough of Haifa after five days.

\*

Mishmar Haemek lay in the foothills of Mount Ephraim, with Arab villages in the mountains above it, the south-east and north-west along the road to Haifa.

Manny could see the scars of battle all around the Kibbutz, which was a hive of activity, with men and women repairing the damage.

They parked their half-tracks, and were about to go in search of Hans and Helga when Hans ran up to them, smiling.

'Aren't you supposed to be in Haifa?'

'We were bored, so thought we'd pay you a visit.'

Hans slapped Manny on the shoulder. 'Helga will be happy to see you.'

They found Helga, a sten gun strapped across her back, in the kitchen with other women preparing the midday meal. On seeing Manny she ran across, hugging and kissing him, eyes shining with happiness. 'Hans told me you were in Haifa.'

Manny smiled down at the upturned face, holding her at arm's length. 'I do believe you've put on a little weight – I'd say a lot of weight.' She tried to kick him, but he was too quick for her and she missed. He laughed, pulling her close and giving her a hug. 'How long have you got to go?'

'Four weeks.' She turned to Sam and Bergman with a smile, pulling away from Manny, giving each of them a peck on both cheeks. 'I'm very happy to see you all; are you staying long?'

'We're going to stay here for the rest of our leave to help with repairs. You took a bit of a—'

Manny was interrupted by Hans entering the kitchen, arm around the waist of a petite woman; her brown hair pulled back from her dirt-smudged face by a red bandana, wearing men's fatigues, a pistol at her hip and a sten-gun slung across her back on its webbing.

'Manny, this is my wife, Eve.'

Eve took Manny's hand, surprising him by the hardness of her skin. She must work in the fields. Her green eyes twinkled, 'At last, we meet the famous Manny. You look as I imagined, maybe a little taller.'

As she was speaking, a man entered the kitchen, walked over to Helga and kissed her cheek holding out his hand to Manny. 'I was told you were here. I've heard so much about you from these two, that it's nice to meet you at last. I'm Yitzhak, Helga's husband and Eve's brother.'

Manny shook the work-hardened hand. Yitzhak had his sister's green eyes and brown hair, but that's where the resemblance stopped. He was as tall as Manny, but not as broad, the army fatigues sweat-streaked, and like his sister there was a pistol strapped around his waist and a sten-gun slung low on its webbing, ready for use. He was unshaven, the stubble rippling across his face as he smiled. 'I was expecting to meet a film star.'

'I'm no film star,' Manny laughed at the comment, placing an arm around Sam's shoulder. 'This is my cousin Sam.' The two men shook hands, as did Eve. Before he could do the introduction, Bergman stepped forward, introducing himself.

The three friends and their men spent the rest of their leave with the kibbutzniks, helping to restore buildings, enjoying the closeness of new friendships. At night they relaxed, singing and dancing traditional songs, not only from Israel, but from places of their birth.

# Chapter 21

Troops and equipment were secretly moved into the Negev for the forthcoming operation, its aim, to conquer the entire Negev.

At noon on 15 October, a notice was sent to UN Truce Supervision HQ, informing them that a convoy was about to set out for Haratiya on its way to the Negev.

When the convoy came in range of Egyptian strongholds they were fired upon and the truce was broken. This was the signal for operations to begin.

*

The new Israeli air force bombed El Arish, the Egyptian air base, which was taken completely by surprise and caught with most of its aeroplanes on the ground. By the following day Israeli air superiority over the Negev was complete.

Manny and Sergeant Major Kraven looked through binoculars down on an Egyptian encampment. 'I can't see any lookouts around their positions, do you?' Manny said quietly.

'No sir.'

'I think,' Manny raised the binoculars to his eyes, sweeping them from left to right, 'we'll attack in two directions.' Dropping the binoculars he turned to Kraven. 'Ivan, you take two section and attack from the south, we'll attack from the north and...' he looked at the luminous dial on his watch, 'I'll give you thirty minutes to get into position, then we'll attack. Set your time to eleven o'clock, now.'

Thirty minutes later, Manny looked at his watch, dropped his arm and yelled, '*Aharay!*'

231

Jacobs gunned the engine and they sped towards the Egyptian encampment, guns blazing, but were unexpectedly met by withering fire from the Egyptians. Friedlander yelled in pain as he was hit, slumping onto the floor of the half-track. The half-track beside Manny was suddenly engulfed in flames, its occupants leaping from their burning vehicle.

Manny yelled at Jacobs, 'Turn around and pick them up!'

Jacobs was about to argue, knowing that once they stopped they would be an easy target, but also knew that Manny would not leave anyone behind. Jacobs weaved the half-track through the sand as Manny leaned over the side, grabbing the arm of one of the men pulling him aboard, and then the upheld hand of the next man, unceremoniously pulling him into the rear of the vehicle, yelling at him to grab Friedlander's gun.

There were two more to pick up, one of them wounded. Jacobs slowed down. Manny leapt from the half-track ignoring the bullets kicking up the sand around him, and knelt by the wounded man, whose name was Krochen. His face was screwed up in pain from a chest wound.

Manny lifted him onto his shoulders, ran to the front of the half-track and got aboard, tapping Jacobs on the shoulder. Jacobs gave a slight nod, putting his foot down and weaving across the sand, heading at an angle away from the bullets flying around them, while Manny gives Kochen a pain killing injection. Suddenly the earth erupted, shells landing close by.

*Tanks, I never saw any tanks!* a voice in Manny's head screamed, a picture of what he'd seen through his binoculars in his mind's eye. He stood, feet braced against the metal sides looking through the binoculars in the direction where the shell had come from as another erupted just behind them, throwing sand and shrapnel into the air as Jacobs wove the heavy half-track through the Egyptian encampment, bullets whizzing through the air, some finding their targets.

'Fuck it!' Manny's mouth drew into a thin, angry line as another of his half-tracks was hit. Then he spotted it; not a tank, but the snout of a two-pounder gun. He yelled at Jacobs, 'Turn to one o'clock.'

Jacobs obeyed the order as the soldier firing Friedlander's gun was mortally wounded.

Manny yelled into his two-way radio, 'Ivan, can you hear me?' Silence. He turned, looking through the binoculars in the direction of where the sergeant major should be, and his heart skipped a beat. Kraven and two of his men were behind their upturned vehicle, firing at Arab troops advancing towards them.

Manny tapped Jacobs on the shoulder, leaning close to his ear and pointing in the direction of Kraven. 'Can you get to him before they do?'

'Yes sir.'

Manny looked once more to where the two-pounder was hidden by a dune as it fired once again, splattering them with earth and bits of metal that bounced off the armour plating. Manny grabbed a handful of grenades, dropped them into a backpack and yelled at Jacobs above the noise of guns and exploding shells. 'Pick them up. I'm going after that fucking gun; once you've got them come back for me.' He looked down at Friedlander. 'Can you fire the Bofors?'

Friedlander, his face a white mask of determination, nodded. Wincing in pain, he hauled himself up grabbing the handles of the twin Bofors looking for a target; gritting his teeth, he fired.

Manny patted him on the back, and then jumped over the side of the vehicle, heading for the two-pounder, holding the Russian Tommy gun in his right hand and backpack in the left. An enemy soldier yelled at him, thinking he was an Arab until seeing the shoulder flashes. Manny fired at him and without breaking stride, hurdled over the dead soldier's body, heading towards the target.

He was furious with himself for not seeing the two-pounder as he zigzagged towards the gun, ignoring the bullets kicking up the sand around him. Now in range, he let go of the Tommy gun, which dropped down his left side held by the webbing over his shoulder. He took a grenade from the backpack, pulled the pin and threw it, at the same time going to ground, throwing four grenades one after the other.

As the last one exploded, he got to his feet, Tommy gun in his hands, running straight towards the two-pounder that had now stopped firing; dropping to the ground, he rolled to his right, crawling a few yards forward and peeped over the rim of the emplacement to see the two-pounder lying on its side, its gun crew dead beside it.

He turned, looking down at the encampment seeing very little confusion amongst the Egyptians. It was as though they were expecting them. Two of his half-tracks and one jeep were now wrecks. Smoke drifted across the battle arena; guns firing, men yelling obscenities at each other, and the wounded crying for help. His men disengaged the enemy, who were heading in his direction.

The Egyptians, wanting revenge for the loss of their gun, moved slowly towards him, some brave enough to charge were soon cut down, while others hoping not to be seen crawled towards him. Manny tossed his last four grenades down on them; those Egyptians that were left retreated.

A half-track pulled up in front of him. 'Need a lift, sir?' said a smiling, dirt-faced Jacobs. Manny leapt aboard and they retreated into the desert, heading towards their headquarters at Mishmar Hanegev. Manny slammed his hand angrily on the metal side of his vehicle, taking no notice of the pain or the scuffed skin, annoyed with himself for not noticing the two-pounder. They had taken a pounding, having lost four vehicles, six men killed and ten wounded; two seriously.

Sergeant Major Kraven leaned across and whispered, 'Sir, it wasn't your fault.'

Manny looked with sad eyes at Kraven, gesturing over his shoulder to the dead and wounded whispering back, 'You're wrong, they're dead because of me. I should have been more careful, I missed something. They must have seen us, probably before we even got there, I should have been more cautious in reconnoitring the area.'

Leaving the wounded in the hospital, he ordered the others to get some rest, and if possible, some sleep. With a heavy heart he handed the dead men to the funeral detail, then trudged wearily to command headquarters.

On the way he met Sam, who had just arrived, also on his way to HQ. Both had casualties and losses of vehicles that the IDF could ill-afford to lose.

Headquarters was a hive of activity. The two cousins were ordered to report to the intelligence officer, a major, who wrote notes as he listened to their reports.

'Get some rest while we decide what to do with you,' said the major.

'Let's see if we have any mail,' Manny suggested to Sam.

'Good idea, I haven't had a letter from Sarah for ages; I wonder if the postman knew where we were.'

There was a bundle of letters awaiting both men. Walking with tired, heavy steps to where they were billeted, Manny uttered wearily, 'As much as I want to read them now, I'm too tired to take it all in, plus we don't know when we're going back into action.'

Sam yawned, 'I second that.'

Manny laughed, 'That's got to be your favourite saying.'

'I was just … oh forget it.'

*

Manny had been asleep for nearly two hours when a corporal shook him awake. 'Sorry to disturb you, sir, but the major would like to see you, and the other captain, Grenfeldt.'

'Thank you corporal, I'll wake the captain.'

As the corporal left, Manny woke Sam. 'The major wants to see us. I'm going to have a shave and shower first.' He sniffed his armpits. 'Ughh, I smell like a skunk.'

'Worse,' Sam smiled gathering up his washbag and towel, adding, 'Did you know you just insulted the skunk.'

Manny threw the towel at him.

\*

An hour later, freshly shaved, showered and wearing clean combat uniforms, Manny and Sam reported to the major, who took them over to a map of the Negev hanging on the wall. 'I want your armour group to do exactly what you've been doing, with raids into the Negev and Sinai Peninsular. While you and your men were resting, I've had your vehicles serviced and re-armed, and scrounged two half-tracks.'

Manny and Sam, with the newly promoted Second Lieutenant Kraven and Sergeant Major Jacobs, inspected their vehicles. The men were tired. They had had very little sleep over the last couple of months, but from experience knew that the end of the war was very near. The Egyptian army, apart from those surrounded at Fulja, were retreating.

He sat in the armoured vehicle, reading Rita's letters over and over again, especially the one saying she was pregnant and the baby was expected in May. He smiled, and lit a cigarette, exhaling the smoke slowly through his nostrils thinking, *no matter what, I must be there.* And read on. *You must ask Sam about his letter.* He did, Sarah was also pregnant and expecting in May. Both knew when that happened.

\*

The following afternoon they joined-up with the rest of the Brigade and met Bergman, whom they hadn't seen for two months, and were told that Dominique was expecting too. May was going to be a busy month for the three comrades.

\*

6 January 1948, and a battle-weary Manny, with Sam, Bergman and their men, waited patiently for a raging sandstorm to abate. News came through that the Egyptians, who a few months before had promised that in two weeks they would eliminate the State of Israel and throw the Jews into the sea, were ready to enter into immediate negotiations for an armistice agreement. There was a shout of joy from the men, who immediately began dancing around their vehicles.

'So, the vanquished meets the victor,' said Manny quietly. But to his disgust, international pressure forced Israel to withdraw from Sinai and Gaza Strip, where they had the Egyptian army surrounded.

The jolting of the vehicle made it hard to read Rita's latest letter as the Brigade raced through the desert towards Eilat with explicit orders not to engage in any battles while the armistice negotiations were going on.

Manny looked across at Bergman as they refuelled their vehicles, 'We're cutting it fine if we want to be in England by May. I promised Rita I'd be home for the birth.'

'You mean,' Sam stated, 'we'd better be there for the births.'

Bergman smiled, 'Dominique told me in no uncertain terms to be there, even if I have to win this war single handed.'

'Oh, the wrath of a woman,' said Manny with a smile.

\*

On 10 March the Negev and Golani Brigades, reached the police station at Umm Rash Rash, known as the resort city of Eilat. Not a shot was fired. It was the last operation of Israel's war of independence.

No one had thought to bring a flag with them, but a soldier, Micha Peri, hand-drew one by pouring blue ink onto a sheet. This symbol of freedom and independence was named the Ink Flag.

*

Between 24 February and 12 July 1949, peace treaties were signed with Egypt, Lebanon. Jordan and Syria, but by then Manny, Sam and Bergman, had additions to their families. Manny and Rita had a boy, naming him Saul, after Manny's friend; Sam and Sarah had a little girl, Lily, and on the same day, Dominique and Bergman also had a little girl, Daniela.

Manny read with trepidation the latest reports in the newspaper from Israel. The Egyptian government would not allow the population of Gaza to become Egyptian citizens or formally want to incorporate them into Egypt.

'This was going to cause big problems,' he said under his breath, as his daughter Miriam tugged at his trousers to be lifted up. Miriam snuggled into his chest, placing her tiny arms around his neck and his heart melted.

# Chapter 22

*May 1955*

THE sun shone in a clear blue sky. The birthday party was in full swing; the proud mothers brought in the birthday cakes, calling to their children who were around the swimming pool, especially those whose birthdays had fallen in May. Everyone cheered and sang Happy Birthday, yelling out the names of the birthday boys and girls.

This had been a tradition since Manny, Sam and their families moved to residences on the outskirts of Tel Aviv. Isaac, now a doctor, and Hannah had immigrated in 1950.

Manny, a broad grin on his face looked around the garden at the happy smiling faces and the laughter of the children playing. This was what he and the others had fought for; somewhere where their families would be safe, without prejudice.

A pregnant Rita wiped the chocolate from around their four-year-old daughter Susan's face and hands. Manny took a photo of the moment, turning the camera onto Joshua, now a major in the Israeli air force, playing with his one-year-old son Abraham; he and Freda had married eighteen months ago.

On returning to England after the 1948 Israeli–Arab war, Manny had thought long and hard about his, Rita and the children's future, torn between staying in the army, and doing something else, but the decision was made for him.

The resignation of many war-weary officers decimated the basic manpower needed to mobilise a sizeable fighting force during a wartime emergency. The Israeli government introduced a three-tier system based on a small standing officer corps, universal conscription and a large pool of well-trained reservists who could be rapidly mobilised.

On his return to Israel, Manny decided to become a reserve officer with the rank of major, and immediately began looking for a house and business premises. Sam and Bergman opted to stay in the army.

Manny found a beautiful property just outside Tel Aviv. It was habitable, but needing restoration, which he left in Rita's capable hands. In the shopping district of Tel Aviv, he came across the business premises he had been looking for, and sent for his father-in-law to get an expert opinion.

Daniel was pleased with Manny's choice. 'I agree this was an ideal spot for the business. Where are we going to get the equipment?'

'You know what to order; I've obtained a list of companies.' Handing the list to Daniel he added, 'We'll go to the bank and open a joint account, and then I'm going back to London to bring Rita and the children over.'

That was six years ago. Rita had added, apart from the original three bedrooms, another two bedrooms onto the house, conservatory and swimming pool. Manny and Daniel's bakery had thrived and they were now employing ten people.

Rosen's perceptiveness of dabbling in the property market had paid off in a big way; they had also obtained shares in US telephone and TV companies. Those ventures had made Manny and the others very rich men.

Their company's name was OZARMA, taken from the initials of each of their names. The group recently opened another property business in Netanya, where they were building holiday apartments, branching out towards Eilat. That was Rosen's job. He hopped backward and forward from Israel to London in his private aircraft. Manny realised a long time ago that Joe loved the challenge of building a business, but even that came second to his wife and family.

Placing another roll of film into the camera, Manny knew he was a very lucky man: all the years of wondering what career to follow, and it had just fallen into his lap. Who would have realised he would become a baker and enjoy it so much? With all his wealth, it still gave him a thrill watching the bread, bagels and rolls coming out of the ovens.

Daniel taught him all that he knew; the rest Manny had done himself. They now supplied bagels, bread and cakes to restaurants and hotels throughout Tel Aviv, and Manny was thinking of expanding their business by buying a bigger property and turning it into a coffee house.

Tomorrow he would be reporting for two weeks' compulsory training, adding more pressure on Daniel, who was not getting any younger: he would be sixty in September.

The training was, to Manny, very essential, as it kept him up to date with the new weaponry the army had obtained, and gave him a chance to meet up with some of his men, especially Jacobs, Friedlander and Kraven.

*

On 29 October 1956, in less than seventy-two hours, over a thousand reservists including Manny had been mobilised. For the commanders of the Israeli Defence Forces, it was a complete success.

Manny, wearing sun goggles, guided Jacobs as their armoured vehicle sped towards Egypt's Suez Canal. So far they had met little opposition and Manny was confident the Suez would soon be in Israeli hands.

The Egyptian President, Gamal Abdel Nasser had nationalised the Suez Canal, which was an essential highway for the world's shipping as it cut the journey through the Cape of Good Hope to Southampton by 6,500 nautical miles. Petroleum accounted for two-thirds of the canal's traffic and was a critical link with the international oil industry.

Nasser's forces had blocked the Straits of Tiran, the narrow waterway that was Israel's only outlet to the Red Sea, and had publicly incited violent hostilities against

Israel by announcing, 'There will be no peace on Israel's borders because we demand vengeance, and vengeance was Israel's death.'

The Israeli government's patience had broken. Now, after trying for a peaceful solution, they had no other option but to attack Egypt.

Covering his face with a kuffiyeh against the swirling dust on the road, Manny was pleased that at last, after years of Arab commando raids into Israel, sponsored mainly by Egypt, they were openly invading the Gaza Strip and the Sinai Peninsula, but he was disappointed by the lack of opposition.

Taking a refuelling stop gave the men a chance to get reacquainted as they ate their rations, talking quietly amongst themselves about family, politics or football, as music, playing softly from their radios, was suddenly interrupted by an announcement.

'British and French bombers have today, 31 October, attacked Egyptian installations. President Nasser has responded by sinking ships in the Canal.'

Manny snapped the last part of his Tommy gun into place after cleaning it, pointed it to the ground and pulled the trigger, smiling at his thoughts. *By tomorrow we'll be in Cairo.* He frowned. *But why aren't we continuing today? We could have crossed the Canal by now.* He shrugged his shoulders. *There must be a reason why...*

*

The following morning, as Israel's Defence Forces attacked, Manny knew the reason for delaying the advance. It was so that Britain and France could invade Egypt and capture the Canal.

To Manny's disappointment, the Israeli army, under pressure from the USA, came to a halt ten miles from the Canal, but before the ceasefire, Israel captured Sharm el Sheikh, and opened up the Straits of Tiran.

Ten days after being mobilised Manny was back at work.

# Chapter 23

*6 October 1967*

T ODAY was Yom Kippur; the holiest day of the year.
Manny walked proudly to the synagogue; with Rita
holding his right hand, and their daughter Josephine,
who everyone called Jo, holding his left. Her name was
Rita's idea, wanting to preserve the memory of Manny's
first love, Joan.

The last ten years had been good to Manny and Rita.
Their children had grown into men and women. David, the
eldest son, who was a lawyer and reserve pilot in the Air
Force, walked behind them, one arm around his fiancée
Daniela, Bergman's daughter; they were to be married at
the end of the year.

Manny and Rita's eldest daughter Miriam walked hand
in hand with Daniela's brother Abe, who was also a pilot;
while her younger sister Susan and their cousin Barbara
chatted away about the latest films, movie stars, music, and
naturally, boys.

Aunt Doris and Uncle Mark had sold their property and
business in London, and retired to an apartment in Netanya.
Rita's father, Daniel now worked part-time, travelling from
shop to shop teaching and making sure they kept up their
high standard of baking bread, bagels and their speciality,
pastries and cakes, which were in great demand, not only by
the public, but by caterers and hotels along the coast. Daniel
had met a widow, Sheila, another refugee from the war.
They had been married a year.

*

The afternoon service was nearly over when the sirens
began to wail. Within minutes the synagogue was virtually

empty as men and women hurried to their rendezvous points.

Manny kissed Rita and their two younger daughters; turning he yelled at David, Abe and Miriam, 'Take no chances,' as they leapt into Abe's car, and at breakneck speed raced towards their airbase, dropping Miriam, an army theatre nurse, at the hospital.

Because of the Sabbath the roads were empty. Manny picked up men thumbing a lift until the car could hold no more, all listening intently to the car radio, hoping to be told what was going on, as the announcer, in a quiet unruffled voice, broadcasted the codewords mobilising various units.

'Fucking hell,' said Manny. 'Of all the days to start a war.'

Reaching his rendezvous point, Manny was told by a lieutenant, 'Sir, Egypt is pouring men and armour across the Suez Canal, in a coordinated attack with Syria, who, with Iran and various contingents from other Arab countries, was attacking the Golan Heights.'

Manny had a worried frown on his face on hearing about the Golan Heights. His son Saul, who had just finished army training, was stationed there. Because of Yom Kippur there was only a small contingent of Israeli tanks facing the Syrians.

In the command post, the officers listened to a report by their commanding officer. 'Thousands of Egyptian troops and armour are at this moment crossing the canal. The information I'm receiving is that the Egyptians have set up a defensive line of SAM-3 surface-to-air missiles protecting the army from attack by our air force, which is, at this moment, unable to do anything against the effectiveness of these missiles. We've been caught completely by surprise. Our job is to stop the Egyptian armour from advancing any further and counter attack.'

Leaving the tent, Manny headed towards his men and vehicles, knowing that it was an impossible task at this very moment in time to counter attack. Gathering the men

around him, he told them in a soft commanding voice what
they had to try and do.

\*

For two days they counter-attacked, which was as Manny
predicted a miserable failure; ten of his men were killed and
thirty wounded; he had lost twenty tanks and ten armoured
vehicles, including his own.

The Egyptians army, using Russian handheld Sagger
anti-tank missiles that could punch a hole through armour
plating, stopped the Israeli armour in its tracks, costing
them dearly in men and tanks.

Suddenly, after four days of heavy losses, there was a
lull in the fighting. Manny received an order to report to his
CO who was standing beside a large map of Israel with
various coloured pins and tapes running here and there.

'Smoke if you want,' he said, lighting up, saying as he
let the smoke trickle from his nostrils, 'As you know we're
fighting on two fronts and now there's a lull…' He took a
puff of his cigarette. 'The Egyptians seemed to be waiting
for something…' he gave a wry smile. 'I'm sure we'll soon
find out, but in the meantime we intend sending
reinforcements from the Sinai to the Golan and push back
the Syrians and Iranians. Once we've accomplished that,
the troops will return to this area.'

He pointed at Manny, 'Your men will stay here using hit
and run tactics, keep the enemy busy.'

'Yes, sir,' Manny could see the sense in High
Command's thinking; all he and those that were left needed
to do was harass the Egyptians for a few days.

With the added reinforcement, individual heroism and
superior gunnery, the Israelis got the upper hand on the
Golan, and the Syrians retreated, leaving behind hundreds
of tanks and other equipment. With the Syrians in full flight
Israel could now put all its attention to the Sinai and the
Egyptian army.

It caught the Israeli High Command by surprise when suddenly Egypt launched an offensive beyond the protection of their SAM-3 missiles, their armour moving rapidly towards the Milta and Gidi passes in six separate thrusts along a hundred mile stretch.

No sooner had the Egyptians moved from their safe defensive positions than the Israeli air force pounced, while at the same time Israeli armour moved to intercept.

Adrenalin pulsed through his veins as Manny ordered his troops to advance. Within minutes their superior gunnery took its toll. Manny's vehicle was hit, again with no loss of life, quickly transferring to, of all things, a tank.

He had decided some time ago that he'd learn all he could about the armour he commanded, working hard in training with Jacobs and the others, plus expert advice from Hans about tank tactics and gunnery. As usual, he made sure that every crew member could do the other's job in case of injury. Now the hours of training paid off; they had already destroyed six enemy tanks.

'Hey, Jacobs, could you make this thing go any faster?'

Jacob smiled, knowing Manny the way he did, he replied with laughter in his voice, 'I'm going as fast as I'm able, sir. If you stopped knocking out so many tanks we wouldn't have to chase those in retreat.'

Manny laughed, and quietly directed Friedlander. 'Tank eleven o'clock.' The turret quickly moved in the direction indicated, stopped, there was a slight shudder as a shell left the muzzle of the gun. Manny watched through binoculars yelling, 'Direct hit.'

Although he was in battle, Manny could not help but think about his children. Saul, he knew, was on the Golan Heights, and David somewhere in the skies above. He, like thousands of other fathers, gave a silent prayer for his children's safety as they fought against staggering odds in manpower and equipment.

*

The following day, Manny was sitting high in his vehicle when it was engulfed in flames from a direct hit. He was thrown to the ground and tried to get up and help his men, but for some reason couldn't. He tried again, falling back onto the sand and blacked out.

He slowly opened his eyes, blinking to get them into focus. He tried to sit up, but fell back immediately onto the pillows, head spinning.

'You're awake?'

Manny wanted to smile at the statement. Of course he was awake; he tried to say something but his mouth was dry, and he made a hand gesture for a drink.

A woman's face appeared in front of him, brown hair tied in a pony tail. She gently lifted his head, helping him to drink; removing his mouth from the glass asking, 'Where am I? What's wrong with me?'

'You're in a military hospital unit, ten miles from the front lines. Colonel, you're one lucky man; a bullet hit your helmet and lodged itself in your temple. There's no permanent damage, you've seven stitches.' She smiled. 'That will give you something to talk about over drinks. You also had some burns to your right side, but they aren't too bad and should heal pretty quickly.'

'What about my men?'

'I'm sorry, I can't help you there. Perhaps the doctor would be able to tell you more, I'll see if he's free to talk to you.'

Manny tried to sit up, but his head felt like it had been hit by a sledgehammer and fell back onto the pillows. After a few seconds, he moved his limbs, they were sore, probably when he was thrown from the tank, but they were all there. He turned his head to the right, seeing rows of beds with nurses attending to patients; then to his left, more beds.

A doctor appeared with the nurse beside him. Before Manny could speak the doctor said. 'I'll answer your questions if I can in a moment, but first let's have a look at your wounds.' Carefully he pulled back the dressing covering Manny's head. 'Mmm, you're lucky. We had to cut your helmet away from your scalp; the impact from the bullet pushed it into your skin, stopping it from entering your skull.'

He pulled back the covers, peeling a dressing from along Manny's right side, looked at the wound and turned to the nurse. 'Some more of the same, give him six-hourly pain killers, and re-dress the forehead.'

'How are my men?'

The doctor avoided the question, patting Manny on the shoulder. 'The headaches should go in a couple of hours, and—'

Manny grabbed the sleeve of his white coat trying to sit up. 'I asked you,' he said between tight angry lips, falling weakly back onto the pillow, 'how are my men?'

The doctor gently took his hand from his sleeve. 'I'm sorry, sir, but we've had so many men through here in the last couple of days, names don't register.' The doctor turned to the nurse. 'When you've finished dressing his wounds, see what you can find out.'

Manny gave the names of his men to the nurse and then the painkillers took effect and he fell asleep. Six hours later, the nurse returned and woke Manny to give him his medication, saying as she helped him take a drink of water, 'Colonel, I'm sorry to tell you that Levene the gunner was killed, Jacobs died on the operating table. Friedlander lost his right leg, and had pretty extensive burns to his body, but he'll be OK given time.'

Manny nodded his thanks, closing his eyes tightly to stop the tears. 'How long before I'm able to get back to my command?'

'I'm sorry, I can't answer that.' She moved away, leaving Manny with his thoughts, as he gradually drifted off to sleep again.

A cool hand touched his arm, he opened his eyes; it was his daughter Miriam. She stroked a tress of hair away from his forehead below the bandages. There were tears in her eyes.

'I'm OK,' he said hoarsely.

She shook her head, the tears streaming down her face, unable to say anything as she bent, cuddling him to her, the side of his face and neck wet from the tears. He knew something bad, must have happened, but didn't say anything, just placed his arms around her.

After a few moments her sobbing stopped, and she gently moved away.

He looked intently into her eyes whispering, 'Who?'

'Saul, he was killed on the 17th.'

'Anyone else?' he asked sadly.

'Barry, he was trying to help some wounded soldiers when a shell landed on top of them. David and Abraham were shot down, but managed to bale out into our lines, they're still flying combat missions. One of the doctors told me you were here. Papa, when will the killing end? Why don't they let us live in peace?'

'I wish I knew.' Manny couldn't hold back his sadness at the loss of Saul. He wanted more than anything to get back into the fight. He tried to sit up, but once again fell back onto the pillows. Between gritted teeth, he said, 'Miriam, help me up.'

'What?'

'Please, petal, help me up.'

'Why, where're you going?'

'Miriam,' he said her name a little too loudly. Heads turned in their direction. She placed an arm around his back, helping him up. A nurse ran across the ward to them.

'What do you think you're doing?'

'Helping me get out of here,' Manny replied angrily.

'You're in no fit state to leave. Anyway, where're you going?'

'To avenge my son, and other fathers' sons,' he said heatedly. Shakily, with Miriam's help, he stood, placing an arm around her shoulder. The room began to spin but he was determined to get back to the fight and took a step forward, but his legs gave way. The nurse grabbed him under his right armpit; pain shot through his body from the burns as she helped Miriam lower him onto the edge of the bed.

'What do you think you're doing?' the nurse said angrily, looked at Miriam, 'and you should know better.'

Inhaling and exhaling heavily tears of frustration at the corner of his eyes, Manny didn't say a word.

'Colonel, if you try that again, I'll have you put in restraints. You're in no fit state to leave here,' And then in a softer voice she said, 'Do I make myself clear sir?'

Manny had no intention of obeying the nurse, but nodded in agreement.

After touching Miriam's shoulder, the nurse moved away to attend to a patient.

Manny looked at his daughter, tears flowing down his cheeks. 'You must help me,' he whispered, fists tightly clenched eyes pleading, fighting the pain from his burns. 'I must avenge your brother, if I don't I'll never forgive myself. Please, I'm begging you; help me get out of here.'

Miriam's eyes showed her anguish, 'Papa, you're in no fit state to—'

'Miriam, if you love me, please let me do this.' He took her hand. 'We never started this war, but I'm damn well going to try and help end it. I need vengeance, I need to look an Arab in the eye and tell him why he's going to die. Please, please, let me do this,' he said vehemently.

For a second she didn't say a word, just looked at his face, the eyes pleading for her help. 'Papa, please don't ask me to do this, I don't want to lose you too.'

He stroked her hair lovingly. 'You won't lose me, I promise.' He pointed to his head and for the first time smiled. 'They've already tried and didn't succeed. I need some clothes, can you?'

Miriam bit her lip and nodded. She looked in the locker beside him, finding socks, combat trousers and boots, and helped him put them on; then without a word she left him, returning minutes later with a shirt and jacket, helping him dress and stand.

Manny swayed for a second, mouth set in a straight, determined line. Steadying himself, he took a couple of tentative steps forward, his arm around Miriam's shoulder, stopping to clear his head and then continued walking slowly and a little unsteadily towards the exit. No one noticed them as they were far too busy: more and more wounded were being brought into the centre. By the time they reached the exit he was able to walk, albeit slowly, without holding onto Miriam.

Outside, the area was buzzing with activity as the wounded were ferried in from the battlefront. A helicopter landed, orderlies ran towards it, taking off the stretchers, hurrying to the tented hospital.

Manny kissed his daughter. 'I love you, see you soon.' Jaw tight with determination, he turned and walked slowly and painfully, though not in a straight line, his body half-bent towards the helicopter and opened the pilot's door. 'I'm Colonel Bergman. I need a lift back to my unit somewhere near the Sinai.'

The pilot was about to say something, but saw the look on Manny's face and nodded. A crew member helped Manny into the helicopter. He waved to Miriam as it lifted off, hovering for a moment; she didn't see him as she was helping the wounded. The sand swirled up from the helicopter's rotors, and it sped away.

Manny stepped gingerly from the helicopter as men carrying stretchers quickly loaded the wounded. A corporal helped an officer from a jeep. Manny, tried to stand upright as he walked over to them, instantly recognising the officer.

'Samson, could I borrow your corporal?' Manny yelled over the noise of helicopter's engines.

The major's pale face turned to Manny, eyes looking at his bandaged head. 'Manny?' He found it hard to speak, 'I thought... you were killed... yesterday. I think... you should... come with me... you don't look to good,' he said between gasps of pain.

'I'm fine; I need to get back to my men, they're in the north somewhere.'

The major turned to his driver, a slight built man with the beginning of a beard on his tanned face. 'Jack, get me on board that helicopter before I bleed to death, and take the...' he looked at Manny, 'this mad Colonel—'

'Thanks, I owe you one,' Manny said. 'I wish you well.' The corporal helped his officer into the helicopter and then moved back to Manny and the jeep, both men turning their backs as the sand formed a cloud from the helicopter's rotors as it lifted off, heading back to the field hospital.

Manny climbed gingerly aboard the jeep, gasping with pain as he picked up a gun lying on the floor. He checked the mechanism and loaded the weapon, turning to the corporal; taking a deep breath and ignoring the pain shooting through his body and throbbing head, he said, 'OK, Jack, let's go back.'

'Very funny, sir, very original,' the corporal smiled, letting off the clutch and they sped away with the sound of artillery fire in the distance. Above them, Israeli fighter planes headed for the canal.

Turning a bend they come across a tank parked at the side of the road with three of its crew beside it. Jack stopped the jeep.

'What's going on, who's in charge?' Manny asked harshly.

A corporal approached the jeep, a frown on his sweat-streaked face, a worried look in his brown eyes as he stood to attention in front of Manny. 'I suppose I am, sir.'

'Have you broken down?'

'Not exactly, sir. Our officer's dead and the driver badly wounded. We sent him in an ambulance to the rear. We're low on fuel and were waiting for instructions, our radios out and we've lost contact with our unit.'

'Have you got a map?'

One of the other crewmen leapt expertly onto the turret, leaned in producing a map.

Manny stepped slowly and carefully from the jeep, opening the map out on the bonnet turning to the corporal. 'How much fuel do you have?'

'Fifteen miles, then we're dry.'

'Can you drive one of these?' Manny asked Jack.

Jack nodded. 'Yes, sir, I have a spare can of petrol on the jeep; that would give us a few extra miles.'

'Great, that's a good idea.' He pointed to a spot on the map. 'We're here.' He moved a finger along a line saying, 'We need to be there; it's about six miles.' He turned to the corporal. 'I suppose you're the gunner, and—'

'That's TJ, he's the loader,' the corporal interrupted, pointing to another man. 'Max Mahoney, machine gunner. No, you don't have to ask where he's from; I'm Frank Katz, sir.'

Manny frowned. 'Why haven't either of you learnt to drive this tank? Surely it's the logical thing to do in case something like this happened?' But before the corporal could reply Manny continued. 'Never mind that now. Jack, pick up the spare can of petrol, and whatever you think necessary from the jeep and let's get going, we've a war to fight.' He climbed painfully, white-faced and feeling nauseous, onto the tank and gingerly into the turret. 'TJ, load the gun,' Manny ordered as they moved off.

They luckily come across a rear supply area. Leaving the others to sort out the refuelling, rearming and a new radio, Manny went in search of someone who knew what was going on, and was soon in front of a colonel.

'I've commandeered a tank, whose officer had been killed and driver injured. Could you please point me in the right direction I want to rejoin my unit?' He rubbed his forehead. 'Have you got any aspirin?'

The colonel looked him up and down. 'You don't look in any state to be joining in the—'

Manny held up his hand, stopping him from saying anything else, and leaned close to the officer, saying quietly in a menacing voice, 'If you don't give me the directions I seek, I'm going to shoot you.'

\*

An hour later, having refuelled, rearmed, with new radio and two packs of aspirin, Manny and his motley crew were on their way to the fighting. Coldly, and with uncanny insight, they joined the fray, and within minutes knocked out four Egyptian tanks. Any Arab crewmen that leapt to safety from their damaged tank were cut down by Manny firing the turret-mounted machine-gun.

They knocked the track off one tank, and as the crew tumbled from it, Manny somehow, without thinking, using all the will power he had, ignoring the pain that shot through him, jumped from the tank charging them, yelling in Arabic and killing each man in a frenzied attack.

Jack and the others were stunned by his behaviour, wondering how with the wounds he had sustained he was able to do what he'd done; until TJ, who spoke Arabic, translated. 'He's saying, this is vengeance for his son Saul, and other fathers' sons.'

\*

As evening approached the five men, who were now on first name terms, battle-stained, but elated with the day's fighting, sat in a circle beside the tank they had named *Vengeance,* which TJ painted on the turret in Hebrew, together with 21 little tanks, their number of kills.

The aspirin had worked; Manny ignored what little discomfort he still had, while Jack looked at his wounds and redressed them.

Frank asked softly, 'Manny, tell us about your son Saul.'

'How do you—'

'TJ speaks Arabic.'

Manny nodded, and in a quiet voice told them about his son, the tears unashamedly streaming down his face. 'He just finished training and was my only child on the Golan. One of my sons is a fighter pilot, and my daughter's a sister in field unit.' Manny looked at each in turn, and was grateful to them for helping him avenge Saul and allowing him to speak about him.

'Do you have children, Jack?'

'Me, no, I'm not married, but I think I've met the one I'll hopefully marry, her name's Mandy.' He took a photo from his top pocket handing it to Manny.

The girl in the picture was posing for the camera; the smiling eyes shining as though she was saying something funny to the person taking it.

'Very pretty,' Manny said, handing the photo to TJ, who held out his hand for it, whistling in American fashion. 'Wow, you're one lucky son of a gun.'

Manny bursts out laughing; only someone like TJ would say it that way and not be offensive.

Frank moved closer handing Manny a photo of a brunette with three children. The two boys have Frank's eyes and nose. The little girl's the image of her mother. 'They are the light of my life; I'm very lucky, I work from home.'

Max Mahoney was thin, like a stick. His bonny face with its beaklike nose never seemed to smile. He hadn't said much all day, and when he had spoken it had been with a quiet, Irish brogue. His eyes and voice were sad. 'I'm divorced, she didn't want to come to Israel, and thankfully my two children did. I live on a kibbutz; she doesn't know what she's missing.' He gave a wry smile. 'Apart from this.'

'Excuse me, sir,' Jack said, 'but do you think we're going all the way to Cairo, we're only a hundred kilometres away?'

Manny didn't answer at once, trying to think what he would do if he were in command, but would Golda Meir, or for that matter the Americans, let them?

'I think, if America and the Knesset don't stop us now, yes, we'll go all the way; for no other reason than to show them we could get to them in their capital city whenever we want. It would frighten the whole Arab world in knowing that we're capable of anything.'

Jack nodded.

Manny pointed a finger at him. 'I personally think that in two or three days' time there'll be a ceasefire agreement. All I hope is that we don't give back the land we've captured, and this surprise attack by the Arabs should never happen again. Let's get some sleep – we've another hard day tomorrow.'

Manny hadn't been able to join up with his unit, but stayed with General Adan's division, reaching the Bitter Lake with the rumour that a ceasefire had been negotiated by the Russians and USA, to begin on 23 October. But both sides ignored the ceasefire. One captured Egyptian officer was angry that the Israelis violated the ceasefire, but shut up when confronted by Manny, who drew his commando knife, placing the point against the Arab's throat, saying icily in Arabic, 'If you don't shut up, I'll shut you up, for good.'

A few days ago Manny would have killed him on the spot, prisoner or not, but he had avenged his son a hundredfold. He turned from the officer, stopping in mid-stride and turned back. 'Do you know many Jews?' he asked.

'No,' was the reply, adding, 'Up until being captured I've never met a Jew.'

Manny and the other men around stared at the Arab in stunned astonishment. 'So how could you hate me and these men if you've never met us?'

The officer didn't reply.

*

An ultimatum was received by the Soviets which resulted in the USA going to DEFCON 3 nuclear alert, which was meant to scare Russia, as their ultimatum clearly read that they were prepared to start World War III. The UN resolution called for an immediate ceasefire by both sides, to begin on 25 October, which Israel and Egypt would adhere to.

Manny looked in the mirror as he shaved, thinking that Israel had, by the skin of its teeth, survived annihilation. They had won a clear battle against the Syrians, advancing to within 20 miles from Damascus. In the Sinai the Egyptian third army was surrounded and they were close to Cairo. With courage, determination and mistakes by their enemies they had survived, but at what cost?

On 22 November Manny, now aged 47, went home to his family and friends, like many others throughout Israel, to mourn the loss of 2,300 loved ones.

Manny was still determined to fight whenever necessary, to uphold the freedom of Israel against its many enemies.

# Chapter 24

*Manny's 50th birthday party, 10 June 1970*

M ANNY was talking to Bergman, who was now a member of the Knesset, and three other members. 'Still, after all these years, I cannot comprehend why the Arabs hate us so much.' His forehead creased in a frown as he continued. 'I wonder what would have happened in 1946, when the head of the Jewish agency begged Rahman Azzam, the Secretary-General of the Arab League, for peace not war. If he had said yes to peace, how different the Middle East and the world would be today.' There are tears in his eyes as he said, 'We, Israel, mourn peace.'

Bergman said, 'Not only that, if Egypt and Jordan, after the Six Day War, had given the people in the Gaza Strip and West Bank the citizenship they asked for, then maybe, just maybe, the refugee problem wouldn't exist.'

'If, and maybe, if my grandfather had been my grandmother...' Manny let the saying hang in the air.

His son, David stood on a chair. 'Family and friends – it's my honour to propose the toast to the birthday boy.' Everyone laughed, and David went on, 'He's our rock, a man to turn to for advice, or a helping hand whenever you need it. Ladies and gentlemen, the toast is: Manny.'

The crowd yelled his name, and toasted him. Someone yelled, 'Speech' and the call was taken up by the other guests.

Manny had no choice but to say a few words. Holding up his hand, he placed an arm around Rita's waist.

'I'm blessed,' he looked down at Rita, 'with a beautiful wife, fantastic children, and children-in-law, my grandchildren, and you—' he swept the hand holding a half-filled glass of champagne '—my wonderful family and friends. What else could a man wish for? Thank you all for coming and making this an occasion I will remember for as long as I live.' He hesitated for a moment. 'If I'm honest, there's another wish – peace, peace in Israel.' Manny raised his glass. 'Family and friends, I give you a toast, peace, and Israel, and a better tomorrow.' Everyone repeated the toast.

Manny was talking happily to Sam, Bergman, and Rosen when his son David stood up in front of the band, saying through the microphone, 'Ladies and gentlemen, my parents will open the dancing with a Viennese waltz.'

Manny took Rita in his arms, and the music began. He hummed to the tune as they moved gracefully around the floor, the people clapping them. Manny laughed, head back with delight as they twirled around the dance floor. The guests joined them, wishing him happy birthday as they passed.

# Epilogue

HE APPEARED from the en-suite bathroom drying his hair with a small hand towel, another larger one wrapped around his waist stopping in front of the dressing table, picked up a comb running it through his steel grey hair. He gives a slight smile at his reflection in the mirror, taking a step back whipping the towel from around his waist turning to a side view of himself, expanded his chest scrutinising his body, muttering haughtily, 'Not bad for an old man of eighty.' He'd lost a little weight, but not as much as they said he would.

Manny leaned towards the mirror; blue eyes staring back as he ran a hand down the side of his face, across his chin to the other side; smooth, the way he liked it. Replacing the comb onto the dresser he reached for his favourite cologne; opening the bottle he sprayed under his arms, then into the palms of his hands, patting it onto his face, closing his eyes, inhaling the fragrance as it drifted around the room.

He opened his eyes and looked thoughtfully through the bedroom window at the blue sky. 'It's going to be a nice day,' he whispered; thinking, *would it be his?* No, he wouldn't think like that. He turned and strode over to the king-sized bed, donned blue silk pyjamas lying on the duvet and got into bed. Reaching for his reading glasses, he picked up the newspaper from the bedside table and opened it at the sports page.

After a few moments he shook his head, dropping it onto the duvet, unable to concentrate, his mind elsewhere. Hearing footsteps on the stairs he looked expectantly towards the open bedroom door. A King Charles spaniel ran into the bedroom, leaping with a delighted bark onto the bed.

'Hey, I've just had a shower,' he said, laughing at the dog's antics, stopping her from licking his face, and then looked up at his wife as the tail-wagging spaniel plonked itself across his lap. 'Hi,' he said.

She smiled. 'You look a lot better, would you like me to make up the settee so you could come downstairs and watch TV?'

'No thanks, I'll, have a snooze up here.'

'OK, it's time for your medicine.'

'Ugh,' he crinkled up his face in disgust.

'You're worse than the grandchildren,' she said scornfully, pouring him a glass of water, handing it to him with two tablets. 'Are you in pain?'

'A little, it's not too bad.'

'The tablets should help; how about a cup of tea, or soup, perhaps a sandwich?'

He absentmindedly stroked the dog's head as she nestled closer to him, sensing his mood. 'Tea would do nicely thanks and a couple of biscuits.' He looked down at the dog as she rolled onto her back to have her tummy tickled. 'You like that, don't you, Rosie?' The dog gave a happy bark, turned and leapt from the bed, following her mistress.

'Thanks,' he said.

She half turned back, 'For what?'

'For being there, marrying me, standing by me, everything.'

'Don't be stupid, I love you; I won't be long.' She turned, tears in her eyes as she left the bedroom.

He must have fallen asleep, but the tinkling of a spoon against the cup awoke him. His daughter Miriam smiled at him. 'Mama said you wanted a cup of tea and some biscuits.' She placed the cup and saucer with a plate of biscuits onto the bedside table and then kissed him on the cheek.

He smiled, 'I'm happy to see you petal.' He reached for the tea. 'I thought you were going to a charity meeting? Something to do with the Anthony Nolan Trust or was it a

Full Monty show for the Ladies Guild?' There was laughter in his voice which brought on a bout of coughing.

Miriam took the cup from him, holding it to his lips, trying to ignore the pain on his face as he took a sip, saying lightly, 'In actual fact the meeting's not until tomorrow.' Feigning anger she said forcefully, 'For your information, we at the Ladies Guild do not put on Full Monty shows.' Unable to keep a straight face any longer, with the pain gone from his face, she said, 'I suppose if we were putting on such a show, you'd want to participate.'

'All you have to do is ask, believe me; once they've seen me in the flesh they'll storm the stage.'

'More likely ask for their money back,' she chortled, giving him another hug. 'You're a dirty old man.'

'Hey, less of the old; I'm happy you're here.'

'I was passing and thought I'd pop in and have a quick cuppa with Mama and see how you are.'

He stroked a blonde curl away from her face, the cobalt blue eyes showing their love for him. 'Me, I'm fine.' He began to cough again.

She quickly poured him a glass of water, placing it in his hands. 'Anything you need, Papa?' she asked as he gulped it down.

Taking a couple of deep breaths, he patted her hand. 'Nothing petal, I'm fine; you being here is all I need.'

'In that case I'm going downstairs to have that cuppa and a chat with Mama. I'll come up again in a little while.'

He smiled wanly, 'OK, petal, I'll call if I need anything.'

She kissed him and left the room.

Tears ran down Miriam's face as she entered the kitchen, just as her mother placed a piece of fish into the frying pan. 'What are we going to do, Mama? His coughing is getting worse.'

'The doctor said there's nothing we could do. We knew this would happen, so let's do the best we can for him, while we can.'

Miriam wiped away the tears. 'When the others get here we should make final arrangements for Papa's surprise eightieth birthday party.'

He lay there for a moment then pulled back the duvet getting out of bed, taking the few steps to the dressing table on the other side of the room and sat heavily onto the stool, leaning forward staring into the mirror. No, those are not the eyes of a killer, but one who had had to kill. Some were people that deserved to die, *Vengeance is mine, sayeth the Lord.* Others were just soldiers obeying orders. Most, if not all, had hatred in their hearts for Jews, and he still asked that question that's never been answered, why do those people hate Jews? His brow puckered into a crease; it was an enigma, especially when many of Israel's enemies had never met a Jew, or even spoken to one. He shook his head; would there ever be peace?

No, he had no regrets; it had been a great life. In the last few years, before the cancer, Rita and he had travelled to many parts of the world. They went to Berlin, and the street where she lived. Her father's bakery no longer existed. They visited Vienna; his father's shop and their home now a shopping mall.

Bergman had gone; killed in a freak flying accident. Aunt Doris and Uncle Mark died within a few days of each other. Mark went first, but Manny was certain Doris died of a broken heart. Daniel followed a year later, leaving a legacy to all those men and women he taught in making fine pastries. Rosen, the man who made Manny rich, had died two years ago of a heart attack, having built a small empire. Both his daughters married astute men who took over from Rosen, adding to Manny's portfolio of shares with those bought in a computer company called Microsoft. Sam retired and lived in Eilat. Isaac and Manny's sister Hannah opened a clinic for underprivileged children, Israeli and Arab. Their grandson Nathan and his wife have taken over.

He kept his promise to Joseph and planted two dozen trees, and also the promise he made himself to find David,

Rothman and Koning's remains, which were now buried in a cemetery in Haifa.

He looked lovingly at the array of photos. His children were married, and three weeks ago he attended the wedding of his grandson Saul. 'No matter what happens to me now, I live on, my blood flowed through their veins,' he said softly.

Manny stood and walked slowly to the bed, pulled back the duvet and lay down, nestling into the pillows giving a sigh of contentment.

Rita entered the bedroom with a cup of tea and some biscuits, placing the tray on the side-table saying. 'The children should be here in a little while; I've brought you a cup of tea—' She knelt by the bed taking his hand, its cold. She kissed it, stood and tenderly placed the duvet over his body, then bent and kissed him.

'Thank you, my darling, rest in peace.'

www.ingramcontent.com/pod-product-compliance
Lightning Source LLC
Chambersburg PA
CBHW050723180626
46814CB00002B/572